This book belongs to:

..............................................................

# You're Strong With Me

## Chitra Soundar & Poonam Mistry

LANTANA PUBLISHING

The rain clouds
were long gone
and the dry season
scorched the land
and browned
the grass.

This was all new for the baby giraffe.
She bounded through the grove and licked
the coarse bark of the acacia tree.

When she was hungry, she looked for her mother in the herd.

"I'm right here," whispered her mother, nudging her from behind.

"Don't wander off on your own too far."

SCRITCH!
SCRATCH!

The baby giraffe stretched up to shoo away the bird that landed on her mother's back.

"Be nice to the oxpecker," said Mama Giraffe. "It eats itchy insects and cleans my fur."

"What is it saying?"

"The bird brings stories from the grassland," said Mama Giraffe.
"The songs tell us about faraway friends."

The baby giraffe fidgeted when the oxpecker flew onto her back.

"Stay still," said Mama Giraffe.

"But it hurts!"

"As you grow older, your coat will get thicker and this will just be a tickle.

Until then, you're strong with me."

HISS! SNAP!

The smell of smoke floated by.
The little giraffe ran to the
edge of the grove in search of
the smell.

"A fire is eating up dry grass,"
said Mama Giraffe. "Before
long, new grass will grow,
inviting new friends to come
and graze."

"It stings my throat," said the calf.

"Close your nostrils," said Mama Giraffe.

"Soon the smoke will call for rain as it rises to the skies."

The baby giraffe
ran around the trees
as she watched the
blaze spread wider.

"Stay close," said Mama
Giraffe, nudging her.

"Can the fire catch us?"

"As you grow taller, your
legs will grow long enough to
outrun the flames.

**STRINK! STRINK!**

The baby giraffe was playing with her friends and didn't hear the sounds.

"Pay attention," said Mama Giraffe. "Every noise and every quiet could be a warning."

"Why are the birds flying towards the fire?"

asked the young one.

"They soar up and swoop down to catch the insects escaping the flames," said Mama Giraffe.

"Often they have to be brave to feed their flock."

The little giraffe lagged behind as Mama Giraffe headed to the creek.

"Keep up," her mother called.

"I'm trying to listen to the sounds of the grassland," the baby replied.

"As you grow wiser, your eyes will spot shadows and your ears will hear the grass rustle.

"Until then, you're strong with me."

SPLASH! WHOOSH!

A school of baby fish leaped in the creek. The little giraffe waited, unsure of taking a sip.

"Drink up," said Mama Giraffe. "We have far to go before sunset."

"I don't know how," said
the baby giraffe.

The water was too far
down.

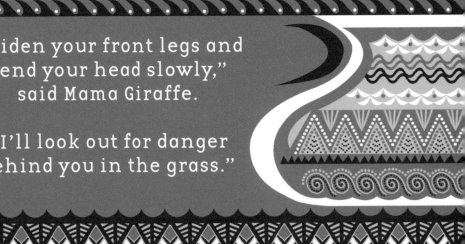

"Widen your front legs and
bend your head slowly,"
said Mama Giraffe.

"I'll look out for danger
behind you in the grass."

Having had her fill, the little giraffe tried to stand up and stumbled a little.

"Watch out," said her mother.

"I don't want to try that again!"

"As you grow bigger, your neck will stretch high enough to reach the dew drops on the trees.

"Until then,
you're strong with me."

That night, under a blanket
of stars, the calf wandered back
from her friends.

"Take some rest," said Mama
Giraffe, moving closer. "You'll
grow a little taller
every night."

She licked her baby's
ruffled skin.

"Until then,
you're strong
with me."

To my family, with them I'm stronger
*Chitra*

To my best friend Sohail
*Poonam*

First published in the United Kingdom in 2019 by Lantana Publishing Ltd., London.
www.lantanapublishing.com

American edition published in 2019 by Lantana Publishing Ltd., UK.
info@lantanapublishing.com

Text © Chitra Soundar 2019
Illustration © Poonam Mistry 2019

Distributed in the United States and Canada by Lerner Publishing Group, Inc.
241 First Avenue North, Minneapolis, MN 55401 U.S.A.
For reading levels and more information, look for this title at www.lernerbooks.com
Cataloging-in-Publication Data Available.

Printed and bound in Europe.
Original artwork created with ink on paper and completed digitally.

ISBN: 978-1-911373-75-9
eBook ISBN: 978-1-911373-78-0

Explore Space!

# Space Walks

by Kathleen W. Deady

**Consultant:**
James Gerard
Aerospace Education Specialist
NASA Aerospace Education Services Program

# Bridgestone Books
an imprint of Capstone Press
Mankato, Minnesota

Bridgestone Books are published by Capstone Press
151 Good Counsel Drive, P.O. Box 669, Mankato, Minnesota 56002
http://www.capstone-press.com

*Library of Congress Cataloging-in-Publication Data*
Deady, Kathleen W.
    Space walks / by Kathleen W. Deady.
    p. cm.—(Explore space!)
    Includes bibliographical references and index.
    Contents: Space walks—First space walk—First U.S. space walk—Weightless walking—What is walking in space like?—Space walking suits—Space walking gear—Space walk training—Future space walks—Hands on—Words to know—Read more—Internet sites—Index.
    ISBN 0-7368-1402-7 (hardcover)
    1. Extravehicular activity (Manned space flight)—Juvenile literature. [1. Extravehicular activity (Manned space flight) 2. Manned space flight.] I. Title. II. Series.
TL1096 .D43 2003
629.45'84—dc21                                                      2001008683

Summary: Explains the history of space walks and describes the type of equipment and
    training astronauts need for walking in space.

**Editorial Credits**
Christopher Harbo, editor; Karen Risch, product planning editor; Steve Christensen, series
    designer; Patrick D. Dentinger, book designer; Kelly Garvin, photo researcher

**Photo Credits**
DigitalVision, 10
Hulton Archive by Getty Images, 6
NASA, cover, 4, 8, 12, 14, 16, 18, 20

1  2  3  4  5  6  07  06  05  04  03  02

# Table of Contents

## Space Walks

A space walk is when an astronaut spends time outside a spacecraft. Astronauts do not actually walk. They float in space. Astronauts take space walks to fix spacecraft or to launch satellites. Astronauts call space walks Extravehicular Activity (EVA).

**extravehicular**
outside the spacecraft

5

## First Space Walk

Alexei Leonov from Russia walked in space first. He spent 12 minutes outside his spacecraft on March 18, 1965. A rope called a tether kept Alexei tied to the spacecraft. The tether stopped him from floating away from the spacecraft.

**tether**
a rope or cord

Ed White tested a new handheld tool during his space walk. It fired jets of gas that helped him move in space.

## First U.S. Space Walk

Ed White was the first astronaut from the United States to walk in space. Ed spent 23 minutes outside the Gemini 4 spacecraft on June 3, 1965. His tether carried oxygen and water from the spacecraft. Ed needed oxygen to breathe. The water kept his space suit cool.

**oxygen**
a colorless gas that people need to breathe

10

## Weightless Walking

Astronauts feel weightless in space. They can float in any position. Gravity does not pull them down toward Earth. Astronauts say walking in space feels like swimming underwater. Some astronauts say walking in space makes them feel carsick.

**gravity**
a force that pulls objects together

11

handles

## What Is Walking in Space Like?

Astronauts float in space. But they cannot swim through space. Astronauts must pull or push against the spacecraft. They must pull themselves from handle to handle to move around.

Astronauts may get thirsty or hungry during a space walk. A drink bag with a straw is attached inside their suit. They also may have a fruit bar.

## Space Walking Suits

Space suits keep astronauts safe for about seven hours. A tank blows air into the suit. The suit has layers of thick rubber and cloth. The rubber holds in air. The cloth protects the astronaut from hot and cold temperatures in space. A helmet protects the astronaut's head.

**protect**
to keep safe

15

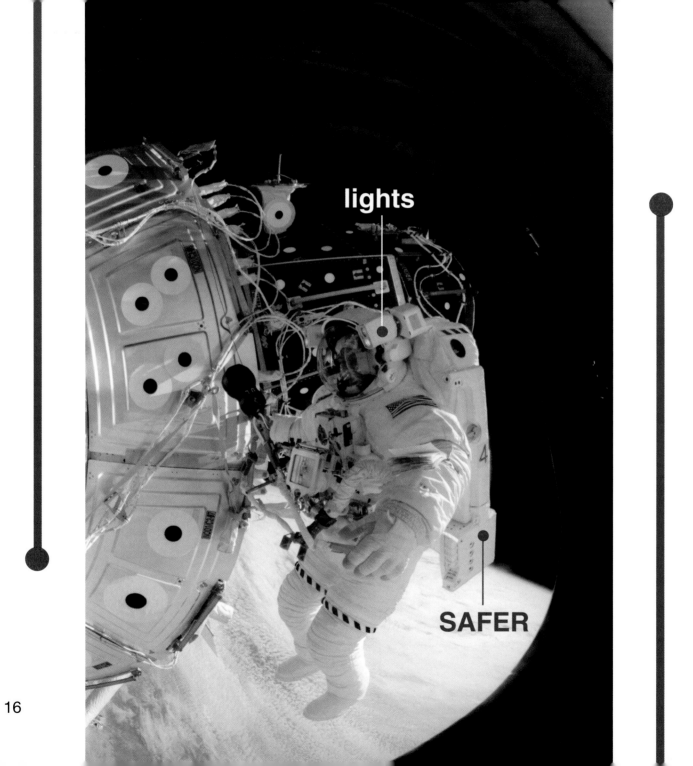

lights

SAFER

## Space Walking Gear

Astronauts need gear to work in space. Radios let them talk to other astronauts. Lights on their helmets help them see. Astronauts sometimes use a SAFER to move without a tether. A SAFER is a rocket-powered backpack.

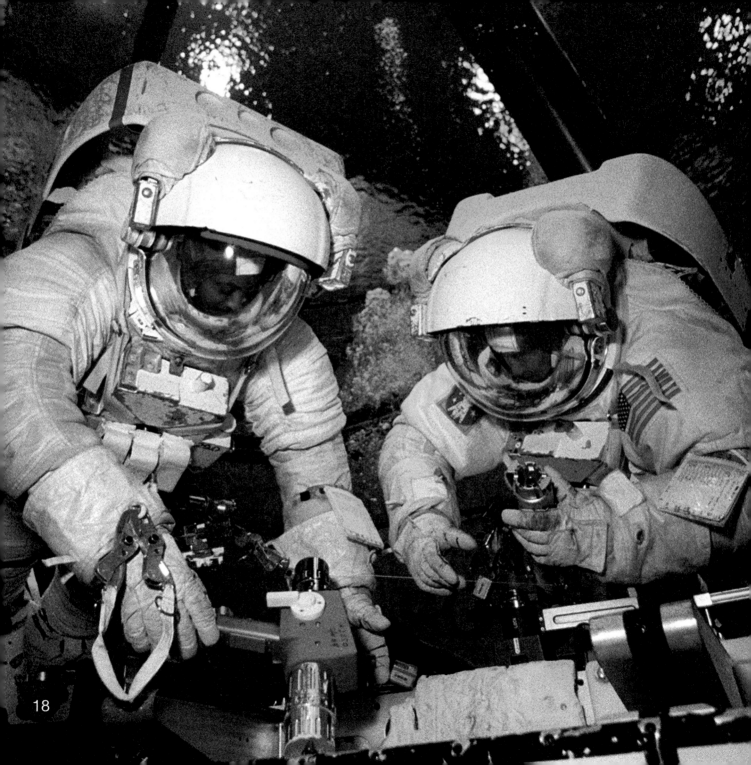

## Space Walk Training

Astronauts must train to walk in space. Astronauts practice space walking with a full-size space shuttle in a deep swimming pool. They learn about their suits and how their gear works. Astronauts practice moving in their suits.

**space shuttle**
a vehicle that carries astronauts into space

Astronauts sometimes hook their feet in place. They then can work with both hands. They will not float away from whatever they touch.

## Future Space Walks

Today, astronauts take many space walks. Sixteen countries are working together to build the International Space Station. Astronauts will take about 160 space walks to finish the space station.

# Hands On: Space Walking

Astronauts cannot swim in space. They must pull or push on something. You can see how space walking feels.

## What You Need
Swivel office chair on wheels

## What You Do
1. Sit in the chair. Lift your feet off the floor. Do not touch anything around you.
2. Try to make the chair move from where it is on the floor. Wave your arms. Shake your legs. The chair may rock and spin. But it will not move from the spot.
3. Think about how astronauts walk in space. Think of ways you can walk your chair around like an astronaut walks in space.

You can pull on another piece of furniture. The furniture is like the handles on a spacecraft. You also can have someone push you in the chair. The other person is like the SAFER an astronaut wears.

# Words to Know

**astronaut** (ASS-truh-nawt)—someone trained to fly into space in a spacecraft

**gravity** (GRAV-uh-tee)—a force that pulls objects together; gravity pulls objects down toward the surface of Earth.

**launch** (LAWNCH)—to send a spacecraft into space

**oxygen** (OK-suh-juhn)—a colorless gas that people need to breathe

**satellite** (SAT-uh-lite)—an object that circles Earth; many satellites are machines that take pictures or send telephone calls and TV programs to Earth.

**tank** (TANGK)—a holder for air or liquid

**tether** (TETH-ur)—a rope or cord; a tether keeps an astronaut close to a spacecraft.

# Read More

**Lassieur, Allison.** *Astronauts.* A True Book. New York: Children's Press, 2000.

**Vogt, Gregory.** *Spacewalks: The Ultimate Adventure in Orbit.* Countdown to Space. Berkeley Heights, N.J.: Enslow, 2000.

# Internet Sites

**How Stuff Works—How Spacesuits Work**
http://www.howstuffworks.com/space-suit.htm
**NASA Kids**
http://kids.msfc.nasa.gov

# Index

**Ronald W. Clark**

# The Scientific Breakthrough

## The Impact of Modern Invention

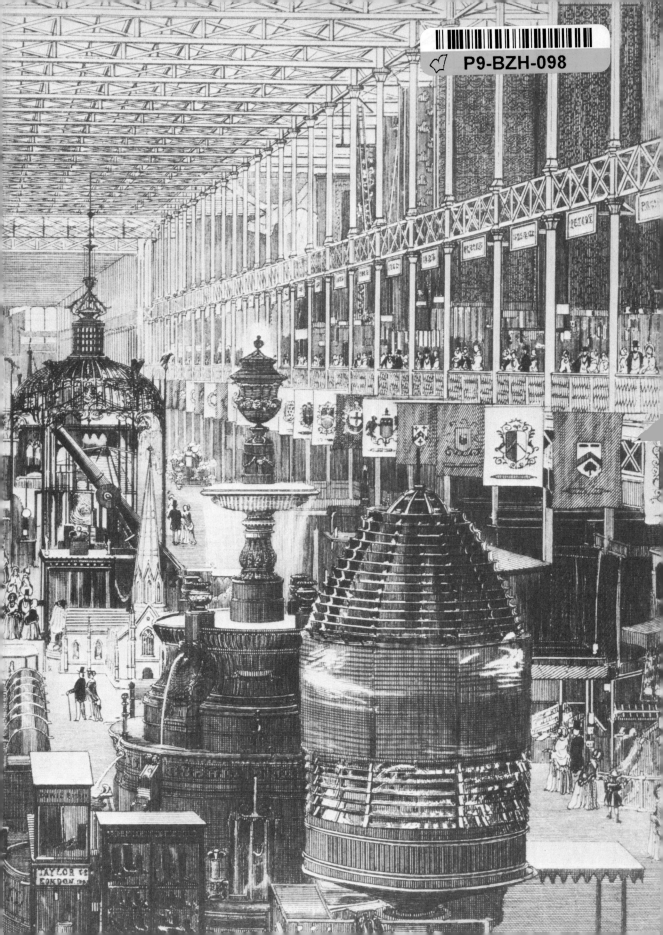

# The Scientific Breakthrough

**The Impact of Modern Invention**

G. P. Putnam's Sons   New York

This book was designed and produced by
George Rainbird Limited,
Marble Arch House, 44 Edgware Road, London W2
for G. P. Putnam's Sons,
200 Madison Avenue, New York, N.Y. 10016

House editor: Peter Faure
Designer: Alan Bartram
Picture researcher: Patricia Vaughan
Indexer: E. F. Peeler

Color printing by W. S. Cowells Ltd, Ipswich
Text setting by Westerham Press, Westerham, Kent
Monochrome printing and binding by
Butler & Tanner Ltd, Frome, Somerset

SBN 399 11179 4
Library of Congress Catalog Card Number 73 78629

Printed in England

Endpapers Illustration:
The Great Exhibition, London, 1851

# Contents

# Acknowledgments

The author wishes to thank the following for help and advice, or for reading portions of the manuscript. However, all opinions expressed are his own, and any errors are his not theirs.

Brian Coe, Curator, Kodak Museum; Louis A. Jackets; C. J. Somers, Ferranti Ltd; G. H. Sturge, BBC; Mrs B. Hance, GEC–Marconi Electronics Ltd; M. Kaufman, Rubber and Plastics Processing Industry Training Board; T. Davies, Plastics Institute; K. B. Bartlett, ICI, Plastics Division; R. W. B. Truscott, UK Atomic Energy Authority; Dr D. M. Potts, International Planned Parenthood Federation; Peter Wymer, Post Office Telecommunications

# List of color plates

# Introduction

An invention is often a dream come true; sometimes it is a nightmare made real. In both cases it will have come to life only after certain conditions have been met. There must first be an ambition of the human race, present in varying degree over the centuries, some constant if unconscious hope which keeps an idea simmering. Thus men dreamed of flight since they first watched the birds; they hoped to unlock the power within the atomic nucleus from the moment they knew it existed; they thought of producing men like gods. But some more localized and more pressing incentive is also needed – what Dr A. P. Rowe, in charge of Britain's radar development at the Telecommunications Research Establishment during the Second World War, has called the operational requirement. In the 1950s poverty and a social conscience combined to produce the first experiments which led to the Pill; a few years earlier the urgent need to create an ultimate weapon before the enemy got it first, alone led to the massive research and development which unleashed nuclear energy.

Yet there is a third essential. When vision and contemporary need have joined up on the field, the catalyst of technology is still required. Powered flight was impossible before the petrol engine. Practical radio awaited Sir Alexander Fleming's thermionic valve, and Air Commodore Sir Frank Whittle's jet was only airborne in the wake of metals capable of withstanding the huge heats of the exhaust gases. These technological advances rested in turn on less publicized developments in many specialities, on the work of engineers and technicians who by their efforts created the *deus ex machina* who made invention possible. Below them, and never to be forgotten in any story of invention or of great scientific discovery, there were the ordinary craftsmen. Clerk Maxwell, one of the greatest theorists of all time and the father of the electromagnetic spectrum, well realized the partnership between his theories and the practical arts. 'I am happy,' he said on taking up his first Chair at Aberdeen University, 'in the knowledge of a good instrument-maker, in addition to a smith, an optician and a carpenter.'

To these requirements of vision, operational need and technological expertise, mixed in proportions that are rarely the same, there must be added luck – 'Chance, Fortune, Luck, Destiny, Fate, Providence,' which as Winston Churchill wrote of the First World War, determines whether you 'walk to the right or to the left of a particular tree, and . . . makes the difference whether you rise to command an Army Corps or are sent home crippled or paralysed for life.' Chance saved the Wrights from destruction and brought them to an appointment with history at Kittyhawk, gave the Americans rather than the Germans the harvest of nuclear fission discovered by Otto Hahn in Berlin. Chance has still to decide into whose hands will fall the possibilities and perils of genetic engineering, the techniques which in the foreseeable future may give mankind the chance of re-creating himself in tailor-made form.

The upsurge of invention of which these are the more sensational illustrations, and which marks the hundred years that began in mid-19th century, almost totally ignored frontiers. It was Lord Rutherford who used to boast that 'science is international, and long may it remain so.' The same is as true with the catalyst of technology, growing at comparable pace in most industrialized countries whatever steps are taken to conceal the growth from commercial or national rivals. Thus inventions tend to be born in different countries, in different forms, at much the same time, often in conditions of commercial or military secrecy which make the task of settling priority a nightmare search, and the problem of patenting and exploitation a rich field for lawyers. That so many of the inventions on which the world now depends began to flower out following the Great Exhibition held in London in 1851 was not chance. But neither was it the result of lonely British supremacy. Rather was it that the Great Exhibition itself reflected the belief that all was possible for all nations in the new confident morning that then seemed to be dawning. Between four and five centuries earlier the Middle Ages had been ended by the scientific revolution which creates the watershed between earlier times and our own. From it there had come in due course the Industrial Revolution. Then, with the ambition surging up within the newly-created United States, and with the long European peace that followed the Napoleonic wars, men turned in a new climate of hope to fulfil their dreams.

These dreams, made real by scientists and technologists, were to revolutionize human existence within the next hundred years with the result that life in mid-20th century is basically different from life in Victorian Britain or Lincoln's America. The advances have come in scores of fields but it is possible to study six main ways in which they have altered day-to-day existence. Photography has provided for the masses what the portrait-painter once provided only for the élite; man-made materials have enabled the many to enjoy the benefits once reserved for the few. Command of the air has effectively shrunk the planet, and control of the electromagnetic spectrum has given men power to disseminate information throughout the world in a way not previously conceivable. Use of the forces locked within the nucleus of the atom has opened up the prospect, if a distant one, of truly limitless energy; and, in a totally different field, new discoveries in biology and genetics now hold out the possibility of man being able to control the destiny of the human race. Among the welter of inventions and discoveries made since the 1850s these can be numbered as the most significant.

# 1 The Picture Makers

The men who came of age in the mid-19th century, as invention and technology began to lay the foundations of the contemporary world, had many ambitions they were eager to fulfil. They wished to create new sources of energy, to fly like the birds, to create for the masses the products which had so far been the prerogative of the rich.

They wished also to do something more human, something closely linked both to the human heart and human pride. They wished to keep some record of the loved one, of a family's daily occupations, or of the property that was the mark of prosperity; some record which would show not only that spirit of a person or a place which eludes all but the exceptional genius of an artist, but also the detail which means so much to those who know its significance.

Artists have benefited from this human wish since the first caveman drew figures on a wall with blackened stick or chipped an outline with primitive chisel. And, despite the urge to interpret rather than depict, to leave a portrait tinted with the artist's feelings rather than an objective record, there was through the centuries a constant demand for portraits, for landscapes, for pictorial accounts of military actions which showed events 'as they were': a demand which in the nature of things could never be fully satisfied but which called for any device which would help create a detailed picture.

To fill this operational requirement there came first the *camera obscura*, or literally darkened room, the ancestor of both the box Brownie and the elegant Hasselblad.

Just when this predecessor of the camera was first used is not clear, but there is considerable evidence that knowledge of the principles involved goes back to ancient times. In the history of photography, as in that of other inventions, it is rarely wise to use the term 'first'. Different definitions, different nuances put on the most innocent words, the genuine wish to claim honest priority and the equally genuine

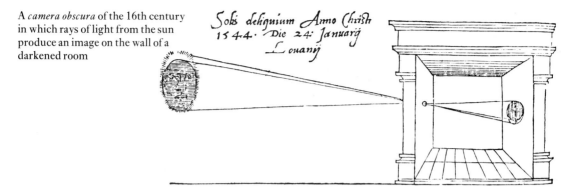

A *camera obscura* of the 16th century in which rays of light from the sun produce an image on the wall of a darkened room

wish to dismiss the holder of a rival theory or the protagonist of a rival school, can restore confusion to the most carefully sorted-out chronological story. But it is at least certain that by the 16th century the *camera obscura* is being described in detail.

The fullest account comes from Giambattista della Porta, a Neapolitan physicist who in the catholic manner of the times wrote also on physiology, gardening and arboriculture. Leonardo had already written several accounts in his note-books, but these were not published until the end of the 18th century. Other Dutch and Italian scientists referred to the ingenious device, which appears to have been well known, but it was della Porta's description, given in his *Magia Naturalis* of 1569, which best explains how it was used by draughtsmen. The principle of the *camera obscura* is simple enough. Light-rays passing through a small hole in the side of a darkened room form an inverted image on the opposite wall of the scene outside. If a sheet of paper is held flat against this wall it will be possible to trace on it, with considerable accuracy, a replica of the scene. That was all: the uncompli-cated conscription of the fact that rays of light shine in straight lines. While this fact, and the possibility of its application, had long been known, it was only in the after-math of the scientific Renaissance that it was developed with speed. Then, in little more than a century, the *camera obscura* was transformed.

First Aniello Barbaro, a Venetian nobleman who was also a professor at the University of Padua, described in *La Pratica della Perspettiva* how the substitution of a glass lens for the pinhole would increase the brilliance of the image. 'Close all shutters and doors so that no light enters the room except through the lens,' he went on. 'Opposite hold a sheet of paper which is moved forward and back until the scene appears in the sharpest detail. There on paper you will see the scene as it really is, with distances, colours, and shadows and motions; the clouds, the water glinting and the birds flying. By holding the paper steady you can trace the whole perspective with a pen. You can shade it and delicately colour it from nature itself.'

But the addition of a lens was only the beginning. It was soon realized that if a concave mirror was added to the optical apparatus the image would be thrown rightside up instead of upside down, while a simple mirror at 45° could be used to throw the image on to a sheet of horizontal paper rather than on to the wall. By mounting the lens in a form of telescope it was possible to bring successive parts of the external scene into view, while different lenses would project different extents of the external scene.

Next, the *camera obscura* became mobile, being adapted to the sedan chair and also to the tent. It was realized that the lens could be housed in a box above a darkened area where the operator sat, and the rays directed down on to a horizontal drawing-board. The next development was construction of a lens plus darkened box with glass top, and before the end of the 18th century there was available a diverse range of small instruments that would produce on a flat surface – sometimes a ground-glass screen – an image of whatever it was pointed at.

By the start of the 19th century nature had thus been induced to provide a picture of itself. The artist producing the family portrait or the panorama of a landowner's property had at his disposal a device which helped him to pin down on paper or canvas a permanent portrait of a transient scene. But, as one artist remarked, the portraitist still had to use the pencil of man; was there no way in which he could use the pencil of nature?

So far, the line of advance was along the path of optics. By various ways man had discovered how to lead light to the surface on which he wished to draw; now, if he wished light to draw for him, it would be necessary for the light itself to affect the substance on which it fell. Thus the chemists were brought in, and were soon making possible photography as the word is understood today, a process in which two lines of improvements can be seen to run parallel. One, from the opticians, brought ever greater control over the amount and kind of light which was used; the other, from the chemists, made the utilization of that light ever more efficient and more controllable.

Man had noticed since ancient times that light changes the colour of certain substances. Many dyed fabrics fade with exposure to the sun while the human skin deepens in colour under its rays. Yet it was not until the early-18th century that the German scientist Johann Heinrich Schulze first noticed, apparently by accident, the light-sensitive characteristics of the salts of silver which form the basis of most photographic processes. Schulze filled a bottle with a mixture of chalk, silver, and nitric acid in the course of routine experiments and left the bottle near an open window. On his return he found that the mixture nearest the window had turned a deep purple while that which had not caught the rays of the sun still remained white. Repetition of the process, but with a bottle of similar material placed by a fire, brought no corresponding darkening; thus it seemed clear that the light of the sun rather than its heat was responsible. To discover whether this was so, Schulze again placed a filled bottle near the window. This time he pasted stencils of opaque paper on the outside. When the bottle was taken down and the stencils removed, their images remained in white on a darkened ground.

Schulze's work was the basis of an interesting parlour trick, but it seemed to be little more. Once the stencils had been removed their images quickly darkened, to disappear in the purple background like Prospero's insubstantial pageant, leaving not a rack behind. Nevertheless, the phenomenon was followed up, notably by the Swedish Karl Wilhelm Scheele who split sunlight up into its component colours with the aid of a spectrum and found that the different colours darkened the sensitive chemicals at different speeds.

One of the next steps forward, an abortive one, was made by Thomas Wedgwood, son of the potter Josiah, who had often seen the *camera obscura* used by artists to paint on dinner services, fired at the Etruria works, the scenery of the great country estates owned by the pottery's customers. If only the scene could be permanently imprinted on the pottery by the *camera obscura*, what an industrial breakthrough this would be!

Wedgwood's experiments were described in the *Journal of the Royal Institution* by no less a person than Sir Humphry Davy in 1802. His paper, *An account of a method of copying paintings upon glass and of making profiles by the agency of light upon nitrate of silver, with observations by H. Davy*, was an account of failure. The images cast by the *camera obscura* were not sufficiently bright to affect the sensitive material used. Furthermore, when bright enough images were created, by placing on sensitized material either bird's feathers, insect's wings, or the paintings on glass that were then the vogue, these images passed away as soon as they were exposed to normal light. No washing of the material was sufficient to remove the traces of silver salt from the parts that had not been exposed to light and these in turn merely darkened, as had the images of Schulze's stencils. Wedgwood's sun-prints could only be looked at by the dim light of a candle.

The first man to overcome this destruction of sun-prints by the light which had made them was Nicéphore Niepce of Chalon-sur-Saône, an irrepressible inventor who with his brother Claude was experimenting with sun-pictures before the end of the 18th century. At one early point in his work it looked as though Niepce would be successful in carrying Wedgwood's work a step further. Using a *camera obscura* he obtained an image on paper sensitized with silver chloride; but attempts to make the image permanent by removing the unexposed portions with acid were only partly successful and the Niepce brothers then turned to a different line. It was already known that light not only darkened certain substances but also hardened others, and the Niepces now sought a substance that would suit their particular purpose. Their aim was to use the *camera obscura* as an aid to the mechanical reproduction of engravings, and both men became familiar with a particular kind of bitumen produced when asphalt was dissolved in oil of lavender. This was resistant to etching fluids but it also hardened under exposure to light. The Niepces therefore coated a metal plate – the earliest ones being of pewter – with the bitumen. In the first experiments the plate was exposed to sunlight by placing it under an engraving whose lines held back the light, and in later ones by exposing it in a *camera obscura*. Time exposures in the latter were considerable and about eight hours were necessary to obtain the photograph

The world's first photograph, taken by Nicéphore Niepce on a pewter plate in 1826 and showing the view from Niepce's window at Gras near Chalon-sur-Saône

from the Niepces' window at Gras – the world's first success-ful permanent photograph which was discovered by Helmut and Alison Gernsheim, the historians of photography, more than a century later. After exposure, the metal plate was im-mersed in a solvent. This removed the bitumen from the parts of the plate on which no light had fallen – the shadows of the original subject – revealing the metal whose tone could then be further darkened. Where light had fallen, the equiva-lent of the highlights in the original, the light-coloured bitu-men had hardened and thus remained. Here then was the first-ever photograph, christened a 'heliograph' by Niepce, a positive rather than the negative produced today in most cameras.

Niepce's success came in the mid-1820s and the view from the window at Gras was almost certainly taken in the summer of 1826 or 1827. Earlier that year he had received the first of many letters from another key figure in the history of photo-graphy: Louis Jacques Mandé Daguerre. Daguerre was a theatrical painter who specialized in the construction of stage sets and of dioramas, popular entertainments in which huge paintings on semi-transparent material were illuminated by moving lights to give an impression of transformation scenes. He had often used the *camera obscura* and in January 1826 wrote to Niepce informing him that he, too, was trying to discover some method of producing permanent images. Niepce reacted cautiously. So, in turn, did Daguerre, not making another approach for a year. Only in December 1829 did the two men become partners and agree that they would pool their knowledge.

Niepce died four years later. Not until 1839, six years later, was the process known as the daguerreotype revealed to the world. And while the invention was bought by the French Government from Daguerre and Niepce's son jointly, it has never been clear exactly how much Daguerre and Niepce *père* each contributed to the first great breakthrough in photo-graphy. Daguerre's name lived on. It still does. And it is certainly true that he had been experimenting for some years before he sought collaboration with Niepce. Nevertheless, there is a strong presumption that the older man was the one more responsible for the new process which was formally made public in August 1839.

The daguerreotype began with a silver-plated sheet of copper. This plate was sensitized by holding it over a saucer of iodine whose vapour formed a thin layer of silver iodide on the plate's surface, and eventually gave it a rich golden colour. At this stage the plate, now in a covered holder, was placed in a

Louis Jacques Mandé Daguerre, the French theatrical painter who invented the daguerreotype process

SOCIAL STRUGGLES.

The use of a head clamp to prevent
movement in early portrait
photography

suitable *camera obscura* – or camera, as the box soon came to be
known. Here the plate was exposed to the light. Next it was
put into a developing box, at one end of which was a yellow
glass window, and exposed to the fumes of a cup of heated
mercury. Immediately after exposure no change could be
noted in the plate; but the mercury vapour condensed on
those portions of the silver iodide which had been affected by
light, and the greater the intensity of light the greater the condensation. Thus an image grew on the plate and to make this
permanent it was only necessary to dip the plate into a solution
of common salt. The result was a one-off photograph, a
unique positive which could not be copied except by re-
photographing and the manufacture of a second daguerreotype. It was extremely delicate, could be damaged by finger-
tip contact, and had to be sealed away from the air to prevent
tarnishing. Therefore the daguerreotype was usually set
behind glass, which was held slightly away from the plate itself,
and mounted on a plush frame. Exposures of five minutes or
more were necessary, and it was customary for the heads of
sitters to be held by discreetly-concealed head-clamps. However, despite these disadvantages, the daguerreotype was an
immense step forward. It could reproduce textures of very
great delicacy, particularly the skin of the human face, and it is
not surprising that when Britain's first Census was held in
1851, more than 50 professional photographers were at work,
almost all of them using the daguerreotype process.

These photographs, produced more than a century ago,
have an almost uncanny way of summoning up the past. The
streets of a Paris almost as remote as the Middle Ages, the
lined faces of the elderly men and women who seem to have
been favourites among early daguerreotype sitters, the calm
beauty of the French countryside, still glow from the metal
plates as though one is looking through a hole into the past.
It is the faces which are most striking of all. For 'photography'
– a word coined only some years later by Sir John Herschel,
the British astronomer who himself pioneered many developments in the art – had achieved one of its inventors' aims.
Memory of the near and the dear could now be supplemented
by something more emotionally satisfying than the artist's
portrait: by the daguerreotype which could bring to life flesh
and blood less artistically but more reliably and more evoca-
tively than all except the rare masterpieces from a small handful of artistic geniuses.

Yet the daguerreotype was still in one way on the far side
of a wide river separating it from photography as the word is
understood today. It was a one-off job. One exposure, one

daguerreotype. To this extent it retained the uniqueness of the artist's portrait. It also retained the same limitation; the family portrait could be cooed over and savoured in only one place at a time.

The first man to remove the limitation was William Henry Fox Talbot, a wealthy Englishman of Lacock Abbey near Chippenham in Wiltshire. Talbot had been born here in 1800 and died in the same great house in 1877. In between he was Member of Parliament in the reformed Government of 1832; became a considerable mathematician; and was led by his interest in archaeology to decipher, for the first time, the cuneiform tablets rescued from the ruins of Nineveh. This man of many parts, so typical of the wealthy Victorians, was also the inventor of the Talbotype or calotype.

During a summer holiday in 1833 Talbot was sketching on the shores of Lake Como. 'After various fruitless attempts I laid aside the instrument and came to the conclusion that its use required a previous knowledge of drawing which unfortunately I did not possess,' he later wrote. 'I then thought of trying again a method which I had tried many years before. The method was, to take a *camera obscura* and to throw the image of the objects on a piece of paper in its focus – fairy pictures, creations of a moment, and destined as rapidly to fade away. It was during these thoughts that the idea occurred to me – how charming it would be if it were possible to cause these natural images to imprint themselves durably, and remain fixed upon the paper.' This of course was just the idea that had come to others, and some years later Talbot regretted what he called the 'very unusual dilemma' which sprang from the fact that both he and Daguerre were working, unknown to each other, along very similar lines.

Talbot was wrong. Far from being unusual, the situation in which men of imagination in different countries – or even from the same country – find themselves independently approaching a great discovery or invention or scientific advance, is very frequent. The climate of the times, the state of the art, and public demand all contribute to this embarrassing state of affairs. Darwin and Wallace separately working towards the outline of evolution; the British, the Germans and the Americans independently developing radar, and the tangled story of the proximity fuse are only three of the more obvious examples.

Talbot returned home and during the rest of the 1830s busied himself with making what he called photogenic drawings. These were on paper which had been made chemically sensitive and then 'exposed' either in the *camera*

A window of Lacock Abbey
photographed by William Henry
Fox Talbot in 1835

*obscura* or, in the case of objects such as leaves or lace, by merely placing the objects on the paper and exposing it to sunlight. The image could be seen on the sensitive paper and was then chemically fixed, although this fixing process was unsatisfactory and most of the original photogenic drawings have by now faded out of existence.

In the first weeks of 1839 Talbot realized that Daguerre was publishing in France the details of a process which he considered similar to his own. The result was a paper giving 'Some Account of the Art of Photogenic Drawing' which he read to the Royal Society at the end of January and a second paper on the same subject read the following month.

The fixing process in Talbot's method was particularly important for one special reason. All his pictures were reversed in tones, the blacks of real life appearing white, the whites appearing black, while those taken in the camera were also reversed from left to right. But once it had been found possible to fix the photograph so that it could be exposed to light once again without fading or disappearing, another process could be carried out. A fresh sheet of sensitized paper could be exposed with the photograph placed face downward on it; and from the original negative the positive appeared with tones correct and with image the right way round.

By 1839 there were therefore two very different photographic processes in existence. Daguerre's produced the finer results, and could be obtained by far shorter exposures, which was all-important to the portrait-photographer. Nevertheless, it still remained a once-only photograph, while from Talbot's paper negatives a large number of prints could be made.

At this stage there seems to have been an explosion of ideas. What in fact happened was that many men who had been tentatively experimenting for years were now encouraged by the success of Daguerre and of Talbot to continue with their work, to reveal ideas in which they had previously had only faint faith. From the spring of 1839 innumerable ways of making it easier to take photographs and to improve the quality of the finished product began to be published in the columns of scientific journals or discussed at scientific meetings. Of all these, two in particular were to help lay the foundations of modern photography.

The first was produced by Sir John Herschel, famous astronomer and son of an even more famous one. Herschel now, at one stroke, initiated one of the important processes in photography which has lasted, virtually unchanged, for more than 130 years. In his diaries, now held by the Science Museum in London, he describes what he did. Many years

William Henry Fox Talbot, the
wealthy Englishman whose work in
Wiltshire was contemporary with
Daguerre's across the Channel

*Below* Photograph on glass by Sir John Herschel of his father's telescope at Slough, taken in 1839

*Right above* Photograph taken about 1845 by William Henry Fox Talbot of his own photographic establishment at Reading

*Right below* Label advertising chemically treated paper for making 'Sun Pictures'

earlier he had found that silver salts – the salts used to sensitize photographic paper – were dissolved by hyposulphite of soda, the 'hypo' that is still linked with the photographic tasks of the amateur's bathroom. 'Tried hyposulphite of soda to arrest action of light by washing away all the chloride of silver or other silvering salt,' he wrote. 'Succeeded perfectly. Papers 12 acted on, $\frac{1}{2}$ guarded from light by covering with pasteboard, were then withdrawn from sunshine, sponged over with hyposulphite of soda, then well washed in pure water – dried and again exposed. The darkened half remained dark, the white half white, after an exposure, as if they had been painted on in sepia.' This is of course the treatment of modern films that are exposed, developed, and put in hypo for fixing, after which the hypo is washed away in running water and the resulting picture left as a permanent image.

During the same summer of 1839 Herschel also created history by making the first photograph on glass, a picture of the 40-foot telescope at Slough, where his father had first set up his observatory on being appointed private astronomer to George III. For the experiment, silver chloride was precipitated on to a circular glass plate $2\frac{1}{2}$ inches across. After two days the water was siphoned off and the plate allowed to dry. It was then sensitized, exposed in a camera or light box, and fixed with hypo, after which the back of the glass was smoked and painted black to give the picture the appearance of a positive print. But the difficulty of making the first emulsion adhere to the glass was very great and, for the time being, glass was abandoned.

Herschel's use of hypo was second in importance only to the discovery by Talbot of a process which drastically shortened exposure time. One says discovery, but application is possibly the fairer word; for the crux of the process was the use of gallic acid to develop the unseen or latent image produced by these shorter exposures, and Talbot was led on to this by the Rev. J. B. Reade, a well-known scientist who had come upon this property of gallic acid some while earlier.

The result was the calotype process, later re-christened the Talbotype, in which ordinary paper was treated first with silver nitrate and then with potassium iodide. The sensitized paper could be kept indefinitely as long as it was shielded from the light. When wanted for use it was treated with gallo-nitrate of silver and would then have to be used within a few hours. But the necessary exposure was of only about a minute, after which development and fixing produced a negative, and from this a limitless number of positives could be made by Talbot's earlier process.

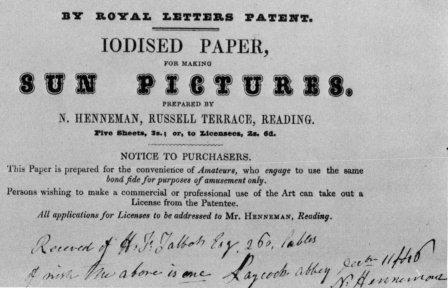

BY ROYAL LETTERS PATENT.

## IODISED PAPER,

FOR MAKING

# SUN PICTURES.

PREPARED BY

### N. HENNEMAN, RUSSELL TERRACE, READING.

**Five Sheets, 3s.; or, to Licensees, 2s. 6d.**

NOTICE TO PURCHASERS.

This Paper is prepared for the convenience of *Amateurs,* who *engage* to use the same *bonâ fide for purposes of amusement only.*

Persons wishing to make a commercial or professional use of the Art can take out a License from the Patentee.

*All applications for Licenses to be addressed to Mr. HENNEMAN, Reading.*

Talbot patented the process but, unlike Daguerre, allowed amateurs free use of it, as is made clear from the packets of 'Iodised Paper' sold in 1846 for making sun-pictures. A notice to purchasers warned that 'this paper is prepared for the convenience of *Amateurs* who *engage* to use the same *bona fide for the purposes of amusement only*. Persons wishing to make commercial or professional use of the Art can take out a License from the Patentee.'

Photography was therefore really born by the early 1840s and for the rest of the decade the story is one of consolidation, explanation and exploitation. But should the application of these simple chemical facts of life be patentable? And, as knowledge increased, would it be practicable to enforce patent restrictions? These were more than purely academic questions as the business of photographic portraiture got into its stride, and while Talbot in effect withdrew most of his patent rights in the early 1850s, he retained their use for commercial portraiture. By this time he had also written the first great classic of photography. In *The Pencil of Nature*, a book in which it is possible to discern a faint trace of the shadow soon to be looming over both artists and book-illustrators, he described and illustrated his early experiments. Many painters had scoffed at the very idea of the objective eye of the camera replacing the subjective eye of the artist. For long it was held that while the painter interpreted, the camera could only portray, an idea belied by the early masterpieces of such photographers as Julia Cameron and decisively refuted by the growth of creative photography during the last third of the 19th century.

In the 1850s photography saw one development even more important than Herschel's discovery that negatives and prints could be fixed by simply soaking them in hypo. This was the collodion process which used glass plates instead of the paper whose texture had been a disadvantage of the calotype. A number of early photographic workers had realized that glass would be an ideal vehicle for the sensitized solution but had failed to discover how this could be made to stick to the glass. Albumen plates prepared with the use of egg white was one solution, but the low sensitivity of these and the long exposures required severely limited their use.

Collodion is a solution of pyroxyline, a kind of gun-cotton, in a mixture of ether and alcohol. When this is poured on to a suitably cleaned glass plate it quickly dries into a thin transparent film. More than one experimenter appears to have considered using it as a basis for photography but it was only in 1851 that Frederick Archer, a sculptor who had been using

Projection of microscopic
dispatches sent out of Paris during
the Siege of 1870

part of photography formed a strong disincentive, and during the two decades that followed Archer's invention many efforts were made to produce a satisfactory dry plate. A Frenchman, J. M. Taupenot, found that if the collodion were coated with a layer of iodized albumen, the plate could be dried and used several weeks later. Other experimenters devised different ways of overcoming the problem presented by the hard surface of the dried collodion, impermeable as it was to the liquid developer. All early efforts foundered on the fact that dry plates were vastly slower than their wet counterparts, in some cases more than a hundred times as slow.

The break-through came in the 1870s with the use of gelatine rather than collodion to hold the sensitizing chemicals. By this time the chemical problems of photography were under constant survey and before the end of the decade dry plates were being made which could be successfully exposed for about 1/25th of a second, the snapshot speed of today's ordinary box camera.

Onward still, and onward still it runs its sticky way
And Gelatine you're bound to use if you mean to make
   things pay
Collodion – slow old fogey! – your palmy days have been
You must give place in future to the plates of Gelatine

wrote the British Journal of Photography's Almanac for 1881.

The overwhelming advantage of satisfactory dry plates was that they could be bought instead of made. When they had been exposed in the camera they could be taken to a specialist for processing. Thus for the first time since Niepce and Talbot had pointed their primitive cameras at the local view, the photographer had become divorced from the chemist. To be successful, a man with a camera had to know the limitations of the materials he was using; for some years yet photographic plates were to lack the uniformity of the mass-production line, and experience of their variations and vicissitudes still helped. But with the arrival of the practicable dry plate, which could be bought from a local shop and taken back there for development when exposed, photography was brought to the edge of the mass-market world.

Only one more development was needed to take it into that world: substitution of the heavy glass plate and its replacement by something lighter and less breakable. The first answer was celluloid, one of the early plastics, invented by Alexander Parkes as far back as 1861, and now coated with a gelatine film. This in turn was quickly replaced by successive developments pioneered by George Eastman, a New York maker of dry plates who in 1888 introduced the Kodak, a word invented by him for its ease of pronunciation in any language, and used to describe the simple camera which was to sweep the world. The new easy-to-use camera was supplied by the factory complete with a roll of film consisting of a gelatino-bromide emulsion on a holding layer of plain gelatine. This was backed by thin paper, soon replaced by a backing much thinner than celluloid. Together with the Kodak itself, the new film provided the basis of the photographic industry as it was to expand during the following century.

A photograph taken in 1888 with the first Kodak camera

The more sensitive emulsions which emerged with the ending of the wet collodion process, and the development of roll films, did more than remove the need for the photographer to be chemist as well: they enabled him to work without a tripod, to hold the camera in his hand. Roll films which occupied little space in his pocket increased his mobility when compared with that of the man forced to carry heavy glass plates. Thus most essentials of the modern photographic world had been created well before the end of the 19th century.

But it was not only the chemists who had been needed. However sensitive they were able to make their photographic plates, there were still three inevitable factors involved in taking a picture. One was the amount of light illuminating the scene to be photographed; another was the efficiency with which this light was transmitted through the lens of the camera; the third was the time during which the light was allowed to fall on the sensitive plate. All three factors were closely linked when it came to photographing moving subjects: the effect of the light on the plate was proportional to its intensity multiplied by the time during which it fell on the plate. The less the intensity, the greater the time for which the shutter would have to be kept open; but the greater this time, the greater the chance that a moving subject would be shown not clear-cut but as a blurred outline – since the image had of course moved on the plate during the fraction of a second during which the picture was being taken.

The use of a lens to concentrate light on to a flat surface had been known since the Middle Ages while methods of dealing with two of a lens' limitations – the formation of an image with coloured fringes due to chromatic aberration, and of a distorted image due to spherical aberration – had been known since the 18th century. The efficiency of such lenses in transmitting light was governed by their diameter and by the distance behind the lens at which they concentrated the light passing through them, and it was found convenient to measure this efficiency by dividing the second distance by the first – the magical 'f' number which decreases as the efficiency of the lens increases. The lenses in the first daguerreotype cameras made for sale had an effective diameter of about 1.1 inches and focused the image on a plate about $15\frac{1}{2}$ inches away, giving a working aperture, as it was called, of about f14. Little more than a year later the Hungarian mathematician Joseph Petzval had designed what is generally accepted to be the first lens produced especially for a camera, one which gave an aperture as large – and as efficient – as f3.5.

With the development of photography after 1840 it was quickly appreciated that certain photographic purposes were served best by certain types of lenses. Speed was only one of the factors involved, and a fast lens suitable for taking portraits might show distortions or aberrations when used for landscape work where a far slower lens might be preferable. Thus from mid-century the evolution of new and more sensitive emulsions, and of more convenient ways of using them, was supplemented by the manufacture of more efficient lenses, this itself being linked with the production of new kinds of glass, and new ways of processing it.

Regulating the time during which the lens allowed light to fall on to the sensitive plate was soon the task of the shutter. In the early days of long exposures, these were made simply by removing a cap or cover from the front of the lens and re-placing it after so many hours or minutes. With the reduction of exposure times first to seconds and then to fractions of a second, something more accurate was required. The answer was given by guillotine shutters, consisting of a plate containing a hole which fell past the lens; by flaps raised or lowered pneumatically; by circular plates with a hole, capable of being rotated at different speeds and therefore of letting through light for different times; and by the shutter which was made up of interleaved blades which could be spring-opened for pre-determined times. There was also the focal plane shutter in which a slit of variable width in a black blind can be made to move across the face of the film or plate.

With the refinement of the shutter there came the variable iris diaphragm, fitted in front of the lens, or sometimes between its individual components. It could be set for any of certain f-numbers, so that whether the diaphragm was opened up – letting in a lot of light and giving a small f-number – or stopped down to provide a big one, it would be possible to work out for how long the shutter should be open to affect, to any agreed extent, a film of any measured sensitivity.

Knowledge of this sensitivity became very necessary as exposures shortened. A minor error in judgment meant little with an exposure of many minutes; it could be ruinous when this was reduced to a fraction of a second. Basically the problem consisted of two halves. First the strength of light in certain specific conditions had to be determined; then it was necessary to assess how much of this light – the 'much' being governed by the size of the lens aperture and the time for which the lens was uncovered – was necessary to affect plates or films of certain speeds. The science of sensitometry, as it was called, was virtually invented by two English workers,

Ferdinand Hurter and Vero Charles Driffield in the last two decades of the 19th century. First they constructed a U-shaped capillary tube filled with a coloured liquid; one of the bulbs was painted red and thus absorbed more light than the other; this brought the liquid in the two arms to different heights and the difference gave a measure of the light-intensity falling on the bulbs. Parallel with scientific measurement of the strength of light there came into existence a large family of devices for showing how lights of differing strengths would affect photographic paper. In the most simple of these a piece of sensitized paper was exposed beneath a series of different-sized holes. From the size of the hole that gave the correct darkening of a test-sheet it was possible to work out the best exposure, and the simple next step was the construction of a calculator, or a set of tables, from which a photographer could find out the correct exposure with a film of any particular speed, under any light conditions.

Refinements of these action meters, tint meters and exposure meters and tables held the field for half a century. Only in the 1930s did they begin to be superseded by meters based on the photo-electric cell. In these the light falling on a selenium or photo-conductive cell automatically swings a pointer to a number from which, with the use of interconnected dials recording film speeds, apertures and shutter speeds, it is possible to gauge exposures for any permutation of conditions.

The last decades of the 19th century removed the worst of the exposure problems; they saw also the development of many different kinds of photography whose seeds had been sown years previously. One, directly linked with fast lenses, shutters and emulsions, was the photography not of the people and cabs of a leisurely world but of birds in flight and racehorses in action. Even before the invention of photography Sir Charles Wheatstone had shown that creation of a bright electric spark in a darkened room 'froze' a moving object as far as spectators were concerned. This principle was used as early as 1851 by Talbot who in a famous experiment in a darkened room attached a page of *The Times* to a rapidly revolving wheel. The lens-cap of his camera was removed, and the wheel lit by a bright electric spark which lasted for only 1/100,000th of a second. The light was brilliant enough, and its duration short enough, to give a sharp image of the revolving page. An alternative to the electric spark was provided from the early 1860s onwards by the intense light of burning magnesium; although its duration was far longer than that of an electric spark its major disadvantage was the cloud of thick smoke

Stereo-photograph of Sir David
Brewster taken by the light of
burning magnesium in March 1864

which accompanied it.

While electric sparks and magnesium were being used to give the intense surge of illumination required for short exposures, complementary efforts were being made to decrease the time for which shutters could be opened when bright sunlight plus a very sensitive plate made this possible. One of the first attempts to solve the problem came from Edward James Muggeridge. He was born in Kingston, Surrey, and renovated his name to Eadweard Muybridge, believing that this was the Anglo-Saxon original. He then emigrated to the United States, and as a photographer went with the official party to Alaska when the Americans bought the territory from Russia in 1868. A few years later Muybridge was hired by an ex-Governor of California to photograph his string of race-horses in action and by an arrangement of spring-released boards managed to take pictures first at 1/500th of a second, later at 1/1,000th and finally at 1/2,000th– pictures which when shown in succession are the genesis of the moving picture.

Shortly afterwards there came E. J. Marey with his photographic gun, a device in which a trigger started a circular glass plate revolving in one direction while a circular metal disc carrying a shutter-hole revolved in the opposite direction. Exposures, which clearly showed the motions of birds in flight, were made only when plate and shutter were moving

Eadweard Muybridge's photograph
of the race-horse in action taken
about 1887

fast, and exposures as fast as 1/25,000th of a second were
finally possible.

Both Muybridge and Marey had built their equipment for
specialist purposes and this was largely true of the other
photographers who from the first years of the 20th century
steadily widened the range of the possible. In the early 1900s
Dr Lucien Bull, anxious to record the wing-beats of small
insects, so arranged his apparatus that an insect emerging
from a closed tube lifted a flap which set in motion a drum on
which film was wound. The drum revolved at 40 revolutions a
second and during each rotation a rotary interruptor fired a
bright spark 54 times. Thus within one second of its emer-
gence the insect had been photographed more than 2,000
times. Multiple lenses mounted on a rotating drum, and
lenses unmasked by a rotating-disc shutter, were later used to
give up to nearly 100,000 pictures a second. More recently the
Kerr Cell, actuated by the momentary application of a high
voltage, allowed exposures of less than one millionth of a
second to be taken of Britain's first atomic explosion.

While the photography of fast-moving subjects demanded
the collaboration of lens-makers, chemists and electrical
experts, the lens-makers themselves, together with the glass-
makers and chemists, were responsible for their own specialist
progress. Lenses which distorted progressively less and which
passed an increasing percentage of the available light were

made throughout the second half of the 19th century, while in
the 1890s J. H. Dallmeyer announced the first telephoto lens.
This was an ingenious arrangement of one convex or positive
lens with a concave or negative lens behind it. The effect was to
give a longer focal length for any particular distance between
lens and film. The size of the image was thus greatly increased
so that the telephoto lens could fill a picture with the weather-
vane on top of a steeple rather than the steeple itself.

High-speed photography, microphotography and tele-
photography were all essentially technical advances. So were
many of the methods by which photographers tried to control
the final effect of light on their medium, although here it was
the photographer-artist rather than artist-photographer who
struggled for improvement. One interesting line of advance
petered out after some decades of popularity, but not before
fathering a family of methods by which prints of quite excep-
tional beauty could be made. These were the various pigment
processes, most of which sprang from the fact that Talbotype
prints, and to a lesser extent the prints made by subsequent
processes, tended to fade. Would it not be possible, it was
argued, to produce an image not in silver but in a permanent
pigment?

A clue to the answer had been found in 1839 by Mungo
Ponton who discovered that when gelatine sensitized with
potassium bichromate was exposed to light it became hard and
insoluble in warm water. As early as the mid-1850s bichromated gelatine containing powdered carbon had been exposed
under a negative and then developed in water which removed
the carbon in the soluble gelatine but left the rest. The process
was developed by more than one worker, but failed to bring
out the half-tones from a negative. It was thus left to Sir
Joseph Swan, inventor of the incandescent lamp, to patent the
carbon process, in which a carbon tissue comprising a layer of
bichromated gelatine on a holding paper is first exposed
through a negative. The exposed surface of the tissue is then
attached to transfer paper, the holding paper is soaked off in
warm water and as the water attacks the unhardened gelatine
the print is revealed in pigment on the transfer paper. Many
variations of this original pigment process were developed
during the last year of the 19th century, but Swan's carbon
process was the most popular, more than 50 different kinds of
transfer at one time being made by the Autotype Company
which bought Swan's patents.

One of the early disappointments about photography had
been its inability to portray people or scenes in colour.
Niepce had confided to his brother how much he wanted to

High-speed photograph of a
dragon fly in flight taken at about
1/2000 of a second by Dr Lucien
Bull in the early 1900s

'fix the colours'. Daguerre and Talbot after him had written in much the same vein and throughout the second half of the 19th century there was a constant succession of photographers or would-be photographers who claimed to have found a way of solving this apparently insoluble problem. Some were optimists but some were charlatans and as late as 1891 *Chambers Encyclopaedia* could state: 'The report that the art of photographing in the colours of nature has been discovered crops up year after year with curious persistency, and may be generally traced to the work of unscrupulous persons who seek to deceive the public for their own advantage. Moreover,' it went on, 'it is difficult to see how the much-talked-of photography in colours as popularly understood can ever be achieved.' The 'as popularly understood' adds the necessary air of vagueness to the statement; but it was in general terms quite true and was to remain so until advances in technology allowed the problem to be solved many years later.

Long before the invention of photography it had been known that white light was made up of three primary colours, a fact which at first led some early practitioners to believe that the problems of colour photography might be solved without undue trouble. What they failed to appreciate – quite

Dr Lucien Bull and the spark drum camera, 1904

apart from the technical problems – was that the sensitive photographic plate or film responded only to some of the colours in the spectrum. Almost all early emulsions were affected only by colours in the narrow blue-violet part of the colour band: the films 'saw' the world differently from humans, a fact which explains the bare featureless white skies of many early landscapes.

The 'first colour photograph' – although hardly one 'as popularly understood' – is generally considered to have been produced by James Clerk Maxwell in 1861. Maxwell had a Scottish tartan ribbon photographed three times on three separate plates, the first time through a filter provided by a blue liquid held in a glass cell, the second time through a green filter and the third time through a red. The three resulting negatives – colour separation negatives as they were soon called – were used to make three separate lantern slides. The slides were then thrown at the same time on to a screen, that taken through the blue filter being projected with blue light, and the second and third with green and red light respectively. The resulting colour image produced by adding together the three primary colours of red, green and blue, was primitive but successful, and during the following years variations of the system were developed by a number of men. Each involved the taking of three separate photographs through different coloured filters, one of the earliest ways of doing this being with the help of a repeating back which could be fitted to an ordinary camera. Thus one-third of a photographic plate was photographed through a red filter. The process was repeated on the next third through a green filter. It was then slid along yet again, and the process repeated once more through a blue filter. An improvement was the beam-splitting colour camera, developed about the turn of the century, using two semi-reflectors set at 45° to the incoming light beam, which was reflected at the first mirror to give a red beam and at the second to give blue. Green was recorded directly. In this ingenious way one exposure could provide three separation negatives. The result of all these devices, however, still had to be projected in a darkened room or looked at through a viewing apparatus.

Attempts to overcome this disadvantage were made as early as 1869 by Louis Ducos du Hauron, who in *Les Couleurs en Photographie, Solution du Problème*, described how prints could be made by the subtractive process. Here the exposures were first made through filters complementary to the primary colours – magenta (minus green), blue-green (minus red) and yellow (minus blue). From the three negatives, prints were

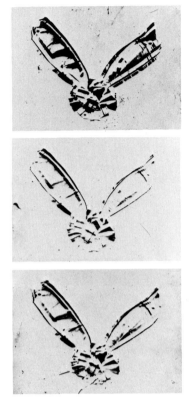

*Additive colour photography.* The first colour photograph was produced in 1861 for a demonstration at the Royal Institution by the physicist James Clerk Maxwell. *Above* The three negatives made by Clerk Maxwell of the tartan ribbon through three liquid filters, blue, green and red in colour (top to bottom: blue, green, red).

1 Subject
2 Blue filter
3 Green filter
4 Red filter
5 Camera
6 Blue filter negative
7 Green filter negative
8 Red filter negative
9 Blue filter positive
10 Green filter positive
11 Red filter positive
12 Projectors
13 Positives
14 Filters
15 Screen with image
16 Clerk Maxwell's first colour photograph

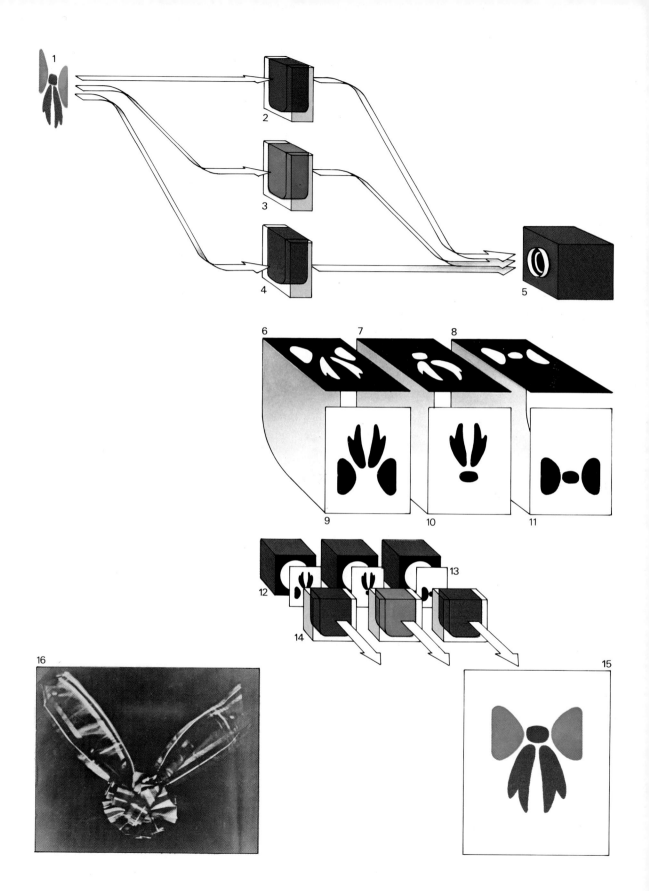

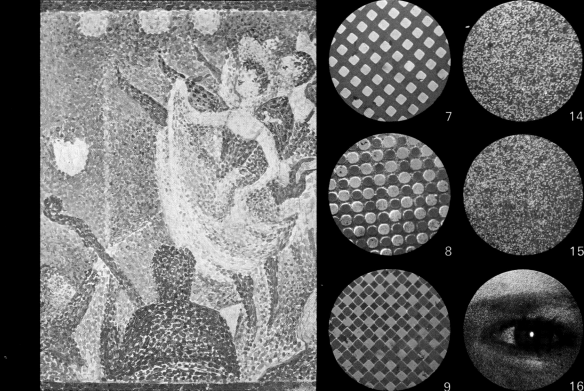

7

14

8

15

9

16

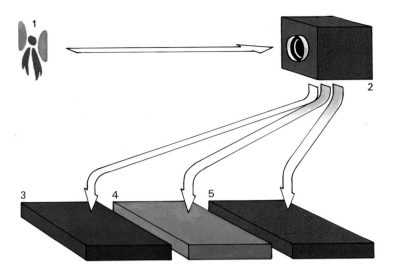

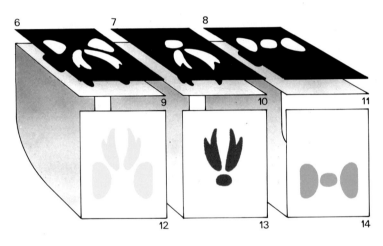

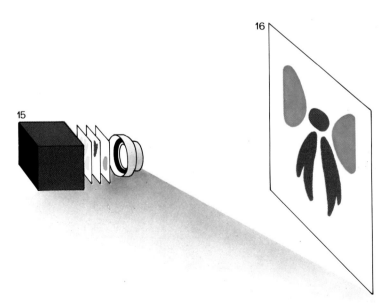

then made on to the three gelatine sheets containing carbon pigments of red, blue and yellow. When the three sheets were mounted together the result was a colour picture – a transparency if the mount was of glass and a print if the mount was of paper.

Ducos du Hauron, like other experimenters of his period, a number of whom produced roughly comparable systems, was handicapped by the response of the photographic emulsions to the colours of the spectrum, so different from those of the human eye. Not until 1873 did Hermann Vogel, a German chemist, find that if the collodion plate were bathed in a certain aniline dye, its sensitivity to green would be increased. Other experimenters went to work, gradually widening the band of the spectrum which would affect the plates. The red end was the last to succumb: only in the first years of the 20th century, following research by I. G. Farben, the German dyestuffs company, was the first plate put on the market which was sensitive to red as well.

However, it was merely one stage, although an important one, in the constant improvement of photographic emulsions throughout the last hundred years. Plates and film were soon made sensitive to infra-red rays at one end of the visible spectrum and to ultra-violet and X-rays at the other. The speed of films was pushed constantly upwards while at the same time the graininess of the emulsions – the size of the individual grains of silver which can adversely affect the print – was steadily reduced.

None of this work, which gradually brought the photographic print more into line with man's accepted view of things, did much to bring nearer the day of the genuine colour photograph. However, it did mean that a panchromatic plate sensitive to all the visible colours was available when means for utilizing it in colour photography at last appeared.

The means were a curious technological adaptation of the method used by the *pointillistes*, painters of the French Impressionist school who achieved their results by using a mass of intermingled coloured points which were merged by the human eye when viewed from the right distance. This principle was utilized by exposing a photographic plate behind a mosaic of extremely small multi-coloured filter elements. When the resulting positive was looked at through a similar screen, a colour picture was seen. The first such process, developed during the closing years of the 19th century, used a screen consisting of fine lines of the primary colours ruled some 200 to the inch on the plate. But this was superseded within a few years by the Autochrome plates which from 1907 onwards were manufactured by the Lumière brothers in France. The plates were first covered with a thin layer of extremely fine starch grains which had previously been dyed green, red or blue, and then been thoroughly mixed. Over this starch layer there was then spread a thin panchromatic emulsion. The emulsion was exposed through the starch grains, each of which acted as an individual colour filter. After development, the plate was re-exposed and re-developed, the result being a colour transparency made up of small grains of the primary colours, the colours being blended by the human eye. For some three decades Autochrome held the field despite the long exposures which its use demanded. Other processes, both additive and subtractive were put on the market, but all failed. Most were unsatisfactory, too expensive, or both.

Then, in the 1930s, the practicability of making extremely thin multi-layer films was married up to the principle of dye-coupling, discovered by Rudolf Fischer in 1912, to produce two very similar films, one made by Kodak the other by Agfa. Both incorporated a triple layer of film whose layers were sensitive to blue, green and red light respectively. After exposure the film was developed, the remaining silver bromide in each layer re-exposed, and the film then re-developed in chemicals that left dye of yellow, cyan or magenta on the three emulsions wherever the silver bromide was turned to silver. All that then remained to be done was for the silver to be bleached away to reveal a bright transparency.

Some years later the next step was taken. It was found possible to convert each of the three emulsions to an image complementing the colour which it recorded. The result was a colour negative unrecognizable by comparison with the original scene, since the negative was in complementary colours, but one from which any number of prints could be made by repeating the process with the use of the same emulsion on a white base.

All these developments had taken the photographer further and further away from the pioneers. He no longer needed to be an able laboratory technician,. competent to handle a number of chemicals; but his choice of lenses, which could offer differing extents of the picture he wished to portray, the wide variety of films from which he could take his pick, and the options offered by lightmeters which suggested how many different pictures might be conjured out of one scene, tended to make him a different kind of technician. The caricature of the photographer begirt with dangling accessories has the truth of all good caricatures. Almost as important as the

Making an instant microscope picture using the Polaroid Land Instrument camera: *Top left* attaching the universal adapter to the microscope and framing the subject. *Top right* placing the focusing tube over the universal adapter and eyepiece, and fine focusing. *Bottom left* placing the camera over the universal adapter and making the exposure. *Bottom right* peeling the finished $3\frac{1}{4}$ by $4\frac{1}{4}$ inch print from its packet after 60 seconds.

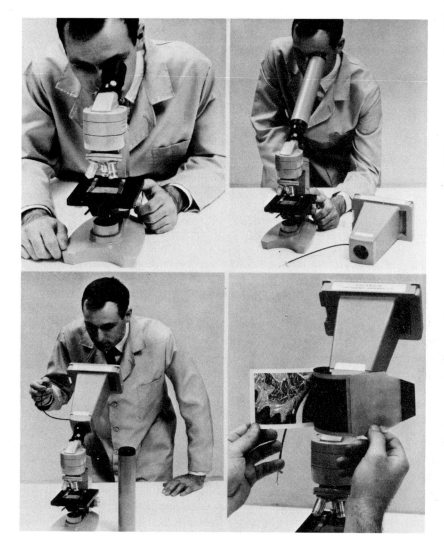

technological barrier which had tended to rise between the photographer and his subject was the long delay between the clicking of the shutter and the first sight of the result. Daguerre, developing his plate and watching the image harden up while his sitter was still on the premises, could see immediately what he had created. Even Bisson on Mont Blanc, plagued as he was by all sorts of problems, could at least set up his camera at a better view-point if his first plate showed it to be necessary. Now the most adept photographer had to wait for the result at least until he got home and it was too late for him to try again.

All this was altered with the introduction of the Polaroid-Land process, invented by Edwin H. Land in 1947 and imaginatively developed during the following years. The

Polaroid camera produces black-and-white or colour prints a few seconds after they have been taken. When Land demonstrated his new system to the Royal Photographic Society in London he said: 'In the earlier arts the artist initiates his activity by observing his subject matter and then responds, as he proceeds, to a two-fold stimulus: the original subject matter and his own growing but uncompleted work. With photography, except for those who combine a long training, high technical ability, and splendid imagination, this important kind of double stimulus – original subject and partly finished work – cannot exist. Consequently, for most people it has been of limited and sporadic interest and has not been a source of deep artistic satisfaction, and there has arisen a gulf between the majority who make snapshots as a record and as a gamble, and the minority who can reveal beauty in the medium. . . .'

The Polaroid system which bridged this gulf, responding with invention to an under-tow of public demand, utilized processing agents in jelly form, held in pods inside the camera. After a film had been exposed it was pulled slowly from the camera. During this operation the unexposed silver salts, normally dissolved and washed away by the hypo, were transferred to a receiving sheet and turned into silver by the developer. Negative and positive emerged together and the positive was peeled from the negative in daylight.

In early models of the Polaroid camera, only this one-off positive was possible, but in little more than 25 years the system has been adapted so that in addition to the positive there is also a negative from which enlargements can be made in the normal way. In addition, a multi-layer colour film has been developed with emulsions carrying yellow, cyan and magenta dyes which are diffused on to the positive as the film is withdrawn from the camera.

At first sight the Polaroid camera has a gimmick value. But it also has far more, a considerable use for architects, surveyors, scientists and many other professional men needing on-the-spot notes. It has also, a fact not commonly appreciated, restored to the artist-photographer the ability to amend and correct on the easel that became the ground-glass screen. In some ways the instant picture camera has given back to the human brain the ability to guide Talbot's 'Pencil of Nature' in a manner that is entirely new. It has also, by making instantly available as well as permanent the scenes which Wedgwood and others had hoped to record in fixed form in their early apparatus, brought photography back full-circle, technologically equipped, to the place where it can satisfy the operational demand.

# 2 Man Takes to the Air

At first glance, successful powered flight during the first years of the 20th century was a direct result of the petrol engine, the comparatively small package which for the first time produced enough power per pound weight to keep a heavier-than-air machine aloft. In fact, it was the outcome of something more complicated.

Men had dreamed of flight since they first watched and envied the birds, wheeling and soaring with a freedom denied to the earthbound; since earliest times the more adventurous

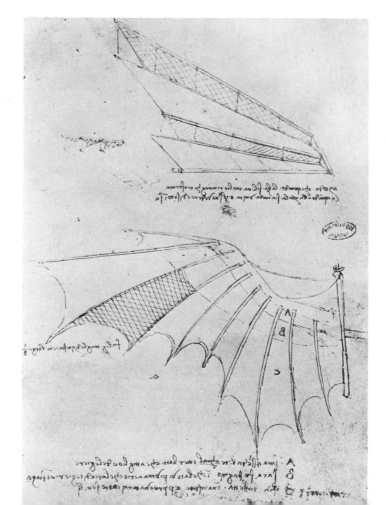

Diagram of ribbed wing, partly covered by silk, by Leonardo da Vinci, about 1486–90

had tried to make the dream come true. Icarus, building wings of feathers cemented with wax but flying so close to the sun that the wax melted, was merely one legend handed down the years and epitomizing the brave men who had leaped from high towers with contraptions strapped to their backs but failed to fly. These adventurers were paralleled by thinkers such as Roger Bacon and Leonardo da Vinci who with greater or lesser success studied the birds, started to work out the principles of flight, and thought up imaginary schemes for translating principles into practice.

The details of these would-be aeronauts are scanty in the extreme. Myth and near-myth are mixed with fantasy. Soldiers quickly grasp how aircraft can be used for bombardment. The physicist Robert Hooke provides a passing reference to the principle of the helicopter. The Swede Emanuel Swedenborg speculates on the possibility of a flying machine. Men continue to watch the birds, and a few of them make models which they hope will imitate flight. Yet there are few links between thought and experiment. In many ways they can be compared to the isolated mountaineering ascents made by a few enthusiasts in the Middle Ages, burning up brightly for only a short while before sputtering out. Not until the latter half of the 18th century does there begin one line of development which was to carry on, without break, towards manned flight more than a century later.

The line was started by the Montgolfier brothers, Joseph Michel and Jacques-Étienne. Intrigued by the idea of Joseph Priestley's 'inflammable air' – later called hydrogen – the Montgolfiers decided to use the gas to raise an airship. The plan failed. But a few years later, on 21 November 1783 the Montgolfiers were in Paris, standing in the gardens of the Royal Château de la Muette in the Bois de Boulogne, watching the inflation with hot air of their giant blue and gold balloon, 50 feet around, 85 feet high. The two men with them, a young doctor, Pilâtre de Rozier, and an infantry major, the Marquis d'Arlandes, climbed into the round passenger car held beneath the airship. A few minutes before two o'clock the ropes were cast off and the balloon, filled by hot air from a fire-grate on which a mixture of wool and straw was burning, sailed up into the Paris skies carrying the world's first aeronauts.

During the next hundred years many men followed the intrepid doctor and major. Balloon ascents in Britain and the United States soon became popular. In 1785 the English Channel was crossed and in 1804 a manned balloon reached a height of 23,000 feet. First hydrogen and then coal gas were used to give lifting power, and both provided greater control

Jean-Pierre Blanchard's balloon crossing the English Channel, 7 January 1785

Mr. Blanchard accompagné de Mr. Gefferies est parti de Douvres à 1 heure precise, il toucha la terre aux environs de Blanay qui est situé entre Calais et Boulogne. C'est le premier qui jouit de l'honneur d'avoir franchi dans un Aerostat le Détroit qui sépare la France a l'Angleterre. Ce fut le vendredi 7 de Janvier 1785 qu'il partit traversa la mer et arriva à 3 heures sur les Côtes de la Pétridie, laissant Calais à une lieue sur la gauche. Il prit terre 3 quarts d'heures après à 2 lieues et demie du rivage ou il fut reçu dans le Château de Mr. d'Honnolam fils. Le même soir après souper les Voyageurs furent conduits à Calais dans une

*Left* Balloon contest at Hurlingham 15 July 1912

*Right* Pilâtre de Rozier and the Marquis d'Arlandes make the first air voyage in history beneath a hot-air balloon sent up from the Château de la Muette in the Bois de Boulogne on 21 November 1783. They travelled the five miles to Paris and landed without injury.

than the uncertainties of a fire. Meteorological records began to be taken among the clouds. Methods of releasing gas from the balloon to make it sink, or dumping ballast to make it rise, were developed. These advances took some of the dare-devil adventure out of ballooning. Ladies made ascents and during the 1800s ballooning became an almost popular sport. Thus when powered flight in heavier-than-air machines became a possibility at the beginning of the 20th century some of the psychological barriers in the competition with birds had already been broken down.

Even so, the balloon was still at the mercy of the winds. It went only where they blew, and it was to alter this state of affairs that men began to experiment with the idea of attaching power units to the lighter-than-air vehicles. Earliest on the scene was Henri Giffard who in 1852 constructed the first genuine 'airship', 'dirigible' or 'controlled balloon' as the machines were later to be variously called. Giffard powered his craft with a steam engine. He was followed, two decades on, by P. Haelin whose airship was driven by a gas engine. Ten years later there came Gaston Tissandier whose slim contrivance, more than 90 feet long, was driven through the air by a screw-propeller driven by a battery-run four-speed electric motor. And in 1896 the German Dr Wolfert used a Daimler internal combustion engine to drive his airship.

From the start it was realized that if a lighter-than-air craft was to be steered through the air, then the circular shape of the balloon would have to be abandoned. During the second half of the 19th century the airship therefore evolved into a long cylinder, the shape of the Zeppelin which was to win notoriety in the First World War and to remain the typical airship shape until the story of the craft was abruptly halted, if not finally killed, by a series of disasters during the 1920s and 1930s.

THE LONDON TO MANCHESTER FLIGHT
DRAWN FOR LONDON & NORTH WESTERN RAILWAY

*Left above* An artist's impression of the 'Aerial Steam Carriage', whose designs were prepared by W. S. Henson in 1842. The model for it was unsuccessful when tested five years later.
*Left below* Louis Paulhan flying a Henry Farman biplane over the London and North Western Railway during the London–Manchester Air Race in April, 1910

*Right* The German zeppelin 'Viktoria Luise' over Kiel Harbour in 1912

Balloons and then airships carried men up into the clouds, and above them. They helped dispel the fear of the unknown which had so constantly been leaning over the shoulder of the first aeronauts. What they did not do was tell men so very much more about the principles of flight which birds used unconsciously and which men would also have to use if they were to fly as and when they wished, rather than with the by-your-leave of the winds.

A great many of these principles had in fact been discovered by one of the geniuses of the 19th century, a man whose real importance has been revealed only during the last few decades. He was Sir George Cayley, a Yorkshire baronet born in 1773 and fascinated ten years later by the story of Montgolfier's flight. Cayley's practical achievements were extraordinary. He built and flew a man-carrying glider, suggested that an internal combustion engine might be the ideal power-unit for aircraft, designed an elementary under-carriage, and used models to test his theoretical ideas.

Even more important – or at least potentially important – he appreciated the basic requirements of heavier-than-air flight. Cayley realized that before a heavier-than-air machine could become airborne it would have to be drawn or thrust forward so that there was a movement of air across an aero-foil or wing; furthermore, this would have to be of such a shape that the airflow across its upper and lower surfaces would create different pressures above and below and thereby

Sir George Cayley's man-carrying glider ('governable parachute') shown in *Mechanics Magazine*, September 1852

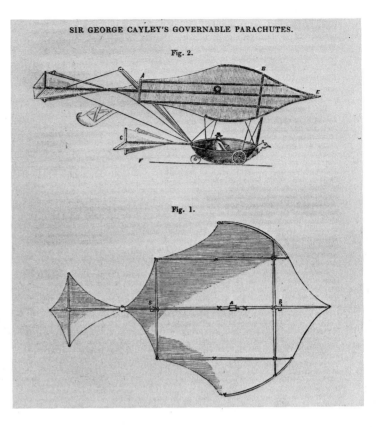

SIR GEORGE CAYLEY'S GOVERNABLE PARACHUTES.

Fig. 2.

Fig. 1.

produce 'lift', the component of the aerodynamic forces which supports an aircraft in flight. Cayley left a sketch showing a single-wing glider on which the lines of lift, thrust and drag, the last being the aircraft's resistance to movement through the air, were all marked.

During the early 1850s at least one and possibly two of Cayley's heavier-than-air gliders took people aloft, the 'lift' being created when the gliders were towed against a slight wind. The first person to be airborne in this heavier-than-air machine was a young and unidentified boy. The second was Cayley's coachman who is reported, possibly apocryphally, to have said after he landed: 'Sir George, I wish to give notice. I was hired to drive, not to fly.'

Cayley died in 1857, before his ideas for a mechanically-propelled aircraft could be tested. But they had already been taken one step further in theory by W. S. Henson – who as early as 1842 had designed an 'aerial steam carriage', a model of which failed to fly five years afterwards – and later by his colleague John Stringfellow. Henson's craft had more than one feature of aircraft to come. His main wing had the cambered profile which it was already known should produce greater lift than a flat surface, while a tail wing with horizontal

and vertical surfaces was similar to that on conventional aircraft two-thirds of a century later. Stringfellow, having built his own monoplane, then constructed a model which followed Cayley's principle of utilizing as great a wing-surface as possible, a triplane whose design did much to influence later inventors.

Henson and Stringfellow, like many would-be aeronauts who succeeded them, were held back by one thing: the steam-engine, then the only means of getting power, was too heavy for the lift which it provided. This disadvantage was only overcome in 1894 when Sir Hiram Maxim used a 320-pound steam-engine to power a tethered test-rig plane with an all-up weight of about 8,000 pounds. As the lift achieved was 10,000 pounds the vital lift-to-weight ratio had been balanced in favour of flight. But Maxim's experiments were suspended. Whether or not his huge and ungainly craft would ever have become successfully airborne is very questionable. In any case the petrol engine was by this time waiting in the wings.

However, before the petrol engine took over, the initiative was to pass for a few years to the gliding enthusiasts, to the Lilienthal brothers in Germany, to Octave Chanute in the United States and to Percy Pilcher in Britain. This was as well.

The model of John Stringfellow's monoplane, the predecessor of his triplane which influenced later inventors

Sir Hiram Maxim's steam-driven
aircraft, built in Kent in the 1890s

Despite the foundations which had been so well laid by
Cayley, the art or craft of aeronautics, the practical business of
keeping a craft stable in the air, was imperfectly understood
until the last decade of the 19th century. It is conceivable that
had the petrol engine been developed only a few years earlier
it might have been utilized not with the spectacular success of
the Wright brothers but in a series of disasters which would
have put back the development of flight a decade or more.
Here perhaps is one of the question-marks of history: if flight
had come too late to be given the spur or operational need
engendered by the First World War, what would its subsequent history have been?

The Lilienthals were the most important of the men who in
the closing years of the century helped to solve the practical
problems of stable flight. They came from Anklam, a small
town on the huge plain that stretches north of Berlin, only a
few miles inland from the Baltic and a staging post for the
thousands of storks who every spring would arrive from their
African homes for a long summer visit. The storks left in the
autumn, circling in scores above the roof-tops, rising higher
and higher until the whole flock would at last wheel and turn
south for Africa.

It was in studying the storks that the Lilienthal boys
learned one of their first lessons about flight. 'It was obvious,'
Gustav later wrote in describing how he and his brother had
tried to approach the birds in the meadows beyond the town,
'that it was easier to rise against the wind than with the wind,
because without some compelling cause the shy bird would
not advance towards us.'

In an effort to emulate the storks the Lilienthals built their own wings, six foot by three foot affairs which they hoped would make them airborne as they ran downhill. They failed, as they failed again a few years later in a more ambitious attempt to fly with home-made wings. Only in the 1870s, when they had started work in Berlin, Otto Lilienthal as an engineer, his brother Gustav as a small businessman, did the brothers build their first real flying machine. This had three pairs of wings; all could be moved up and down by an operator pedalling bicycle-wise. In addition, the contraption incorporated an ingenious device which enabled air to pass through the wings on the upstroke but arrested it on the down-beat. Perhaps most important of all, the Lilienthals supported their machine by rope and pulley and found that with the aid of only 40 pounds at the other end of the rope they could raise the 180-pound weight of their loaded machine by energetic pedalling. This was a scientific answer to the amount of lift required – even though it seemed to rule out any hope that man could ever fly by his own unaided efforts.

This first, and unsuccessful, phase of their efforts was ended by the Franco-Prussian War. The second, which covered the building of further wing-beating flying machines, was no more successful. One machine, whose wings were moved by spiral springs, was launched from a fourth-floor window down an inclined plane. Another had wings built in as close facsimile as could be to an actual bird's wing. 'They were moved partly by springs, partly by steam power,' Otto later wrote. 'We succeeded in making them fly freely at various speeds, but we did not succeed in establishing what we really wanted. We could not prove that forward flight saves work.'

Both men were now approaching middle age. Then they separated, Gustav emigrating to Australia and not returning to Germany until 1886. But both continued to think about flying. The permanent refusal of the born inventor to accept failure kept nagging away at them. On the ship to Australia Gustav had studied the albatross, marvelling at its skill in gliding through the rigging with only an inch or two to spare. In Germany, Otto had continued to study the storks, 'our constant models' as he called them, and had started to keep the birds as pets.

And now, as the 1890s approached, the two brothers re-united and began their decisive work. In 1889 they published what was to become one of the most important of all books on flying, *Bird-flight as the Basis of Aviation*. The titles of its chapters – *The Force Which Lifts the Bird in Flight*, *The Energy Required for Wing Motion*, and *The Wings Considered as Levers* – indicate its nature. The Lilienthals had realized one thing: that although man could not produce enough lift by beating wings with his own efforts, he could run or jump into a headwind and create enough lift on a pair of stationary wings to get him off the ground. Once in the air, he might be able to keep head-on into the wind and continue gaining height; lose it by turning out of the wind; then gain it again by turning into it once again.

Some of the first experiments with this new technique were made with a 40-pound wing of more than 100 square feet strapped to Otto's back. With this he would run along an inclined board and leap off the end into the air. 'King of the air in calm weather,' was how he described the state of the art after some hundreds of experiments.

But this was only one stage. Both men were now comparatively well-off. So much so that they were able to have a special hill built for their experiments at the Reinersdorfer Brickworks outside Berlin. Fifty feet high, the hill was crowned by the shed in which the brothers kept their wings, and by experimenting here when the wind was strong enough they found that they could become airborne for as much as 100 yards.

The next move came in 1895. In that year the Lilienthals moved out to the Rhinow Hills whose heather-broken slopes rise for 250 feet near the little town of Rathenau on the River Havel. Here improved versions of their gliders – for the early wings soon developed into something identifiable as such – did not merely become airborne. They flew 250 feet, 500 feet, eventually more than 1,000 feet. The brothers stayed in the air, under control, for as long as a quarter of a minute and when the air currents were right they were even taken up higher than their launching-point. Man was now 'flying' for the first time in the heavier-than-air machine.

Otto Lilienthal, immaculately-clad in white knicker-bockers, controlled his machines mainly by swinging his body from side to side, changing the glider's centre of gravity and, thereby, the effect on it of the headwind. This primitive method was eventually improved. There was, for instance, a form of crude elevator, to which Lilienthal was attached by a harness. By lowering his head, he could raise the elevator and cause the plane to sink. Neither was this all. 'I am now engaged in building an apparatus in which the position of the wings can be changed during flight in such a way that the balance is not affected by changing the position of the centre of gravity of the body,' he wrote in April 1896. 'In my opinion this means considerable progress, as it will increase the

safety. This will probably cause me to give up the double sailing surface as it will do away with the reason for adopting it.'

By this time the Lilienthals had shown that manned flight was possible, given the movement of air across an aerofoil. So far the flyer depended entirely on the winds, but the petrol engine was now beginning to offer the chance of an aircraft being pushed or pulled through the still air – a process which would of itself generate lift since it was immaterial whether the air was moving over the aerofoil or the aerofoil was moving through the air.

Otto Lilienthal was in fact considering the addition of an engine when, in August 1896, he made his last flight. Once again, he sailed out from his launching site on the Rhinow

One of the last flights of Otto Lilienthal, made in 1895

Hills. But when the wind dropped the glider did not, as usual, sink gradually; for some reason that was never discovered it plunged to the ground. Lilienthal died from his injuries the following day, after significant last words: 'Sacrifices must be made.'

In England Percy Pilcher, who was in correspondence with the Lilienthals, made a number of successful gliding flights, developing his machine by the addition of tail plane and undercarriage until it began to look like the early powered aircraft which were to come a decade or more later. In the latter half of the 1890s he was, like the Lilienthals, preparing to add a petrol engine. Then in 1899, having been towed off the ground by a team of horses near Market Harborough, Pilcher crashed and was killed.

Meanwhile in America Octave Chanute, a successful railway engineer, was also experimenting. Like Lilienthal, whose designs formed the basis of his early gliders, Chanute became convinced that movement of the body was no way in which to alter the aerodynamic characteristics of an aircraft; instead, he proposed wing-warping, changing the shape or camber of the wing by pulling on wires or strings. Chanute, who was in his 60s, flew only rarely but in 1896 and 1897 his colleagues made more than 1,000 successful glider flights from a launching site outside Chicago.

Thus in the final years of the century only one thing was needed for powered flight: a successful marriage between the glider and a power-pack that would produce sufficient lift for its weight. This was to be consummated by the Wright brothers, two young men from Dayton, Ohio, who as the 20th century approached prepared for their appointment with history.

Octave Chanute's 1896 glider being tested on the shore of Lake Michigan with A. M. Herring, a fellow engineer, as pilot

Wilbur Wright was born in 1867, his brother Orville four years later. They were of the pioneering American generation, ready and able to turn their hand to anything. Orville bought a printing press and started his own business while still in his teens. His brother, not to be outdone, launched his own weekly paper and the following year Orville, going still one better, started a daily paper with a third brother. Yet a third newspaper was later published by the family who shortly afterwards started the Wright Cycle Company and devised and put on the market the 'Van Cleve' bicycle, named after one of their mother's ancestors who had arrived in America two hundred years previously.

What lines this irrepressibly fecund family might have followed but for the attraction of flight no one can tell. But the catalyst came in 1896 with the death of Otto Lilienthal. News of the accident arrived on the telegraph which served the Wrights' papers. Then Wilbur, learning that Lilienthal's success had started with his study of bird-flight, took down from the shelves of his home library a copy of *Animal Mechanism*. Written by the Professor Marey whose photographic gun had first revealed the wing-movements of gulls, *Animal Mechanism* stimulated the Wrights to ask the age-old question: if a bird's body can be supported by wings, why cannot a man's?

For three years they studied all the information they could lay their hands on. Then they wrote to the Smithsonian Institute in Washington, which they found was also scientifically investigating the possibilities of flight, and were put in touch with its Secretary, Samuel Langley, whose steam-powered models were already making flights of more than three-quarters of a mile. But Langley, who can claim the first sustained powered flight with *un*manned heavier-than-air machines, was unable to scale up his work before the Wrights had leap-frogged into the lead.

The two brothers quickly saw that better control in the air should be achieved before the problem of lift-to-weight ratio was successfully tackled. Like the Lilienthals, they turned to the birds. But whereas it was storks who had given the Germans the essential clue to 'lift', it was the humble pigeon who suggested to the Wrights the form of aeronautical control which Otto Lilienthal was possibly contemplating at the time of his death. Pigeons, the two brothers noticed, would sometimes oscillate their bodies rapidly from side to side, tilting one wing up and another down, then rapidly reversing the process. 'These lateral tiltings first one way and then the other, were repeated four or five times rapidly,' Wilbur later said; 'so

The Wright brothers' no. 2 glider
at the Kill Devil Hills in 1901

rapidly, in fact, as to indicate that some other force than gravity was at work. The method of drawing in one wing or the other, as described by Chanute and Louis Mouillard, was, of course, dependent in principle on the action of gravity, but it seemed certain that these alternate tiltings of the pigeon were more rapid than gravity would cause, especially in view of the fact that we could not detect any drawing-in first of one wing and then of another.'

They concluded that pigeons exercised control by using the dynamic reactions of the air rather than by shifting the centre of gravity. At first they proposed copying this by the use of what were later called ailerons, trailing flaps on the wings which could be raised or lowered by wires. As this was found to be too mechanically difficult in the current state of the art, they investigated wing-warping, as Chanute was also investigating it.

The method was tested on a model kite and found to work.

The next step was to try it out on a man-carrying craft, an experiment which the Wrights realized would demand a strong headwind if sufficient lift were to be created. Their chosen site, picked after taking advice from the US Weather Bureau, was on the coast adjoining Kitty Hawk, an isolated fishing-village standing on a long sandy spit thrusting into the Atlantic from the mainland of North Carolina. Kitty Hawk was some 800 miles from the Wrights' home in Ohio, and their first journey took them a week during which a railway trip was followed by a steamer-voyage, followed by a small-boat trip, followed by a four-mile walk.

To the lonely testing-ground on the sandhills the brothers brought in the summer of 1900 the sections of their man-carrying glider which they then assembled on the spot. The results were satisfying if unspectacular. 'These experiments,' Wilbur later said of the flights, 'constituted the first instance in the history of the world that wings adjustable to different angles of incidence on the right and left sides had been used in attempting to control the balance of an aeroplane. We had functionally used them both when flying at the end of a rope and also in free flight.'

The following year they were back again, and this time they were visited at Kitty Hawk by Octave Chanute. They glided more than 300 feet and they made numerous alterations to the machine which was kept in a small wooden hangar. But their attempts to stabilize the craft were less successful than the previous year and they returned home disillusioned. 'When we left Kitty Hawk at the end of 1901,' Wilbur later said, 'we doubted that we would ever resume our experiments. Although we had broken the record for distance in gliding, so far as any actual figures had been published, and although Mr Chanute, who was present for part of the time, assured us that our results were better than had ever before been attained, yet when we looked at the time and money which we had expended, and considered the progress made and the distance yet to go, we considered our experiments a failure. At this time I made the prediction that men would some time fly, but that it would not be within our lifetime.'

But now luck took a hand. Or, more accurately, a chance suggestion came at the right moment of technological progress; the suggestion was made, moreover, to men who despite their apparent pessimism, still nourished that reluctance to accept defeat which is the hallmark of the pioneer down the ages.

Chanute proposed that Wilbur should lecture on his problems to the Western Society of Engineers in Chicago.

Wilbur agreed, somewhat reluctantly, but decided that he would first have to check many facts and figures. To carry out the checking he built in his Dayton workshop one of the first wind tunnels to be built in the United States, six feet long, only 16 by 16 inches in section, and equipped with various devices for holding different aerofoils in the stream of air which could be pumped through it.

In this apparatus the Wrights now tested more than 200 different kinds of aerofoil, keeping accurate results of exactly what happened.

And once the two brothers had accumulated their long columns of figures showing how different shapes reacted to different conditions, one thing became obvious: they had to test their fresh information. Thus it was back once more to Kitty Hawk, on its windswept spit of land where the US National Monument now stands.

They arrived at their former camp-site on 25 August. With them, prepared for assembly, were the parts of a biplane 32 feet from wing-tip to wing-tip. This glider – for they had not yet tackled the problem of power – had a front rudder, a vertical tail plane consisting of two parallel sections, and a wing-warping device which was operated through a harness worn by the pilot.

Throughout September and October the craft was dragged up one of three hills on the dunes – 30-foot Little Hill, 60-foot West Hill or the 100-foot Big Hill. At the top they would wait until the wind blew strongly enough. Then the brother holding down the plane would let go and the glider would sail into the wind, gaining height as it did so. More than 700 flights were successfully made. More important, the wing-warping mechanism did give better control than before.

The Wrights had, moreover, built in one major innovation before they left Kitty Hawk in the autumn. They had replaced the double tail-fin by a single fin which could be turned left or right as the wing-warping mechanism was operated. Previously, wing-warping had produced its own difficulties, but the Wrights now found that if the fin was moved as one of the wings was warped, then the result was to take the glider round left or right in a smooth turn. They had therefore not merely solved the problem of balance in the air but the riddle of how to turn away from the headwind, left or right.

These experiments of the late summer and autumn of 1902 marked a turning-point. Previously, it is clear, the brothers had looked on their flights as an adventurous hobby. Now, out of the future, they saw the beckoning shadow of man piloting himself through Tennyson's central blue. They saw also the potentials of the dream and quickly applied for a patent which covered their linking of wing-warping and rudder control.

Between the autumn of 1902 and the autumn of the following year the Wrights hoped to do two things. They had to design the right kind of propeller and they hoped to find a suitable engine to power it. Eventually, they had to design the engine as well. The propellers, two of which were fitted to the plane they took to Kitty Hawk in the autumn of 1903, were long, slim, and of a kind totally different from the marine propellers with which engineers were alone familiar. These two propellers, mounted behind a double wing and driven by two chains, one of which was crossed so that the propellers revolved in different directions, were powered by a four-cylinder petrol engine based on the single-cylinder gas engine which they had been using to pump air through their wind tunnel. The petrol was vaporized as it passed over the heated water-jacket, and the only way of controlling the engine speed was by adjusting the ignition timing, a job which obviously had to be done before take-off. Thus the engine was set 'by guess and by God' and the only change that happened later was due to pre-heating of the inlet air by the water-jacket which reduced the initial output of the engine from about 12 horse-power to about 9.

It was late in September before the Wrights arrived at Kitty Hawk, with their new machine and their 1902, un-powered, version which they assembled first and used for a number of test glides. From the start, nearly everything seems to have gone wrong. There was a 75-mph gale. Some of the shafting on the powered plane broke during ground tests and had to be replaced. It was December before the brothers were able to make the final adjustments on the powered craft and then, when they had hoped to make their first flight with it, the headwind which they still felt was necessary died away to a complete calm.

Not until 15 December was everything ready. The craft was held back on the long launching track as the engine was revved up. Then it was released. It rose for some 15 feet. Then the nose dropped – because, as the pilot Wilbur quickly realized, he had first brought the nose up too quickly and the aircraft had then developed what would now be called a stall.

Three days were needed to make the necessary repairs and it was the morning of December 17 before the brothers hauled out their machine and assembled the 60-foot wooden launching rail. There was only a week to go to Christmas Eve and with a lengthy journey back home they were greatly tempted to hold over further effort until the coming year.

Orville Wright making the first
powered, sustained and controlled
flight in history, on 17 December
1903

Since Wilbur had been at the controls three days previously it was Orville who now lay horizontally on the lower wing as the engine was revved up and the plane held back by a taut checkwire. Around the track which pointed straight into a 25-mph wind there were half a dozen spectators from the nearby fishing hamlet. Further off a few coastguards looked through their glasses and no doubt wondered what was to come next.

At about 10.30 Orville slipped the restraining wire and the 'Flyer' as it had been christened shot forward down the wooden rail. The aircraft had gone some 40 feet when it eased itself up from the rail and slowly rose to a height of about 10 feet. Orville kept it on course, flying into the wind at a ground speed of about 10 mph.

This first powered, sustained and controlled flight lasted a mere 12 seconds and covered about 120 feet. Then the aircraft was dragged back to the track, Wilbur lay at the controls, and the 'Flyer' made a second flight, going slightly farther this time. Both brothers made further flights that morning, the final one lasting nearly a minute and covering more than 800 feet.

Then, just about mid-day and as they and their helpers

*Above* Santos-Dumont flying his
14-bis in France in 1906

*Below* S. F. Cody in his Cody
Biplane, 1912

were discussing the next move, a sudden gust of wind turned
over the craft. Damage was not severe but it was enough to
persuade the Wrights that enough was enough; to pack up and
set out two days later for Dayton.

Nevertheless, man had flown at last under his own power
and control. The Wrights, confident now that they were on
the road to success, tried for good business reasons to make
little of the fact for the time being. But the story leaked out
and by the beginning of 1904 it was clear that the previously
impossible had been made possible.

The repercussions of Kitty Hawk were to be world-wide
but they did not come immediately. Five months after the
Wrights had been granted their patent in 1906, Alberto
Santos-Dumont, the rich and colourful Brazilian living in

Paris, made the first powered flight in Europe with his extraordinary '14-bis', an aircraft resembling a collection of box-kites strung together more by chance than design. The following year Henry Farman, artist turned car-racer turned aeronaut, began flying the first of the truly successful biplanes built by the Voisin brothers. Louis Blériot, preparing for his own appointment with history, flew the predecessor of the monoplane in which he was to cross the Channel two years later. Even so, in Europe as well as in the United States, experiments continued much as though the Wrights had not given a clear lead to the way that must be followed.

All this was dramatically changed after 1908. In that year the Wrights came to Europe and had soon flown in France, Germany and Italy. They flew for up to two and a half hours at Pau, in the French Pyrenees, and they began to train French pilots to fly the Wright aircraft that the Government was by this time buying. Later in the year Wilbur Wright flew publicly in France and his brother flew in public in the United States. In England, S. F. Cody flew at Farnborough the British Army Aeroplane No. 1, while numbers of passengers had flown for the first time in the two-seaters that the Wrights were now building.

The next year, 1909, Blériot flew the Channel, Orville Wright flew at more than 1,000 feet, and the world's first aviation meeting was held outside Rheims. Here 23 planes were airborne and Farman stayed in the air for more than three hours during which he covered more than 100 miles.

Within two years it had become clear that flying was no flash-in-the-pan development but a new method of transport with immense, if ominous, possibilities. Little time remained before the outbreak of the First World War gave its formidable impetus to the development of aircraft.

During those years, flying moved out of the experimental stage into that of the near-sporting. The planes themselves could now be flown with predictable results and the experiments lay rather in the extension of their use. The first seaplane was flown successfully, and then the first amphibian. In the United States the first take-off and landing was made from the deck of a ship. Men flew over the Alps and with the use of the first rudimentary air-to-ground radio there came the possibility of wider knowledge about the weather conditions which were now becoming an important limitation of an aircraft's use. In Britain the Short brothers built the first craft that could fly under the power of either of its two engines, the Gnome rotary power units which were themselves a considerable advance on their predecessors. In Russia Igor Sikorsky,

A Hawker Siddeley Harrier vertical take-off and landing multi-purpose combat aircraft landing on the supply ship Green Rover, moored in the Thames at Greenwich in 1971

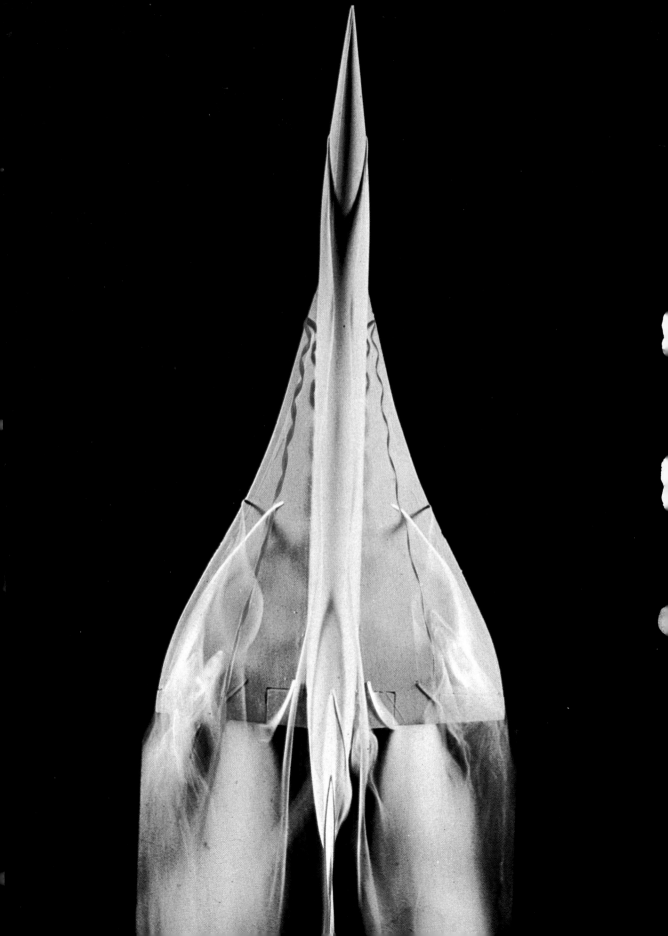

A scale-model of the Concorde undergoing a water-tunnel test in the laboratories of the French Office National d'Études et de Recherches Aérospatiales. Airflow characteristics are indicated by confetti-like streamers caused by dye released into the water.

later to become famous for his development of the helicopter, produced what was for those days a giant biplane. With a 92-foot wing-span it had the distinction of being the first aircraft with an enclosed passenger cabin.

This period also saw the world's first monocoque fuselage, an omen of things to come. So far, fuselages had consisted basically of a skeleton of longitudinal wooden members, held together at intervals with transverse braces. On to this there was then added the covering of the fuselage, usually of canvas, but it was the skeleton alone which bore the strains and stresses of load-carrying. In the monocoque fuselage – first used in the Monocoque Deperdussin which in 1912 won the Gordon Bennett Cup – the skeleton was replaced by the wooden, or later metal, shell forming a single integral unit.

Such advances had steadily made flying a practical proposition during the first decade and more of the 20th century. The World War, which broke out in the summer of 1914, decisively altered the pace of this steady progress, as the Allies and the Central Powers both desperately struggled to win the mastery of the air without which, it was already being dimly seen, victory on the ground or on the oceans would only be temporary.

The changing roles of aircraft in war did much to govern the route which progress took. In the early days planes were used largely for reconnaissance – much as balloons had been used during the siege of Paris in 1870. This demanded aircraft which could be slow but which had to be relatively stable so that the observers had time in which to notice and record what they could see on the ground. The need for stability increased as photographic reconnaissance became more general and the photographers required a more stable platform from which they could operate.

Reconnaissance aircraft were soon being shot down, by ground fire and later by enemy aircraft whose armament at first consisted of little more than revolvers and sporting rifles. Thus there grew up a demand for aircraft which could fly faster; which had a higher operational ceiling and could keep above the range of accurate ground fire; and which had the increased rates of climb which enabled them to gain, with the minimum time, the higher positions which gave the advantage in air combat. While the demand for faster and more manoeuvrable aircraft was increasing, the development of bombing from the air called for planes whose first operational requirement was the carriage of heavy loads.

These varying demands on aircraft-designers and aircraft-

The first passenger aircraft with enclosed cabin, the Sikorsky Grand, built in Russia in 1913

builders were in general met by two complementary lines of research. In Britain at the National Physical Laboratory and the Royal Aircraft Factory at Farnborough, in Germany at the aeronautical research institute at Göttingen, scientists probed the fundamentals of aerodynamics, producing more efficient wing-sections, one of the most important keys to an aircraft's efficiency, and discovering in other ways how the maximum use could be made of the power available from improved aircraft engines. Engineering research into the problem of extracting more power from less weight was the second factor which helped to give temporary advantage in the air, first to one side and then to the other.

During the war many daring experiments were made. As early as May 1916, a Bristol 'Scout' was launched from another plane in mid-air. In the United States a radio-guided flying bomb was developed which could automatically be directed on to its target. In Russia, Igor Sikorsky successfully designed the huge Ilya Mourametz bomber, powered by four engines each of 100 horse-power, carrying a bomb-load of 600 pounds, and serviced by a crew of up to 16 men who could carry out minor repairs while the giant plane was in flight.

In most of these developments, designers among the Allies

and among the Central Powers pushed ahead at much the same pace. But the Germans succeeded in gaining one major advantage for a considerable while and also in introducing a virtually new type of aircraft construction which was to have great repercussions when the war was over. The advantage came from the Fokker synchronizing gear, designed by a Dutchman and introduced by the Germans. Once aerial fighting became common it was clear that the ideal would be to have a machine-gun fitted along the main axis of an aircraft. All a pilot would then have to do would be to aim the aircraft at the enemy and press the trigger. At least, that would be the case were it not for the propeller. This seemed to rule out that type of armament for the 'tractor' plane, in which the propeller was at the front of the aircraft, and limit its use to the less efficient 'pusher' type in which the propeller was at the back. Anthony Fokker had a solution. 'The obvious thing to do was to make the propeller shoot the gun, instead of trying to shoot the bullets through the propeller,' he said. The outcome was the interruptor gear, an early crude version of which was used in a French aircraft captured by the Germans, which synchronized the firing with the swiftly-turning propeller and gave the Germans a considerable advantage until the Allies, recovering an interruptor gear from a crashed German aircraft, were able to devise something similar.

The other development pioneered by the Germans was to have a much longer-lasting effect. Thus far, a majority of aircraft conformed to a pattern. They were built largely of wood and canvas. From their central fuselage there spread a pair of wings strutted and braced with wire and wood to give them the necessary rigidity. They looked, and they were, fragile contraptions which tore and broke with little provocation. Some aircraft, such as Blériot's classic No. XI, had boasted a single wing, but they too gave the impression of being held together largely by glue and good faith.

Now the pattern was dramatically altered by the perseverance of one man, pushing against the conservative opinion of his Government. This time it was the German Government. The man was Professor Hugo Junkers, a Rhineland engineer whose successful business had brought him the money for aeronautical research. Early in 1910 Junkers had filed a patent for a 'flying wing' which would house engine, fuel, payload and crew. It was never built but five years later it provided the key to a revolutionary aircraft. This was the J1, a plane with a single cantilevered wing – a wing, that is, supported at one end only, and without any external bracing. The whole aircraft was, moreover, built entirely of metal. The initial plan had

Experimental Junkers-built iron
wing being tested at the Junkers
factory, July 1915

been to use aluminium, but when it was found impossible to
release supplies of the scarce material Junkers used sheet iron
to cover the framework of iron tubing. The 'Tin Donkey' flew
for the first time in December 1915, the predecessor of a long
line of all-metal monoplanes. Later the sheet iron gave way to
ribbed duralumin, the hallmark of the Junkers for years to
come.

The struggle to win mastery of the air during the First
World War dramatically speeded up the evolution of aircraft.
In 1914 top speeds were about 80 mph and by the end of the
war they had almost doubled. The practical ceiling for aircraft
was raised from 7,000 feet to nearly 30,000 feet. Engines that
weighed about 4 pounds per horsepower in 1914 had been
fined down to weights of less than half that by 1918, while
wing-loadings, which averaged about 4 pounds to the square
inch when war broke out had roughly doubled by 1918. In
addition the very number of men who flew during the war
years, or who were brought into direct contact with aircraft,
did much to transform flying from the rarity of pre-war days
to the near-commonplace of the 1920s. After all, there had
been only about 300 British Service aircraft in existence in
1914. When the war ended there were more than 22,000.

The main repercussions of the aeronautical advances spurred
on by the war were to be felt on civilian flying during the next
two decades. Speed, ceiling, range, carrying capacity, comfort

and safety were all increased and utilized by the civilian air-lines which now sprang up. Radio began to diminish the hazards of long-distance navigation. The Atlantic was flown for the first time. Regular air services between the capitals of the world became commonplace and as commercial airports were set up on the fringes of the big cities flying began to assume the shape and the importance which it occupies today.

Even so, one of the most significant post-war pointers to the future of air power concerned the Services. It came in 1921 when, in tests off the coast of the United States, Martin bombers sank the 22,800-ton German battleship *Ostfriesland*, which had been brought there for the experiment. Although the Admirals were reluctant to admit the fact, the world's navies would no longer have the freedom of the seas unless they first gained mastery of the air – a lesson which was to be rammed home off the coast of Norway in the spring of 1940 and less than two years after that when the great battleships *Prince of Wales* and *Repulse* were sunk with ease by Japanese planes off the coast of Malaya.

The twenty years between the two World Wars witnessed the increasing threat from the bomber. It saw also the rise and fall of the airship, the civilian version of the Zeppelins which had raided London between 1914 and 1918. As early as 1919 the British R34 made a double crossing of the Atlantic, sug-gesting that these vast cylindrical ships of the air might well offer a new and civilized means of air travel. But the destruc-tion of the R34 two years later, when she broke up over the city of Hull with the loss of more than 40 lives, was an omen of things to come. The Graf Zeppelin made its first passenger carrying transatlantic flight in 1928 and both Britain and Ger-many had ambitious plans. But in 1930 the huge British R101 crashed in France on a planned flight to Egypt and India with the loss of nearly 50 dead. It was the first of a succession of air-ship disasters, and work on her sister-vessel, the R100, was abandoned. Inflammable hydrogen, the gas used to lift air-ships, was already being replaced by the far safer helium, but the series of tragedies, culminating in the destruction of the Hindenburg as she came in to her mooring mast in New Jersey in 1937, put paid to the world's airship plans. A third of a century later it seems possible that they may be revived.

The inter-war years also saw the practical introduction of rotorcraft. As with so many other ideas, this one can be traced back to Leonardo da Vinci, whose notebooks reveal that about 1500 he had envisaged an aerial craft with rotating wings which would give it lift. More than 300 years later the British inventor W. H. Phillips devised and built an unmanned model

The Hindenburg bursting into
flames on preparing to land at
Lakehurst, New Jersey, 6 May 1937

aircraft whose rotary blades were propelled by wing-tip
steam-driven jets. Another half century passed before two
separate inventors in France, and Igor Sikorsky in Russia,
began to experiment with full-scale aircraft incorporating
rotors.

Such aircraft are of two kinds. There is first the autogiro
in which a conventional propeller is powered by a conventional engine. But the autogiro is also equipped with freely-rotating rotors mounted above the fuselage; as the propeller
pulls the plane forward through the air, the impact of air on
the rotors causes them to revolve and thus provide the necessary lift to take the plane off the ground. The helicopter is a
more complicated affair although today a far more practical
one. Here the rotor blades are revolved by the engine which is
thus used directly to provide the necessary lift. Once the helicopter is airborne forward flight is achieved by varying the

incidence to the air of the rotating blades. From the earliest days, one of the main problems with the helicopter was the torque reaction effect exerted by the rotors. The fuselage tended to twist in a direction opposite to that of the rotors and was counteracted, in the earliest machines, by a small propeller fitted to the end of the fuselage and so designed that its only job was to keep the craft on an even keel.

The pioneer of the autogiro was the Spaniard Juan de la Cierva whose main aim was to provide a safeguard against the stalling of aircraft at the low forward speeds of take-off and landing. Cierva's first autogiro was demonstrated in England in 1926 and was steadily developed during the next few years. It was soon overtaken by the progress of the helicopter.

Igor Sikorsky, whose giant bomber had been built in Russia from 1915 onwards, had constructed an experimental helicopter as early as 1910. Emigrating to the United States, he developed his ideas between the wars and by 1939 had produced his first successful helicopter. In Germany the Focke-Wulf company had been doing the same, and both the Allies and the Axis powers continued during the Second World War to improve an aircraft which could use a field of cricket-pitch size for take-off and landing. Today the helicopter runs shuttle-services into city centres, evacuates mountaineers from inaccessible places, and is even used as an industrial load-carrier from which heavy pieces of machinery can be winched down on to a construction site with the minimum of trouble; and has been evolved for Services into what is in practice a new military weapon. First developed as a light gad-fly of an aircraft, it is today something very much more – the Russians have a craft with twin rotors of 240 feet span, 200 feet long and capable of lifting a 34-ton payload.

The years between the wars saw a host of technological improvements. One was the use of geodetic construction for the building of aircraft fuselages. This is a basket-work or lattice-like structure of such a design that the compression loads induced in any member are braced by tension loads in crossing members. It had been used by Barnes Wallis to contain the gas-bags of the ill-fated R100, and was later used by him in the design of two British bombers, the Vickers Wellesley – the first aircraft in the world built entirely on the geodetic principle – and the Vickers Wellington.

The aircraft propeller was also revolutionized between the wars. From the earliest days of powered flight it had been realized that to gain the maximum efficiency from an engine the propeller which it turned would need to meet the air at one angle during take-off or landing, and at another angle during

steady flight. The engineering problems involved were very great and it was only in 1924 that two British designers, Dr Hele-Shaw and T. E. Beacham, working privately but with the help of Government funds, patented a variable-pitch propeller which could be adjusted to meet flight needs. A decade later means were devised of linking engine-revolutions with propeller-pitch, thus further improving the aeronautical efficiency of aircraft.

Another technical innovation was the use of slots to raise the efficiency of the wings. A quarter of a century earlier the Wrights had found that wing-warping, which increased the camber of the wing, also increased the craft's lift as well as enabling the pilot to guide it in the air. The principle had been developed by Henry Farman who provided the trailing edges of his wings with ailerons – or little wings – consisting of flaps which could be raised or lowered independently to give lateral control. For technical reasons these flaps were of comparatively little use on biplanes and although they were fitted on the SE4 biplane which was made at the Royal Aircraft Factory at Farnborough from 1914 onwards, they were not much liked by pilots.

Like many other aeronautical innovations, the idea of slotted aerofoils, through which air passed from the lower to the upper surface when the slots were open, came to more than one man at roughly the same time. Certainly a German pilot, G. V. Lachmann, thought of the idea in 1917 while recovering in hospital after a crash brought about by a stalling aircraft. Lachmann reasoned that during level flight air would pass across the upper and lower wing surfaces without passing through the slots. When, however, the nose of the aircraft went up in the first movement of a stall, wind would begin to pass through the slots and would have a counteracting effect. In England, workers at Handley-Page came to much the same conclusion after wind-tunnel tests of aerofoils, while in Germany Hugo Junkers also conceived the idea of slotted wings. They came into use during the 1920s, finally growing into a large family of types incorporating slots which were permanently open or could be closed either manually or automatically.

This particular increase in aerodynamic theory and practice was accompanied by the development of streamlining. Today, when it is widely appreciated that the smallest excrescence on a moving object will effect its movement through the air, the aircraft of the immediate post-war years have an extraordinarily shaggy look. As two experts have written, 'until the early 1930s designers lived split lives, especially in Europe, in

*Above* An illustration of geodetic construction: fuselage of the Wellington bomber

*Below* Wing construction showing aerofoils

one of which they recognized that the reduction of drag was the simplest way of making aeroplanes more efficient, while in the other they designed airplanes which were box-like in shape, hung about with such excrescences as fixed undercarriages and festooned with bracing wires. The wires might be of stream-line section, but this was virtually the sum of the genuflection made towards streamlining.' Only in the later 1920s – partly under the influence of the British aeronautical engineer, Professor, later Sir, Melvill Jones – did designers begin to give streamlining its due importance.

Among these was R. J. Mitchell, leader in the British efforts to win the Schneider Trophy and a good deal more besides. The race had first been flown in 1913 when the French winner averaged about 45 mph. By the time that the Italian Major Bernardi won the Trophy in 1926, the speed had crept up to nearly 250 mph. This victory faced the British with a problem since the Trophy was to be won outright by the first country to gain it three times in succession or four times in all – and the Italians had already won it in 1920 and 1921.

To the rescue there came Vickers-Supermarine of Southampton, and Mitchell, their chief engineer and designer. For the 1927 contest Mitchell designed the S5 which won the race at 281.65 mph. His S6 won the next race, two years later, at 328.63 mph and a development of this, the S6b, won the following contest in 1931 at 340.08 mph, thereby gaining the Trophy outright for Britain. The importance of this triumph was to be considerable. For one of the 1931 machines had flown at more than 400 mph, a feat which induced Air Marshal Dowding, then the Air Council's Member for Research and Development, to suggest that two British manufacturers should produce prototypes of different aircraft. Each should have the highest possible performance and should be able to take off not from water, as did the Schneider Trophy float-planes, but from the small airfields then in use. From Vickers there eventually came the Spitfire, a superb example of aero-dynamic knowledge wedded to engineering skill. From Hawker's there came Sydney Camm's Hurricane.

Both the Spitfire and the Hurricane exemplified the stream-lining, made possible by ingenious design, which was excep-tional for its time but which was to become commonplace after the Second World War. As in other spheres, the demands of war – or in this case the expected demands of the expected war – were to have a drastic effect on civilian practice.

The effects of the Second World War on aviation were naturally enough comparable in many ways to those of the 1914–18 war. Planes became faster. Their operational heights

*Above* The Supermarine section of the British team for the 1927 Schneider Trophy with the Supermarine S5. R. J. Mitchell, the chief designer of all the Schneider Trophy aircraft and of the prototype Spitfire, is fifth from the left in the front row. Flight-Lieutenant Webster, winner of the 1927 trophy, is standing on the aircraft.

*Below* A Spitfire Mk XIV

were pushed up, one result of this being that pressurized cabins, only built in the later 1930s, had become commonplace by the end of the war. New metals were produced, new methods of manufacture employed. Yet despite the importance of the technological advances which so increased the efficiency of planes and the top performances of which they were capable, all were overshadowed by two almost self-contained developments. One was the coming of radar, the latest utilization of the radio-waves of the electro-magnetic spectrum, introduced as a device to give early warning of the approach of bombers but quickly spreading into a huge range of devices which revolutionized both long-distance navigation and the problems of landing in bad weather. The second device was the jet, the new form of propulsion which has transformed civilian flying from a sometimes bumpy journey 'below the weather' to the tea-table smoothness of flying in the stratosphere.

Only towards the end of the war did aircraft begin to utilize this innovation, as revolutionary as the all-metal construction with which Junkers had changed the face of flying 30 years before. In the first half of the 1940s all aircraft were still using the same basic method of moving a plane forward through the air that had been used by the Wright brothers almost half a century earlier. An internal combustion engine was used to turn a shaft which turned a propeller. The propeller might be a 'pusher', mounted behind the engine and wings, or a 'tractor' which was mounted in front of them, but in both cases the result was the same: the aircraft was moved forward through the air and this in turn created the necessary lift to make the craft airborne.

As aircraft flew higher it became increasingly clear that this system suffered from a double built-in disadvantage. For the higher the altitude, the less dense does the air become. One result is that the propeller finds it more difficult to 'bite' and its ability to move an aircraft forward is thus affected; in addition, the efficiency of the engine itself is affected by the lack of air. This second disadvantage can be counteracted by the fitting of a supercharger, which will supply the engine with air at a pressure higher than that through which it is moving. It also means increased weight, more complexity, and more things to go wrong.

The jet engine, whose basic principle had been known even to the Ancient Greeks, consists essentially of a chamber open at the forward end. A compressor draws air into the chamber and compresses it in one or more combustion chambers into which fuel is injected. The mixture of air and fuel is ignited; it burns; it expands and, since it is prevented from moving forward, is thrust out through the rear of the chamber, passing, as it does so, through a rear turbine which drives the compressor. The result of this violent ejection of burned fuel backwards is to drive the engine forwards. The movement is in no way governed by the density of the surrounding air, being simply an illustration of Newton's law of equal and opposite reaction.

The advantages of the jet were numerous and obvious. The engine was simpler in construction than the internal combustion engine. It could use a wider variety of fuels, and it produced no vibration, while the fact that no propeller was required in itself eliminated a number of design problems.

With all these things to be said for the jet, it is natural to ask why it had not appeared sooner on the scene. The answer is the simple one of technological limitation. The temperatures of the ejected gases are very great, and it was only during the years between the wars that the manufacture of special alloys made it possible to conceive of a practical jet engine. Then, as with many other revolutionary inventions dependent on technological advance – notably radio, radar and the use of nuclear energy – the possibility of utilizing it began to be investigated independently in a number of countries.

As early as 1920 Dr A. A. Griffith of the Royal Aircraft Establishment at Farnborough had proposed that a gas turbine of the kind finally utilized in the jet-engine might turn a propeller – an idea which evolved as the turbo–prop engine after the Second World War. The following year the Frenchman Charles Guillaume patented the design of a jet-engine, although no progress appears to have been made in developing it. A new theory of turbine design from Griffith in 1926 renewed interest in the possibilities of the jet and research work continued at Farnborough, although with only slight interest from the authorities. Meanwhile, and quite independently of Farnborough, Frank Whittle, a young Flight-Lieutenant in the Royal Air Force, was working on the same problem. In 1930 he patented with money from his own pocket, his own design for what was to be the prototype of the jet engine which has today almost totally taken over in the air from the internal combustion engine.

The essential simplicity of the Whittle engine was summed up in his own words at the time. 'Reciprocating engines are exhausted. They have hundreds of parts jerking to and fro, and they cannot be made more powerful without becoming too complicated. The engine of the future must produce 2,000 hp with one moving part: a spinning turbine and compressor.'

Even so, it was not until six years later that Whittle's idea

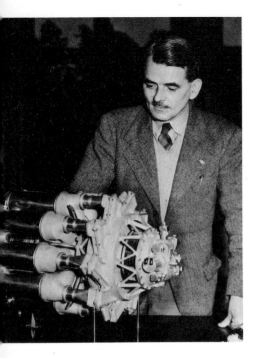

Air Commodore Sir Frank Whittle
with a model of his prototype jet
engine

began to be taken seriously by the authorities. Sir Henry
Tizard, then Chairman of the Government's Aeronautical
Research Committee, was the man who finally persuaded
Britain to pour into the necessary research the huge sums that
were needed. 'I knew it would cost a great deal of money,' he
said later; 'I knew that success was not certain; and yet I felt
that it was of great national importance to spend the money.'
As it was later written – 'to every Whittle his Tizard.'

By this time, with war only a few years away, the Germans
were also at work on the same idea. A jet-engine similar to
Whittle's was patented in 1935 by Hans von Ohain and two
years later Heinkel's began to develop it. Simultaneously a
turbo-jet programme was started by Junkers while the Italian
Caproni Company began to work on a pseudo-jet which used
a piston engine to operate a compressor.

By 1939 the British and the Germans were thus running
neck-and-neck in a race for use of an engine which with its
promise of increased speed and higher operational ceiling
might well give command of the air. The story is one of leap-
frogging records – the Germans putting the He176, powered by
a liquid fuel rocket, into the air in June 1939, following this two
months later with the He178, the world's first turbo-jet to fly.
The 178 used the Ohain engine that had first run on the test-
bench two years previously. The British followed in May 1941
with the test-flight of Whittle's jet, fitted to the experimental
Gloster E28/29. The next year the Germans put into the air
the remarkable Messerschmitt 262, powered by twin wing-
mounted jets which gave it a top speed, at 20,000 feet, of
540 mph and a service ceiling of 40,000 feet. It was followed
in 1943, by the Gloster Meteor, the production model of the
E28/29, and the British can claim to have beaten their
enemies to the post by getting the Meteor into squadron
service with the RAF before the Germans got the Me262 into
similar service with the Luftwaffe.

The jet-propelled Meteors were used effectively to combat
the German flying bombs launched against Britain during the
summer of 1944, their speed of 480 mph giving them the edge
over the robot-weapons which they shot down in numbers.
Despite this, the jet came too late to play any significant part in
the Second World War. But British jets were shipped to the
United States while the war was still on and from these were
derived the first American jet-aircraft, notably the Lockheed
Shooting Star which was used in the Korean War – where it
was completely outclassed by the MiG-15, built by the
Russians.

On parallel lines to the 'true' jet, went the development of

Griffith's idea for the turbo-prop. This, it was hoped, would claim the best from both worlds, since at lower altitudes it would have the advantages of a propeller-driven aircraft while having the smooth running characteristics of the jet. The Rolls-Royce Welland engines, the first of the 'River Class' of jet engines, named to give the idea of flow associated with jet propulsion, powered the first RAF Meteors in 1945. They were followed by the Derwent, the power unit used in the Meteors which set up new world speed records in 1945 and 1946. Next came the Trent, an adaptation of the Derwent which became in September 1945 the first airscrew gas turbine to fly. But although two Trent units were flown in a Meteor for the first time in that month, the engine was used mainly as a research engine.

The Dart, which could be run for as long as 5,000 hours – representing 1,500,000 miles – before an overhaul, was the first engine designed as a prop-jet to fly, making its initial flight in the nose of a Lancaster in October 1947. The Vickers-Viscount, fitted with four Dart engines, was the first prop-jet powered airliner.

With the aid of the jet, planes at last broke through 'the sound barrier', that concentration of air which begins to form up before a plane as it approaches the speed of sound. With the aid of the jet, passenger aircraft flying above the weather brought to the trans-world flight a new standard of comfort and safety. And with the aid of the jet supersonic planes have now been brought to the point where, for better or for worse, they seem likely to enter commercial service.

The jet, which has created its own pollution in the form of noise, is likely within the next few years to help solve the very problem it has created. This solution will probably be the aircraft designed for vertical take-off and landing, a characteristic which would confine the major noise nuisance to a small area instead of spreading it across a wide swathe of country below the conventional flight path. The idea of non-conventional take-off was developed immediately after the Second World War in a variety of aircraft which used combinations of rotating vanes, rotatable wings and propellers whose thrust could be changed at will from the horizontal to the vertical. Most were experimental aircraft and most of them, at best, produced only STOL, or short take-off and landing, rather than the ideal of vertical movement.

The break-through came in the 1950s with the use by Rolls-Royce of the turbo-jet engine in what was called the 'Flying Bedstead' – officially the Rolls-Royce TMR, or thrust-measuring rig – a device that gave man a new means of getting airborne. Until the Rolls-Royce engineers perfected the equipment it had been possible to rise into the air either by the use of lighter-than-air machines such as airships or balloons, or with the help of the aerodynamic lift given by the movement of air over a wing or aerofoil. Whittle had provided the key to a third door more than a decade earlier when his first jet-engine, weighing 560 pounds, had produced a thrust of 850 pounds and during the war much effort had been concentrated on the design and production of military aircraft which could best utilize this new method of propulsion. During the first years of peace, however, it was realized that once the thrust became considerably greater than the weight of the thruster it was theoretically possible for an engine to lift itself vertically from the ground – and, by a cut-down of power, to land in the same way.

The limitation was suggested by the word 'theoretically'. Jet-engines themselves presented a large enough bag of problems. When designers contemplated using jet-thrust not to drive an aerofoil plus fuselage horizontally through the air but to raise it vertically off the ground, it became evident that there would be difficulties of control. These began to be solved in the 'Flying Bedstead', an ungainly-looking contraption which in essence was little more than a test-bench carrying two Nene engines. The 'Flying Bedstead' weighed 7,200 pounds but the two engines between them developed a com-

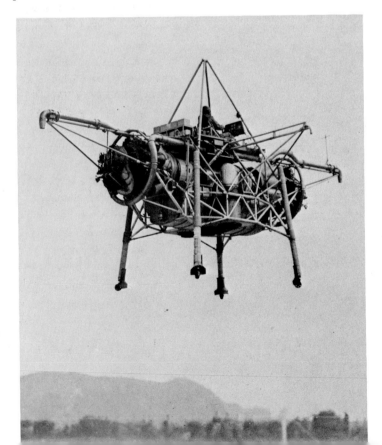

The Rolls-Royce 'Flying Bedstead', predecessor of the vertical take-off aircraft

bined thrust of 7,700 pounds. When both were operating all-out the three-and-a-half-ton monster rose slowly but steadily off the ground, hovering in the air above a torrent of jet-stream. Four subsidiary control jets, fore and aft, port and starboard, were used to maintain equilibrium, while by tilting the rig slightly the 'pilot' could produce forward movement.

It was clear that if a plane could be designed on this principle it would need no hard runway for take-off or landing. This would obviously have immense advantages in a commercial passenger-carrying aircraft. A Service aircraft utilizing the same principle would offer equal benefits, since the ability to land in little more than an open field – a characteristic of the first aircraft that had quickly disappeared with increasing sophistication – would give massive operational advantages. Smaller aircraft presented fewer problems of development and this fact, together with the Cold War climate of the 1950s, brought numerous kinds of VTOL Service aircraft into the air within the decade.

The simplest system was that used in the Hawker Kestrel – later developed into the Harrier – which was powered by a Bristol Siddeley Pegasus engine. The jet-stream was led out through four rotatable exhaust nozzles. With the aircraft on the ground, the nozzles pointed down and in the first moments of operation took the aircraft vertically off the ground. The jets were then slowly turned to the horizontal position to provide forward movement.

A second system, used in the Dassault-Sud Balzac among other aircraft, employed one engine, or set of engines, for vertical lift, and a separate engine or engines to give forward movement, the two groups being started up or shut down as required. A combination of both systems is also used in some designs – one set of engines is used for vertical lift, and then shut down; a second set is used first to assist the vertical take-off and then swivelled horizontally to provide forward movement.

It seems likely that during the 1970s the first VTOL passenger aircraft will come into commercial service – possibly the Breguet 941S capable of carrying 100 passengers at 400 mph; so also, in all probability, will supersonic transports flying at more than 1,400 mph. These figures suggest that on a small planet such as the earth, the lines of aeronautical advance are soon likely to be changing direction and emphasis. It is already being asked whether clipping an hour or so off the Atlantic crossing is worth either the expense or the drain on scarce men and materials that supersonic planes demand. In all the developed countries the menace of aircraft noise is increasing,

A Boeing Jumbo Jet, capable of carrying 363 passengers and more than 17 crew, at London Airport

as are the problems of siting airports to ensure that they cause minimum environmental pollution. Thus the problems that the new pioneers of flight have to solve are rather different from those of three-quarters of a century back. It is now possible to go as far, or as fast, as man in his present state of development normally needs. Pioneers will still, restless human nature being what it is, try to push back the frontiers of knowledge still further, as they are already doing by space travel. But an increasing number will be diverted to the task of producing, with existing knowledge, aircraft that serve mankind more efficiently.

# 3 The Magic Spectrum

While the camera was being transferred into the plain man's instant recorder of events and flight was being made an everyday affair, a totally different field of scientific endeavour was being probed and exploited for the first time. The camera was conscripted for a score of unexpected tasks, industrial as well as artistic; the jet plane brought every country on the planet within little more than a day's flight of any other; yet during the first three-quarters of the 20th century the electromagnetic spectrum helped not only to create vast new industries but to alter communication between humans more radically than they had been altered since Gutenberg set up the 42-lined pages of his Bible in movable type.

Most great scientific discoveries, as well as most inventions, can be traced back through the generations; the tracks grow steadily fainter rather than suddenly stopping so that it is easier to say that records have disappeared than that they never existed. Leonardo, sketching an armoured machine that the 20th century knows as the tank, may well have elaborated an earlier thought; the early Greek atomists, picking by chance on a theory that Dalton created with intent, were merely speculating on riddles that had entranced even earlier men. So too with the discovery and investigation of electromagnetic radiations, that huge spectrum of waves of which only a small part, covering visible light, has been known for more than a century.

Knowledge of magnetism, if not understanding of it, starts back in pre-history. From Thales, who was traditionally the first man to note that some rocks attracted iron, through Petrus Peregrinus who devised the pivoted compass needle, the line leads to William Gilbert who in the first Elizabeth's day brought the study of magnetism into the era of numerical experiment – and is remembered for his efforts in the 'gilberts' of magneto-motive force. Gilbert not only refuted such superstitions as that garlic destroys magnetism, but discovered the 'dip' of the magnet. He also put forward the idea that the needle did not point to the heavens but to the magnetic poles of the earth which he saw as a single giant spherical magnet. Almost as significantly, Gilbert discovered that a variety of gems, as well as amber, attracted light objects when rubbed, and christened them 'electrics' after the Greek word for amber.

For long after Gilbert's day, knowledge of electric phenomena advanced on lines parallel to research into magnetism but unconnected with it. Only in 1819 did the Danish physicist Hans Oersted, demonstrating to a class in the University of Copenhagen, bring a compass needle close to a wire through which an electric current was passing. The needle twitched, then turned at right-angles to the current. When he reversed the current, the needle swung round south to north, still at right-angles to the current but pointing in the opposite direction.

André-Marie Ampère, Georg Ohm and Charles Augustin de Coulomb are three of the men who in the first third of the 19th century began to disentangle the links between electricity and magnetism. Then, in 1831, Michael Faraday showed that the movement of a magnet relative to a coil of wire outside it produced an electrical current in the wire – thus presenting evidence for his belief that the phenomena of electricity and magnetism could best be considered in terms of fields, or areas of space over which their forces were exercised. With the links between electricity and magnetism increasingly recognized, the stage was set for Maxwell.

James Clerk Maxwell was the Edinburgh physicist and mathematician who in less than two decades used Faraday's experiments to furnish equations linking the two sorts of

Michael Faraday lecturing at the Royal Institution in December 1855

phenomena, boldly claimed that light itself consisted of electro-magnetic waves, and forecast the future discovery of invisible waves of the same sort. These were in fact the radio waves of Heinrich Hertz, first revealed in his laboratory 25 years after Maxwell had died of cancer at the age of 48.

Maxwell's revolutionary theory was finally described in *A Dynamical Theory of the Electromagnetic Field*. The paper declared that neither electricity nor magnetism existed in isolation and gave a simple set of equations which linked their various phenomena. The nub of the theory was that oscillation of an electric charge produced an electro-magnetic field which spread outwards at a constant speed from its source. Maxwell's equations showed this speed to be roughly 186,300 miles per second. This was approximately the speed of light, a fact which Maxwell felt was unlikely to be a coincidence. Thus light, he concluded, must itself be a form of electro-magnetic radiation, an idea which on the face of it settled a scientific argument that had been raging for years.

Since Newton's day, theories of the nature of light had fallen into one of two groups: those which descended from the Greek belief that it was composed of minute grains in rapid movement, a theory that with some reservation was supported by Newton himself; and the newer idea put forward by Christiaan Huygens which considered light as waves propagated through an all-pervasive ether much as ripples are transmitted through a shaking jelly. The Frenchman Augustin Fresnel had experimentally done much to support the wave-theory. Now came Maxwell, boldly claiming that all light, whether from a candle, a fire, the sun or one of the new electric lamps, was electro-magnetic radiation.

Maxwell predicted the existence of other electro-magnetic waves also travelling through space with the velocity of light, and acceptance of what was still a theory hung largely on their discovery. This came in 1887 from Heinrich Hertz in Karls-ruhe. Hertz used an electrical circuit that built up a charge first in one then in another of two metal balls, the charge jumping the gap between them each time it had built up sufficiently. According to Maxwell, each oscillation should start off an electro-magnetic wave. To detect it, Hertz set up a simple wire-loop with a gap in it. The apparatus worked. The sparks in the first piece of apparatus were matched by smaller sparks in the second, the waves that had been started by the oscillating apparatus creating a complementary but smaller current in the receiver.

Thus were created the world's first man-made radio waves. Experiments quickly followed which showed that they were

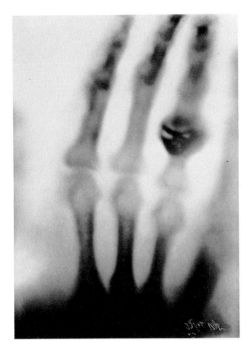

X-ray of a hand taken by
W. C. Roentgen

radiated at the speed of light, and could be reflected and refracted in the same way. All this was further support, if it were still needed, for Maxwell's conception of a whole spectrum of radiations of which visible light formed only a small part. Further evidence came a few years later when Wilhelm Roentgen produced from a high voltage discharge in an evacuated tube a new type of radiation which he called X-rays. Still more evidence came early in the 1900s when radio-active materials were found to be emitting gamma rays. Thus the existence of large segments of the electro-magnetic spectrum was known before its exploitation by inventors and technologists began in earnest at the turn of the century.

In many ways, electro-magnetic waves can be likened to waves on a pond, even though they spread in three rather than in two dimensions. They can, in particular, be described in terms of wavelength and frequency, the first being the distance between the crests of successive waves and the second being the number of cycles of the wave motion in any particular time. The huge differences in these wavelengths and frequencies are among their most curious characteristics. Thus at one end of the spectrum there are the gamma rays, with only $10^{-12}$ to $10^{-10}$ centimetres between crests, created from $10^{20}$ to $10^{22}$ times per second. At the other end there are the radio waves, up to $10^6$ centimetres in length and produced $10^3$ times per second. Thus the range runs, in simple terms, from gamma rays only trillionths of an inch long to radio waves up to thousands of feet. In between, increasing in wavelength from the gamma rays, there are X-rays; ultra-violet waves which play an important part in fluorescence; visible light, increasing in length from the blue to the red; the infra-red – below the red – or invisible heat rays; and finally the radio waves, which fill a big sector of the spectrum ranging from the EHF or extremely high-frequency radiations to the longer VLF or very low frequency, a contrast emphasizing the fact that high frequencies are matched by short wavelengths.

The great potentials of Hertz's experiments, which finally put the existence of the electro-magnetic spectrum beyond doubt, were appreciated only slowly; and before wire-less transmission was exploited the scientific world was startled by announcement of a new radiation that had obviously immense possibilities.

It came from Wilhelm Roentgen in the Bavarian city of Würzburg, where he was head of the university's department of physics. Roentgen was experimenting with the luminescence produced in certain chemicals by the use of a cathode ray tube, a device in which an electric discharge takes place in a partial vacuum. On 5 November 1895, Roentgen darkened his laboratory to observe results better and turned on the tube, still enclosed in black cardboard. What he saw to his surprise was that although the tube was still covered, a sheet of nearby paper coated with barium platinocyanide was glowing. When he turned off the current the glow ceased; when he switched on, the glow returned. Taking the paper into the next room he found that when the tube was switched on it continued to glow even there.

Roentgen's astonishment comes up through the sober scientific words of the report he wrote after testing the powers of the new rays. 'Paper is very transparent,' he said; 'behind a bound book of about one thousand pages I saw the fluorescent screen light up brightly, the printer's ink offering scarcely a noticeable hindrance. In the same way the fluorescence appeared behind a double pack of cards; a single card held between the apparatus and the screen being almost unnoticeable to the eye. A single sheet of tinfoil is also scarcely perceptible, it is only after several layers have been placed over one another that their shadow is distinctly seen on the screen. Thick blocks of wood are also transparent, pine boards 2 or 3 centimetres thick absorbing only slightly. A plate of aluminium about 15 millimetres thick, though it enfeebled the action seriously, did not cause the fluorescence to disappear entirely. Sheets of hard rubber several centimetres thick still permit the rays to pass through them.'

More important were the different extents to which the rays penetrated human flesh and bone. Roentgen was quick to see the immense medical value of the discovery and his anxiety to announce it was equalled by the need to have as many facts as possible verified. Only on 28 December, after seven weeks of constant experiment, did he finally submit his first paper on the new phenomenon to the Würzburg Physical Medical Society. News of its contents quickly reached Berlin and Vienna, then other European capitals, and by the evening of 23 January, when he lectured to a packed auditorium in the university, he was famous.

One point that Roentgen had already confirmed was that the new rays affected photographic film, and his lecture concluded with an impressive demonstration. Would Professor Albert von Kolliker, the university anatomist, care to have his hand photographed? The professor stepped up, and placed his hand on the sensitized film before the tube was switched on. Shortly afterwards, Roentgen held up the developed film which clearly showed the bones, the soft tissues of the hand, and the firm image of a metal ring on the professor's third finger.

Kolliker then proposed that the new phenomena should not be called X-rays, as Roentgen had so far called them, but Roentgen rays. But much of the world was unable to deal easily with the 'oe' of the German name and by the turn of the century it was X-rays whose fame had become firmly established. Roentgen himself did not apply for the use of the 'von' granted to him by the Prince of Bavaria in honour of his achievement and he did not attempt to make a penny from his discovery. 'According to the good tradition of the German University professors,' he said, 'I am of the opinion that their discoveries and inventions belong to humanity, and that they should not in any way be hampered by patents, licences or contracts nor should they be controlled by any one group.'

The use of X-rays as an aid to medical diagnosis quickly swept the world. Location of bullets in a soldier's leg, of objects swallowed by children, were among the first and most obvious applications. Later, as the nature of X-rays came to be better known and understood, it was found possible to photograph with them tumours inside the human body that could not otherwise be located, to record with their help the metabolism of the human body, and to use them in numerous other ways as a new medical tool.

Some time passed before that tool was properly understood. But eventually it was realized that X-rays were produced when the electrons forming the stream of electricity from the cathode in the tube were suddenly stopped by contact with the metal of the anode. When this happened, the electrons gave up some of their energy in X-rays much as a bullet stopped by a wall will give up its energy in the form of infra-red rays recognized as heat. It was found that when the voltage applied to the tube was increased the resulting X-rays had greater penetrating power; further experiments showed also that the greater the penetrating power of the rays the greater their frequency.

While the medical applications of Roentgen's new rays were being investigated and exploited, Heinrich Hertz's discovery in Karlsruhe was not going unnoticed. His rays had been electrically produced, they travelled at the speed of light, which for most practical purposes meant that they spread instantaneously, and they created a complementary current at a distance, without the aid of any linking wires. These facts naturally titillated the men who were already using electricity to transmit messages with the aid of wires.

As far back as 1844 Samuel Morse had used his eponymous code to send the words 'What hath God wrought?' along a 10-mile telegraph line between Baltimore and Washington. As far back as 1876 Alexander Graham Bell had patented a device in which sound-wave vibrations were turned into a fluctuating electric current which was sent along a wire before being converted back into sound waves. Now Hertz's discovery seemed to offer immense new possibilities: the transmission of messages across estuaries and channels, from ship to shore, and in dozens of other situations where the laying of a cable would be either impracticable or impossible.

First, however, a multitude of questions had to be answered. How far could these mysterious waves be made to travel? How could they be increased in strength so that they were easily detectable? How could it be certain that radiations of one wavelength would not become mixed with those of another? And even if it were possible to send the dots and dashes of the Morse system, would it ever be possible to superimpose the human voice on wireless waves in the same way that it had been successfully superimposed by Bell on an electric current?

All these questions pointed towards tremendous commercial possibilities in a booming world crying out for better communications. The result was that throughout the 1890s and the first years of the 20th century scientists in countries as distant as the United States and Germany, Russia and Britain, struggled to solve them. The basic tools of knowledge with which they worked – Maxwell's equations and the papers of Hertz and the others who had followed in Maxwell's footsteps – were available to all. The technologies available to workers in the laboratories of Washington and Cambridge, St Petersburg and Berlin, were roughly comparable. Thus it is not surprising that the record of inventions that helped transform radio from a dream to a practicality is one of competing priorities, of claim and counter-claim, usually put forward in good faith but making it unwise to give more than a measure of credit to any one man. An exception can fairly be made of Guglielmo Marconi, driving forward through the difficulties with the single-mindedness of genius.

One of the first advances was an increase in the sensitivity of the detector for picking up the wireless waves. This came with the development of a device known as the coherer. The Frenchman Édouard Branly had already noted that when a spark from an electric machine or from an induction coil was created near an exhausted glass tube in which metal filings were packed between silver electrodes, then the conductivity of the filings suddenly increased by as much as a thousand-fold. In the 1890s Sir Oliver Lodge showed that the device also responded to wireless waves and by connecting it to a circuit incorporating a bell or a Morse instrument he was able to record the arrival of wireless waves by bell or by buzz. The

Sir Oliver Lodge in his laboratory
at Liverpool in 1892

improvement in reception was again increased when the Russian scientist Alexander Popov heightened the sensitivity of the receiving device by attaching the Branly-Lodge coherer – so called because at the moment of reception all the finely divided metal filings cohered together – to a long metallic rod called an aerial.

It is at this stage that Marconi enters the story. Heinrich Hertz died on 1 January 1894 and some months later the young Marconi, just 20 and holidaying at the Oropa Sanctuary in the mountains above Biella, read Hertz's obituary notice in an Italian electrical journal. It was written by Augusto Righi, the Italian physicist whose experiments on the reflection of Hertzian waves had helped to show their electro-magnetic nature, and whose lectures Marconi had attended in Bologna. Marconi, fired with the idea of applying the new waves to communication, returned home for long uninterrupted months of experiment. Having read everything available he got to work, improved Branly's coherer, utilized an 'aerial' for reception, and then found that if he used another aerial for transmission this increased the range at which the wireless waves could be detected. In the hills around his home at Pontecchio, 11 miles from Bologna, he was soon receiving signals sent from two miles away and had confirmed the enormously important fact that they could be received 'from the other side of the hill'. Then, anxious to serve Italy, the young Marconi wrote to the Italian Minister of Posts and Telegraphs in Rome. In the manner of Governments, Rome was uninterested. Marconi, thinking of ship-to-shore communication, turned to the leading maritime nation. In the first months of 1896 he arrived in England.

The record of Marconi's early years in England is one of almost continuing success and of the gradual improvement of wireless transmission and reception by a multitude of small details. These did not take the idea beyond the reception, at a distance and without intervening wires, of a signal which could be produced by switching an electric current on or off. But this on–off signal allowed the transmission of messages by means of the Morse code; Marconi's determined improvement of range was, moreover, matched by his vigorous and imaginative demonstration of what his new system meant in practical terms.

He was first encouraged by a far-seeing General Post Office, whose engineering chief, William Preece, was himself a pioneer of telegraphy. His first demonstration between the GPO building in St Martin's-le-Grand and the Savings Bank Department 300 yards away was followed by experiments on Salisbury Plain. Here, before Army and Navy officers, he sent signals first 2 miles and then nearly 5. Early in 1897 the demonstrations were repeated from South Wales across the Bristol Channel to Brean Down in Somerset, $8\frac{1}{2}$ miles away.

At this point Marconi formed his own Wireless Telegraph & Signal Company, soon re-formed as Marconi's Wireless Telegraph Co. Ltd which set up a permanent transmitting station near the Needles on the western end of the Isle of Wight. From the 15-foot high mast near the Needles Marconi kept in constant touch with a receiving station on the mainland near Bournemouth, about $14\frac{1}{2}$ miles away – and, more significantly, with vessels passing up the packed shipping lanes of the Solent which had been equipped with his receiving apparatus. By this means passengers on board were able to receive messages, in good weather or foul, some time before docking at Southampton.

Using a 65-foot transmitting aerial on a steam tug, Marconi sent the world's first radio sports news, relaying details of the Kingstown Regatta in southern Ireland to a mainland receiving mast. He helped to keep the Queen at Osborne in touch with the Prince of Wales, cruising off the Isle of Wight in the Royal Yacht. And on 27 March 1899 Marconi in Wimereux, near Boulogne, sent the first of a stream of signals across the English Channel to Dover.

Post Office officials examining Marconi's apparatus used to communicate by wireless eight miles across the Bristol Channel in 1897. The upper two pieces are a Righi spark gap (*left*) and an induction coil; *below* a Morse inker and relays

By the start of the new century Marconi's first works at Chelmsford, in the south-east of England, was making in quantity the 10-inch induction coils for transmission of wireless waves and the coherers for reception, equipment already in use by the British, German and Italian navies and by a number of commercial shipping companies. And by now he had found a method of controlling oscillation frequency, which meant that transmission and reception could be made on a predetermined wavelength. This increased the efficiency of reception and made it possible to rule out chance interference by other broadcasts.

Hertz's wonderful waves had by this time been received more than 50 miles from their transmission point; it seemed as though Hertz and Maxwell had been right in their assumptions that such waves, once produced, went on indefinitely. Marconi was determined to find out if this were so. By 1901 he had set up a transmission station at Poldhu, Cornwall, on the western tip of southern Britain, and what was in his mind must have been clear to all from the moment that the tall radio towers began to rise on the coast: transmission across the Atlantic.

There was still one thing that seemed to rule out wireless messages to America. This was simply the curvature of the earth. For it was known that light travels in straight lines and it was equally certain, furthermore, that radio waves did the same. But the curve of the earth raises a giant 150-mile hump of ocean between Britain and America, and a straight line extended across the Atlantic would end up hundreds of miles above the US coast, a position where no receiver had ever been.

Marconi in the room at Signal Hill, Newfoundland, with the instruments with which he received the first trans-Atlantic wireless signals on 12 December 1901

Despite the head-shakings of those who knew better, Marconi pressed on with his preparations.

After more than one set-back, and the destruction of the aerials at his first reception site on Cape Cod, Massachusetts, all was ready. Marconi had found a new site above the port of St John's in Newfoundland and here he prepared his equipment early in December. At Poldhu, more than 2,000 miles away in Cornwall, the pre-arranged letter S in morse was tapped out automatically.

'It was shortly after mid-day (local time) on 12 December 1901 that I placed a single ear-phone to my ear and started listening,' Marconi later wrote. 'The receiver on the table before me was very crude – a few coils and condensers and a coherer, no valves, no amplifier, not even a crystal. I was at last on the point of putting the correctness of all my beliefs to the test. The experiment had involved risking at least £50,000 to achieve a result which had been declared impossible by some of the principal mathematicians of the time.'

Suddenly he heard the sharp click of the 'tapper' as it struck the coherer.

'Unmistakably, the three sharp clicks corresponding to three dots sounded in my ear; but I would not be satisfied without corroboration. "Can you hear anything, Mr Kemp?" I said, handing the telephone to my assistant. Kemp heard the same thing as I.'

The 'impossible' had in fact been achieved with the help of the as yet undiscovered ionosphere, the envelope of ionized particles surrounding the earth like the skin surrounding the flesh of an orange. Only a year after Marconi's epoch-making trans-Atlantic experiment the first of the layers making up the ionosphere was discovered by Oliver Heaviside and A. E. Kennelly who showed that wireless waves would not shoot off into space but would be reflected back and forth between the ionosphere and the earth's surface.

The repercussions of Marconi's success were immediate – and not all of them were pleasant. More than a dozen telegraph cables were already in operation across the Atlantic, and radio communication was obviously a threat to the companies which owned them. Considerable efforts were therefore made to throw doubt on the success of Marconi's work. However, the opposition was fighting a losing battle and Marconi now went on from one triumph to another. First he showed that shore to ship transmission was possible at a range of more than 2,000 miles. Then he replaced the coherer with a magnetic detector which was not so vulnerable as the coherer to the rollings of a ship at sea. A 'Marconigram' service which regularly supplied news to ocean liners came next and, soon afterwards, the first impressive demonstration of how radio could bring vital help to a sinking ship. Then, in 1905, reception of signals was made immeasurably easier by Marconi's discovery that a horizontally bent aerial would send out waves most strongly in one specific direction.

So far, however, Marconi – and the many others who were by this time following him – was still creating radio-waves by the unaided spark method used decades earlier by Hertz. The powers which he could draw upon were vastly greater but basically the system was just as inefficient. And, far more important, it was still only possible to transmit and receive wireless waves in bursts; short and long bursts could be distinguished with the result that the dots and dashes of the Morse code could be utilized to send information. But this was still a long way from the time when 'nation shall speak peace unto nation'.

During the first decade of the 20th century two main lines of invention began to transform the primitive wireless of the dot-dash era to those of the contemporary world. The first, and potentially the most important, came from John Fleming, the man who can without qualification be called the inventor of the wireless valve. Fleming found that when a current was passed through the heated filament of a lamp bulb then negative charges – but *only* negative ones – would stream from the filament on to a cold plate inside the bulb. This characteristic, it was quickly realized, could be used to turn the oscillations of the radio-waves hitting an aerial into a continuous current, a more useful transformation than could be provided by the coherer, by the magnetic detector or by the crystal detector which had by this time become a further alternative.

But although the valve quickly became a more valuable detector of radio-waves, it was to be given an even greater importance by Lee de Forest, an American radio expert who was eventually to have more than 300 patents to his name. The most famous was his development of Fleming's two-element diode valve into the triode. The third element was a grid interposed between the heated filament and the cold plate. The importance of this was that the charge placed on the grid controlled a stream of electrons passing from the filament to the plate; more significantly, variation of a very weak potential on the grid produced an electron flow that was similar but very much stronger. In other words, the triode valve could be used to amplify a weak current into a strong one. Furthermore it was discovered, some years after the first triodes were produced, that they could also be used for the generation of currents.

It was the valve which mainly helped to make possible as a practical reality the broadcasting of human speech and of music. Priority is unclear, but certainly Reginald Fessenden, a Canadian-American physicist, was one of the first to conceive the idea of using a continuous stream of radio-waves as a carrier on which a pattern of sound-waves could be imposed. Graham Bell had already shown that the fluctuations of a sound wave could be turned into a correspondingly fluctuating electric current and turned back into speech at the end of a wire. Was the same thing possible without the wire? Fessenden answered this question in the early 1900s. He did it by producing a continuous stream of waves, all of the same length and thus of the same frequency. But before transmission the stream of waves was modulated by an electric current that fluctuated according to the rising and falling of a human voice. Thus the wave-pattern transmitted was that of the carrier-wave modulated in a way that corresponded to the irregularities of a sound wave. At the receiving station, the fluctuating current corresponded, just as it would had it been sent by wire, with the original human voice and was almost as easily transformed back into sound waves. Fessenden's early broadcasts were later repeated by de Forest with his new triode and in 1910 he broadcast the voice of Caruso, an event which did almost as much for the future of radio as the inception of Marconigrams.

The fact that the sound of Caruso's extraordinary voice could be brought into the living-rooms of men and women miles away from the concert hall was technically unimportant but psychologically significant. The risings and fallings of the human voice had been sent without wires almost a decade earlier. But now, all at once, the potentialities of the radio portions of the electro-magnetic spectrum became evident. Not only voices without wires but music without wires! From 1910 until the present day progress in broadcasting has been made up largely of technical advances which have added refinements to this existing possibility. More powerful transmitters have vastly increased the area within which their transmissions can be picked up. Methods have been discovered of eliminating the crackling interference of atmospherics, the natural electrical signals of the universe. Perhaps most important of all, the aural quality of radio reception has been immensely improved.

This development sprang not only from improved equipment but from increased knowledge of how radio-waves are transmitted through the atmosphere and reflected back from the various layers of the ionosphere. The knowledge began to accumulate in the 1920s after radio, which like most other technical developments had benefited from the spur of the First World War, was launched on a commercial basis in Britain, the United States and a number of European countries. During this decade, which witnessed the first important steps to transmit without wires not only sound but also vision, research into the ionosphere was carried out primarily to improve radio reception; but it also paved the way for radar, after radio and television the most important of all techniques for using electro-magnetic waves. The story has a unique interest, partly because of the leap-frogging developments made in different countries and laboratories, partly because of the decisive part which radar was to play in the Second World War.

As early as 1887 Hertz had shown that radio-waves were reflected by metallic objects. But the power of his primitive equipment was small, the reflecting surfaces were only a few feet away, the reflections were recorded only with difficulty, and neither Hertz nor his immediate successors regarded the phenomenon as much more than an interesting fact of nature to be duly recorded and filed away. In 1904 the German physicist Christian Holsmeyer was granted a patent for an anti-collision device for use at sea which depended on the use of radio echoes, but it was not until 1922 that Marconi, accepting the Medal of Honour of the American Institute of Radio Engineers, openly speculated along the lines that the pioneers of radar were to follow.

'In some of my tests', he said, 'I have noticed the effects of reflection and deflection of these [electric] waves by metallic objects miles away. It seems to me that it should be possible to design apparatus by means of which a ship could radiate or project a divergent beam of these rays in any desired direction, which rays, if coming across a metallic object such as another steamer or ship, would be reflected back to a receiver screened from the local transmitter on the sending ship and thereby immediately reveal the presence and bearing of ships, even though these ships be unprovided with any kind of radio.'

*Left* Christian Holsmeyer's device of 1904 for preventing collisions at sea by the use of radio echoes

*Right* Dame Nellie Melba, the famous Australian prima donna, broadcasting from the Marconi works in Chelmsford on 15 June 1920 – the first advertised programme of broadcast entertainment

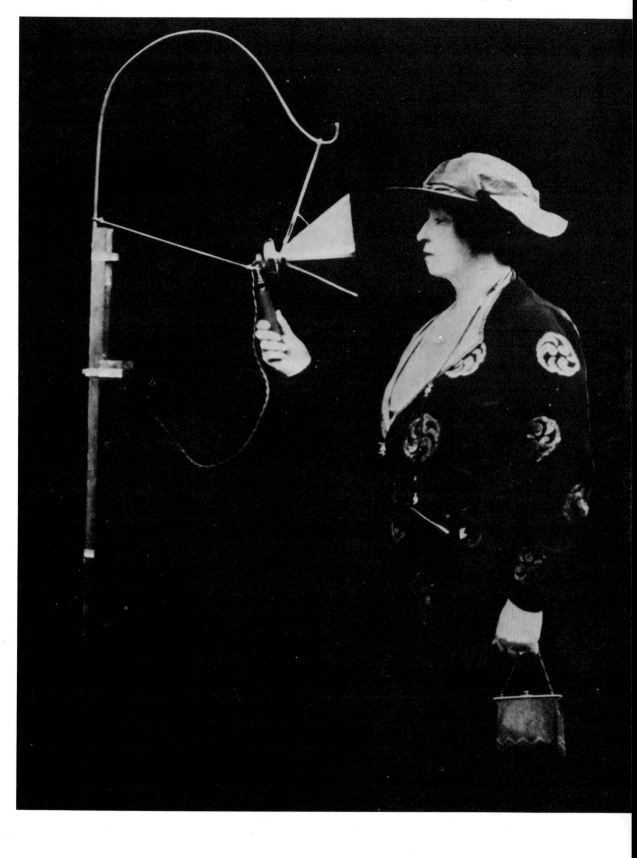

The idea of a ship, or for that matter a plane, sending out radiations and receiving back echoes, lay many steps ahead in the history of radar. But Marconi's statement is typical of the way in which men were thinking; during the next few years more than one scientist and inventor proposed that radio reflections might be conscripted to locate objects. In 1923 and 1936 Heinrich Lowy of Vienna filed two patents for 'measuring the distance of electrically-conductive bodies', one being a form of radar altimeter. In the United States one inventor lodged a patent for a form of radar signalling system, while A. H. Taylor and L. C. Young suggested that the interruption of radio-waves could reveal enemy vessels 'irrespective of fog, darkness or smoke-screen'. In Britain two workers at the Admiralty Signal School, Portsmouth, filed a secret patent as early as 1928 for what was later to be called 'a complete patent for radar'. At the Army Signal Establishment a few years afterwards two scientists devised a system for recording reflected radio pulses. But neither the Army which still believed the cavalry to be Queen of the battlefield, nor the Navy which still pinned its faith on the battleship, was interested in new-fangled detection devices, and two great opportunities were lost.

Many of these plans, patents and ideas were only in the laboratory or drawing-board stage and at first glance it is easy to understand the sceptical view of the Services. However, by the 1930s one man had in fact shown the practicality of using radio reflections. He was Edward Appleton, a Cambridge physicist who in 1924 had discovered the height of the ionosphere, the layer of ionized particles which envelopes the earth. Appleton had used a receiver to pick up radio transmissions sent out a known distance away. Some of the received waves came along the straight path from transmitter to receiver and some came a longer route by travelling up to the ionosphere whence they were reflected down to the receiver, thus covering two sides of a triangle instead of one. Appleton arranged for the wavelength on which the signals were transmitted to be varied and when the difference in length of the two routes travelled was a whole number of wavelengths these would combine to produce a loud signal; when the difference was equal to an odd number of half wavelengths the signals would tend to cancel one another out. A simple equation which used the mean wavelength, the small change in wavelength, and the number of 'fadings', enabled the difference in length of the two routes to be easily worked out; and this gave the height of the point of reflection, or in other words the height of the ionosphere.

This was Appleton's first way of doing the trick. But soon afterwards he repeated the experiment using the system of pulse transmission which had been devised in the United States. Short sharp bursts of radio energy were sent out and reflected back from the ionosphere whose height was then discovered by recording the time taken for the journey up to the ionosphere and back again.

It was still all rather esoteric viewed in practical terms. But a further, and key, step was taken by Appleton in 1932 when he led a party to Northern Norway to make observations during the International Polar Year. His main work was concentrated on discovering how thunderstorms affected the ionosphere. However, as far as the future of radar was concerned the important thing was that he recorded radio reflections on the cathode ray equipment with which he – and others – had long been experimenting. Earlier, reflections had been used to make a photographic record with the aid of a galvanometer. Now something very different was achieved, for the incoming pulses were utilized to affect the steady horizontal line on a cathode-ray tube. Each time a pulse arrived there was a small 'blip' on the line, and the position of the 'blip' gave an indication of the distance away of the reflecting layer.

At this point it is useful to summarize exactly what had been achieved. Appleton checking his thunderstorms – and the workers in the Admiralty and Army Signals Establishments who had produced their own versions of embryonic radar – had been adapting the old trick of the sailor caught in thick fog off a rocky coast. The sailor shouts or whistles and by noting the interval before he hears an echo is able to work out his distance from the cliffs of the coast. The forerunners of radar were using the same technique; but they were using radio-waves which travel a million times faster than the sound-waves of the sailor's voice and they were using a reflecting layer about which comparatively little was yet known. What they had done was to show that there lay to hand a new scientific tool which could be turned to good effect under certain conditions, by skilled operators, for limited purposes. But even this had little resemblance to a practicable weapon. It is not as surprising as it seems at first that the birth of radar itself still hung fire. As with so many inventions, what was needed was the operational requirement.

In Britain this necessary spur was administered by the Air Defence Exercises of 1934. At that time early warning devices consisted only of acoustic shields, designed to magnify the hum of approaching planes (and pointing, incidentally towards France) and the exercises underlined that for all practical purposes London was defenceless – 'the greatest target in the world, a kind of tremendous fat cow, a valuable fat cow tied up to attract the beasts of prey' as Churchill described it. An Air Ministry Committee – the famous Tizard Committee – was set up to decide what should be done, and before it met the chief scientific adviser to the Air Ministry, H. E. Wimperis, decided once more to investigate the 'Death Ray', that device which rose as a spectre at regular intervals. To make quite sure that the Death Ray was an impossibility, Wimperis sought the help of Robert Watson-Watt, then Superintendent of the Government's Radio Research Station.

The next few steps are well known. Watson-Watt ruled out a Death Ray. But simple computations worked out by his assistant, A. F. Wilkins, suggested that broadcasts at the powers then practicable might produce detectable reflections from the kind of aircraft then flying – a case of theory confirming what had already been noted. Post Office engineers had recorded a few years earlier that passing aircraft caused a fluttering of their radio signals while Appleton himself had noted more than once how planes flying over his laboratory had interrupted his work. Now, however, something else was envisaged.

On the morning of 26 February 1935 a Heyford heavy bomber, a biplane with a top speed of 131 mph, flew over Daventry, passing through the transmissions from the town's BBC station. On the ground a small group including Watson-Watt, Wilkins and A. P. Rowe, an Air Ministry observer, watched a green blob on a cathode-ray tube expand and shrink. The range at which the reflection could be picked up on the screen was only 10 miles. But it justified Watson-Watt's exuberant words: 'Britain has become an island once more.'

In this early stage of development it was merely planned that a series of radio towers should be set up round the coast to transmit overlapping spheres of radio-waves. Planes approaching the coast would reflect the waves and these reflections would be picked up by stations which would thus be given advance warning of enemy raiders. Although the distance of the approaching planes could be calculated from the position of the blob on the radar screen, nothing more could at first be learned from it. But during the following months the equipment was refined and improved to show first direction and then height. Finally it was possible to tell from the green blob on the screen whether the radar echoes were being produced from one plane, from a few or from many. And before the outbreak of war British planes had been fitted with a simple device which enabled the radar watchers round the coast to

One of the radar towers which formed part of Britain's early warning system when war broke out in 1939

German shipping at Oslo seen with the help of the radar device H₂S. The coastal area can be compared quite easily with a map of the same area. No echoes are received from the water, but the presence and location of shipping is indicated by quite strong 'echoes' or 'blips'.

tell immediately whether echoes were coming from friend or from foe. All these developments were built into the series of radar stations which by the outbreak of war ringed Britain. They not only gave advance warning of enemy aircraft but by indicating the size of individual formations enabled Fighter Command to husband its severely-stretched resources during the Battle of Britain.

The Germans also developed radar along very similar lines, and in the early days their equipment was often as good as the British and sometimes better. Their failure sprang primarily from lack of liaison between the Luftwaffe and the scientists – and from a misplaced German confidence that scientific aids were not needed for victory.

As soon as the vital importance of radar in the war was appreciated, development went ahead in Britain, in Germany, and in the United States where American defence scientists were in the autumn of 1940 told of the British work by members of the Tizard Mission.

One of the first and most important steps forward was the production of the cavity magnetron valve. Its value stems from the fact that as shorter and shorter wavelengths are used, so does the potential operational usefulness of radar increase. The original experiments had been carried out with 5,000-centimetre waves and by the autumn of 1939 wavelengths down to 50 centimetres were being discussed. There seemed, however, to be one insuperable limitation. For as the wavelengths grew shorter so did it become more and more difficult to provide them with sufficient power. It was not, it appeared, possible to solve one half of the problem without correspondingly increasing the other half, and the indissolubility with which the two halves were linked looked like a permanent limiting factor to those who were developing radar.

The problem was solved in Birmingham by Professor J. T. Randall and Dr H. A. Boot. Together, they developed the magnetron, a valve devised some years earlier and utilizing a magnetic field to produce its effects, into something radically better. Their cavity magnetron had, as its name implies, a number of long cavities machined in a solid block of copper. The electrons from the cathode were carried round in a magnetic field past a number of oscillatory circuits in these cavities which became sources of very short waves. When the first valve was tested in February 1940 the wave lengths were found to be shorter than 10 centimetres, while 400 watts was being generated, a power much greater than anything previously produced in this way.

Short waves were an essential of many other applications of radar which came into operational use as the war went on. A centimetric radar set on the Dover cliffs in the summer of 1941 detected ships 45 miles away. Large vessels could be seen leaving the enemy-held port of Boulogne in all weathers, while even the small German E-boats could be tracked more than 17 miles away. Very soon, British radar had 'closed' the narrows of the English Channel.

Before the end of the war the reflections of radio-waves were not only enabling gunners to 'see' invisible targets but were giving their missiles a new order of deadliness. This was provided by the proximity fuse, a device built in to the head of a shell and incorporating a radio transmitter and receiver. The waves sent out were reflected back from the object aimed at; when the receiver indicated that the target was a certain pre-arranged distance away the shell was automatically exploded, thus ensuring the maximum damage.

There were many other ways in which the principles of radar were exploited, particularly by those who fought the war in the air. Airborne radar sets were built and with their help pilots were able at night to 'home' on to enemy planes. Two important navigational aids known as 'Gee' and 'Oboe', were developed and enabled radar transmitters on the ground in England to guide pilots accurately to positions directly above targets in Germany. More important still was $H_2S$. This was not a navigational aid but a system which gave the pilot a picture of the ground over which he was flying. It was achieved by utilizing the fact that short radio-waves give a different kind of reflection when they are thrown back by open country, by water, or by built-up areas, of particular use in the war against

Inside Bawdsey Research Station,
operational from early 1936

Germany since so many of the main targets were close to large areas of water – Hamburg being on the Elbe estuary, Berlin almost surrounded by big lakes, and various other cities easily identifiable by the shapes built up by the pattern of radar reflections.

These wartime uses of radar paved the way for the numerous post-war navigational and blind-landing systems without which the growth of the world's air routes during the last quarter-century would have been impossible. Today the multiple applications of radar allow planes to take off in safety in quick succession from busy airports, enable a pilot to check his position on a journey across the world, and then pick up a radar-landing device which will lead him down onto the runway in the worst weather.

The last quarter-century's growth of commercial flying which has so changed the business and the holiday patterns of the world would have been impossible without the guiding hand of radar, itself the direct outcome of the frantic need to win the war in the air. By contrast television, that other technical marvel of the electro-magnetic spectrum which makes the post-war world so different from the pre-war, has grown up despite the hiatus of the war years during which research was pressed ahead on devices of more direct Service significance.

It is the use of electro-magnetic waves to transmit pictures which has made contemporary television possible, but the idea of sending images from one place to another by electrical means goes back not only beyond the birth of radio but beyond even the discovery of electro-magnetic waves. In fact Morse had been sending messages by wire only a few years when various ingenious ways of using electricity to send pictures were being proposed. Most of them depended for their practicability on the light-sensitivity of selenium, the rare element first isolated by Jöns Berzelius in the early years of the 19th century. One form of the element, the so-called 'metallic' selenium, was being used in the early 1870s by Joseph May, at a cable station off the coast of Ireland. May noted that unexpected variations in the readings of his instruments were caused by the effect of light on the selenium; for some inexplicable reason, he found, light changed the electrical resistance of the material. More important, it seemed clear that the variation in resistance was proportional to the intensity of the light. Thus light itself could be made to create an electrical signal.

A decade after this discovery of what was to be one of the essentials of television, the German engineer Paul Nipkow patented his scanning disc, a device which used another principle basic to television: persistence of vision, the characteristic of the human eye which presents to the brain as one moving image the multiple static, and slightly different, images of the cinema film. Nipkow made use of this by piercing in a disc a series of small holes arranged in a spiral. If the disc were rotated between a light source and an object the whole of that object would be scanned by light through the holes after one revolution of the disc. The darker and the lighter portions of the object would reflect different amounts of light and if these reflections were thrown on to a succession of selenium cells, the cells could be used to send a series of electrical impulses along a wire. At the receiving end the impulses could be used to produce signals corresponding to the brightness of the individual parts of the object lit up at the transmitting end of the line. If the signals – the turning on, for instance, of individual lights in a mosaic of lights – were viewed through a second Nipkow disc, then the eye would briefly receive a series of transitory images corresponding to the parts of the object being scanned. If the wheel were

Karl Jansky pointing in 1933 to the position on a chart where radio noises from space were first heard. While trying to pinpoint the source of noise interfering with the radiotelephone service, Jansky detected a peculiar hissing sound coming from the area of the Milky Way, later identified as radio signals generated by the natural processes in stars and galaxies. His work resulted in the new science of radio astronomy, in which the heavens are studied by listening to radio waves rather than by looking through an optical telescope.

revolved fast enough the eye would transmit these parts to the brain as a single image.

The basic idea of activating in succession the individual items in a mosaic of photo-electric cells was first conceived for use by means of the electric telegraph. However, even 'wired vision' as it might have been called, was ruled out for practical purposes by two things. One was that the process of scanning the mosaic of photo-electric elements by mechanical means was too slow; the separate images did not follow one another fast enough and the result was not a composite picture that could be properly recognized. The other was that while mosaics of separate elements could produce rough patterns, much as the lighting-up of separate bulbs in a mosaic of bulbs can produce numbers or letters in a display sign, the elements were neither small enough nor numerous enough to represent acceptably the infinitely numerous lights and shades of everyday scenes.

With the birth of radio, and the ability to send electrical signals through space by the use of a carrier wave, much that

was possible by wire became possible by wireless. Before this,
however, the key to television as it is known today had been
provided by the cathode-ray tube, which was steadily improved. John Fleming discovered that the stream of electrons
pouring down the length of a cathode tube could be focused
by an encircling electrical current on to a target at the end of
the tube – a target which if coated with a flourescent material
would be made to glow at the spot hit by the focused electron
stream. Subsequently it was found that an external magnetic
field could be made to deflect the electron stream so that it hit
any desired part of the target.

At this point, the major essentials of modern television had
already been produced in embryo, although few men realized
the fact. One who did so was Archibald Campbell Swinton, an
electrical engineer who had already impinged on history at
two points, by producing the first X-ray photograph in
Britain in 1896 and by giving Marconi his vital letter of
introduction to William Preece of the Post Office in the early
years of the 20th century. In 1908 Campbell Swinton wrote an
extraordinary letter to *Nature*, the British scientific journal.
Describing what was called 'distant electric vision', he outlined a system strikingly similar to that used in television today. The transmitter incorporated a screen painted with
fluorescent material on to which a scene was focused much as
it would be focused on a photographic film in a camera. The
screen, glowing with a fluorescent image, was scanned by a
cathode-ray tube in the same way that the human eye scans the
type on the written page, moving from left to right along a
succession of horizontal lines which followed one another in
succession down the page. The stream of electrons in the
scanning tube, passing across the light and dark portions of the
fluorescent image, was used to trigger off a series of electrical
impulses which corresponded to the light and dark of the
image. These impulses, transmitted to a cathode tube in the
receiver, were in turn to trigger off a stream of electrons
which, as it was scanned across a screen similar to that in the
transmitter, produced on this screen a fluorescent image
whose light and dark portions matched those of the original.
The replica was made up of a succession of images, glowing as
the electron beam continuously swept across the target from
left to right, returned to the left a little lower down and
continued the process until the whole screen had been
scanned, when it returned to the top of the screen and began to
repeat the process. The action was so quick that the human
eye retained the first of the images until the scanning process
had covered the whole screen and begun again, thus providing

the brain with an unflickering picture analogous to that produced on the cinema screen.

At least, that was the idea behind Campbell Swinton's plan. But in the early years of the century neither methods of sufficiently amplifying the signals nor of moving the scanning beam across the target screen were developed far enough to make practical television possible. Better amplification came first, and the first television transmissions were made with the help of mechanical scanning systems based either on Nipkow's wheel or on mirror-drums whose mirrors created a succession of overlapping reflections of a subject as the drum was revolved.

During the 1920s and 1930s these systems were extensively experimented with both in the United States and in Britain. As early as 1923 a scanning disc system was used to send a picture of President Harding from Washington to Philadelphia; four years later the Bell Telephone Laboratories

Research apparatus used in the development of television. The scientist on the left is observing the image re-created through the rotating disc. The scanning disc at the other end of the shaft intervenes between an illuminated transparency and the photo-electric cell, housed in the box visible beyond the driving shaft

supported experiments which enabled pictures to be sent by radio from New York to Washington; and in 1928 a radio station in Schenectady began half-hour transmissions that were probably the world's first, even if they were only experimental. But these transmissions gave only 24 lines per picture and although other experimenters were getting 50 lines this still produced far too coarse-grained a picture to be acceptable.

The same was at first true of the system introduced in England by John Logie Baird, a Scot who is important in the story of television not so much for his technical innovations as for his introduction of television to the general public. Baird, an inveterate inventor responsible not only for a television system but for a chemically treated damp-proofed sock and a new method of jam-manufacture, started work on his apparatus in 1922. He was poor, and the state of his finances is indicated by the components of his first television transmitter which used a form of Nipkow disc and was assembled on a washstand. 'The base of his motor was a tea-chest, a biscuit tin housed the projection lamp, scanning discs were cut from cardboard, and fourpenny cycle lenses were used,' it has been written. 'Scrapwood, darning needles, string and sealing-wax held the apparatus together.'

John Logie Baird's early television apparatus dated about 1925

Baird developed his device for three years and in 1926 was able to demonstrate it before some 50 members of the Royal Institution in London. He used a revolving mirror drum which in conjunction with a spotlight projector scanned the subject being televised with a concentrated spot of light. The spot was picked up by a mosaic of photocells whose output made up the initial currents transmitted. Baird's picture had a definition of only 30 lines, his scanner covered the subject area only five times a second, and the picture itself was only two inches high and an inch and a half wide. Despite the primitive character of the picture, Baird pressed on, and by 1929 was able to persuade the British Broadcasting Corporation to start a regular series of television transmissions, the second in the world. They were something more than the purely experimental transmissions which had been started the previous year in the United States. Baird's Televisor, as he called his receiving apparatus, was now capable of producing $12\frac{1}{2}$ pictures a second and was put on public sale and within three years thousands of the British public had, for instance, seen the Derby televised from the race-course at Epsom in 1931.

However much Baird and his colleagues improved their apparatus, they were handicapped by the comparative slowness of the mechanical scanning device. Something dramatically better than this became possible during the 1930s as there emerged various practicable methods of using an improved cathode-ray tube to replace mechanical scanning. The key figure in this development was Vladimir Zworykin, a Russian electrical engineer who settled in the United States after the Revolution. In 1928 Zworykin patented the idea of using a cathode tube to scan a television screen, and during the next decade developed what he called the iconoscope, the first practical television camera.

By the early 1930s a number of companies were pressing forward with research in Britain. Baird was experimenting with 120-line transmissions, Cossors were finding what could be done with 180-line pictures, while EMI and Scophony Ltd were other firms in the field. By 1936, when the BBC began regular transmissions from Alexandra Palace in North London, two systems were used on alternate weeks – a Baird System by this time giving 240 lines, with 25 pictures a second, and a Marconi-EMI System giving 25 405-line pictures per second. The arrangements continued for only a few months, after which the Marconi-EMI system alone was used. The impact of television during these years immediately preceding the war should not be over-estimated; nevertheless,

some 10,000 sets for picking up the 405-line services were sold
in Britain between 1936 and 1939.

The outbreak of the Second World War put a temporary
stop to anything not directly connected with the Services but
the development of electronic techniques during the next six
years, particularly for such war-winning devices as radar,
brought forth the tools which soon turned the television
images of the late 1930s into the pictures of today.

Most contemporary systems use hundreds of lines per
picture (405 and 625 in Britain, 525 in the United States, 625 in
Europe) and in Britain they provide 25 complete pictures per
second, with interlaced scanning giving double that number
of frames. Twenty-five pictures per second is not, of itself,
good enough to eliminate flickering, a problem which is overcome by the ingenious interlacing method. In this, lines 1, 3,
5, 7 and so on are scanned first, followed by lines 2, 4, 6, 8 etc.
This is done at twice the normal speed, thus producing two
fields of $202\frac{1}{2}$ lines each on the 405 system, which are merged to
produce 25 complete pictures every second, thus eliminating
flicker.

Operation of most systems is basically the same. With the
use of one typical camera tube an image is focused on to a
light-sensitive screen in the camera. The dark parts of the
screen retain all their electrons but the parts hit by light from
the image lose some of them. When the beam of electrons in
the scanning tube hits a dark part of the screen, already full of
electrons, it is reflected back to a collecting plate and sends out
a pulse. When the beam hits a light part of the screen, which
has given off some of its electrons, the beam is absorbed and
fails to return to the collecting plate. Thus a 'pulse' and a 'no
pulse' signal is obtained, is transmitted by a carrier wave just
as a sound signal would be transmitted, and is then reconsti-
tuted on a picture tube in the receiver.

The huge expansion of television in the post-war years was
not only a demonstration of man's growing understanding of
electronics and his mastery of electronic techniques. It was
also a response to a demand, in many ways a fulfilment of
A. P. Rowe's 'operational requirement', providing a more
affluent world with time on its hands with a new kind of mass
entertainment. The demand for colour soon came.

Crude systems for sending colour-pictures by wire had
been proposed since the early years of the century, most of
them using a prism system to break up into the primary
colours the light from an object being mechanically scanned.
However, a practicable colour system had to await the coming
of electronic systems, and several arrived simultaneously in an

attempt to satisfy the demand. Various methods are used for sending out from a camera three sets of signals, each linked to the amounts of the three primary colours present in the different parts of the image being scanned. With few exceptions, however, these signals are translated back into a coloured image by what is basically the same method. This relies for its operation on a receiving screen which is coated not with the usual photo-sensitive material responding to white light but with a pattern of red, green and blue phosphor dots, arranged in triangular units. Behind this mosaic there is stretched a shadow mask pierced by thousands of small holes. During reception three electron guns, each responding to the pattern of impulses produced by the red, the blue or the green parts of the original image, scan the screen simultaneously, each beam being so positioned that signals from the red parts of the original pass through holes behind the red phosphor dots, blue signals fall on the blue dots and green signals on the green. The signals are so fast and the dots illuminated are so

Drs William Shockley (*seated*), John Bardeen (*left*) and Walter H. Brattain, at Bell Telephone Laboratories in 1948 with the apparatus used in investigations that led to the invention of the transistor

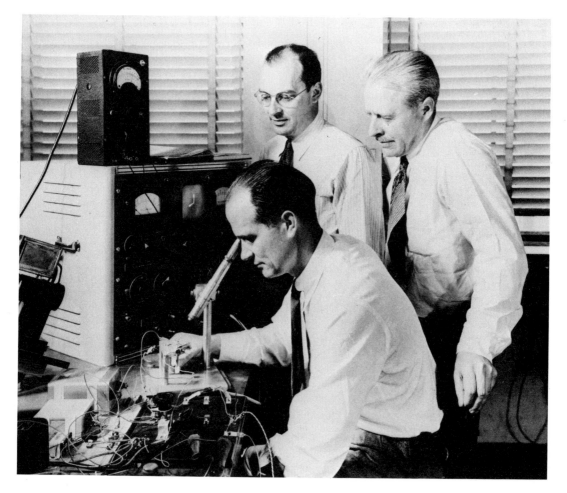

small and so closely-spaced that the eye is deceived into seeing an unflickering colour image of the original.

During the last quarter-century television – as well as radio – has been the object of extensive technological research which has steadily increased the quality of reception and the convenience of equipment. The physicists, the chemists, the metallurgists have all contributed, and television itself has become a good illustration of the way in which inventions and advances in a number of fields are closely inter-related.

Few single inventions had a greater effect than that of the transistor which from 1948 began to transform not only radio and television but a host of other equipment which depended for its working on the control of electrons. Many men contributed to its creation, and important among them was the English-American physicist William Shockley. Some years earlier Shockley and his fellow-workers in the United States had discovered that crystals of the rare metal germanium would, if they contained minute quantities of certain impurities, act like the crystals of the early radio sets: they would work as rectifiers, passing on surges of current in only one direction. They would, however, do the job far more efficiently. In 1948 Shockley discovered how to combine two slightly different sorts of crystals in such a way that they would not only act together as a rectifier but would also amplify a current. The device – soon called a transistor because it transferred current across a resistor – would do all that a radio valve would do. It had, moreover, immense advantages, since it was smaller, lighter and more rugged than a valve. In addition it would start work without any of the preparatory warming-up period that was needed with valves.

The use of transistors – whose development was speeded-up a decade later with the need for miniaturizing equipment in satellites – spread quickly throughout the radio and television industries. It also spread in other parts of the electronics industry which had been developing along parallel lines.

One spectacular example of the way in which technologists in the industry have utilized the fresh knowledge of the electron, acquired as men discovered more about the electromagnetic spectrum, is the contemporary electronic computer. Its importance springs basically from one fact: that in carrying out calculations it employs not the human hand, as in an abacus, not a physical mechanism as in a mechanical computer, but an electric current that allows information to be sent from place to place in a minute fraction of a second.

It was in the 1930s that American researchers first pointed out the similarities between the on-off states of an electric

Colour television transmission

1 Dichroic mirrors
2 Image orthicon
3 Blue signal
4 Red signal
5 Green signal
6 Early synchronizing pulses
7 Encoder
8 Synchronizing generator
9 Synchronizing pulses
10 Chrominance signal
11 Luminance signal
12 Transmitter
13 Receiving aerial
14 Receiver
15 Video panel
16 Decoding panel
17 Deflection yoke
18 Radial convergence magnet
19 Electron guns
20 Magnetic shield
21 Shadow mask
22 Phosphor dot screen with image

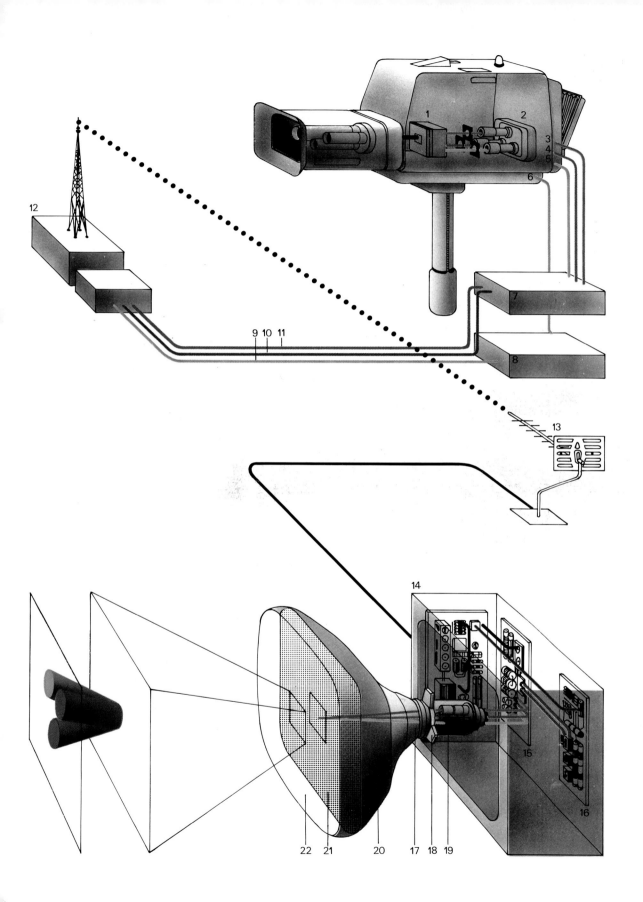

An experimental laser being used by Montague Burton, the tailors, to cut through thick piles of cloth without distorting them

circuit and the basic twin alternatives of logic. From here the next step was the combination of the binary system, in which all numbers can be expressed in a two-symbol notation, and the operations of mathematical logic. This enabled the most complicated sums and calculations to be carried out at what would previously have been unimaginable speeds.

One of the disadvantages of the new electronic computers which began to be built soon after the end of the Second World War, was their size. Thus the American machine ENIAC weighed 3 tons, and used 130 Kw – largely because it was packed with thousands of valves. It was these valves which were eliminated in later computers by transistors, the devices which, as much as any other single item, transformed the prospects for the new electronic machines which within two decades became an almost everyday feature of business and commercial life.

# 4 Man Makes Materials

Man's use of the electro-magnetic spectrum had one thing in common with the development of photography and the conquest of the air: it enlisted in its service a new class of artificial material which man began to make during the closing decades of the last century. These were plastics. The first may have evolved directly from research into photographic plates, the evolution of others was encouraged by the growing demands of the electrical industry, while later plastics were tailor-made by chemists specifically to treat the fabric which covered the wings of early aircraft. Invention, like peace, seems indivisible.

Since the earliest times man had not only used such naturally occurring materials as wood, stone, minerals and animal and vegetable fibres. He had also learned how to process some of them into metals such as bronze and into brittle amorphous mixtures such as glass. These materials, though literally man-made, were different in one very important way from the huge family of plastics which evolved from the pioneer work of the mid-19th century. For they were produced by men who learned, very largely by trial-and-error, how to create materials with whatever characteristics of hardness, malleability or transparency they required. They got the right end-product but they rarely knew why.

This hit-and-miss method changed as during the first half of the 19th century the science of chemistry finally burst away from the tendrils of alchemy which had continued to hold it back. But it was a gradual process; although public display of the world's first plastic articles came only at the 1862 International Exhibition in London, their story can be traced back for at least three decades. In 1832 Professor Henri Bracconat of Nancy discovered that if he poured concentrated nitric acid on to cotton or wood fibres he got a hard water-resistant film which he called xylodine. A few years later Professor Théophile Pelouze of Paris found that the same materials could be used to produce an explosive substance. However, neither Bracconat nor Pelouze thought it worthwhile to follow up their work and it was left to Christian Schönbein, a German-Swiss chemist, to take the next step a decade later. One story is that Schönbein, experimenting in his wife's kitchen, spilled some acid, mopped up the mess with a cotton apron, began to dry the apron over a stove and then saw the apron disappear with a smokeless bang. Whether or not the story has the mythological quality of Newton and the apple, Schönbein certainly arrived at Woolwich Arsenal to demonstrate the new smokeless powder that might revolutionize warfare. What he had produced was cellulose nitrate, commonly called guncotton; he had, moreover, discovered how to make it under controlled conditions. These conditions governed the characteristics of the new material, and a letter Schönbein sent to Michael Faraday at the Royal Institution in 1846 gave a hint of things to come. 'To give you some idea of what may be made out of vegetable fibre I send you a specimen of a transparent substance which I have prepared from common paper,' this went. 'This matter is capable of being shaped into all sorts of things and forms, and I have made from it a number of beautiful vessels. The first perfect one I obtain is destined to be sent to the Mistress of the Royal Institution.' There were other possibilities, and Faraday soon gave Schönbein an introduction to John Dickinson, the founder of the famous firm of paper-makers. Would not the new substance be suitable for the making of bank-notes? This was not the only idea floating through the minds of the inventive 19th-century chemists and another who was sent a specimen of Schönbein's material commented: 'The glass-like paper is indeed very beautiful, and I wish it could be obtained sufficiently thick to be used for windows.'

Alexander Parkes, inventor of 'Parkesine', an early plastic

However, Schönbein's main concern was with the explosive potential of nitrocellulose, and its development into the world's first useful plastic was left to Alexander Parkes, a Birmingham metallurgist and one of those typical Victorians with brain never very far from a new idea and energy always on hand to exploit it. Parkes used to claim that he was first an artist and only secondly a metallurgist or chemist, a claim that sprang from his first patent which covered the 'Electro-deposition of Works of Art'. While the idea of electro-plating was not entirely new, Parkes refined it to new levels. When Queen Victoria visited his Birmingham works she was presented with electro-plated roses. When Prince Albert did so, something more extraordinary was produced: an electro-plated spider's web, every strand of which was coated with the thinnest covering of silver. Parkes was also the pioneer of the cold vulcanization of rubber, while as early as 1843 he patented a process for waterproofing fabrics with a solution of rubber in carbon disulphide, an idea later sold to a firm which founded not only an industry but a word: Charles Macintosh & Co.

Just what led Parkes into the world of nitrocellulose is not clear, but it has been suggested that Schönbein's English patent agent discussed the subject with him. Parkes was attracted to new ideas for their own sake but in this case he already had certain links with the subject. One of his earliest patents concerned improvements in the photographic uses of collodion; and collodion, it will be remembered, is a solution of cellulose nitrate in alcohol and ether. One of Parkes's ideas was to prepare a layer of collodion so thick that no glass would be necessary to support the sensitive photographic emulsion, and it is possible that this interest led him on to production of 'Parkesine'. There was also his hobby of moulding objects in sealing wax – a figurine of Napoleon made by Parkes was for years in the Birmingham Art Gallery – and this also played a part in his development of a cheap colourless material which passed through a plastic stage during its production.

From the start, Parkes had a number of problems. The cotton material, he soon discovered, had to be less heavily nitrated than if it was destined to be guncotton. Once he considered making a material in what would now be called production quantities, rather than the small one-off amounts made by Schönbein, he had the problem of raw materials. There were various qualities of cotton and only some of these fitted his purpose. There was also the question of cost. Parkes lived in that curious world between science, technology and business, but he knew that it would be useless to consider commercial possibilities until he could think in terms of practical prices.

Some of his early processes were sophisticated and in-genious, although one of them opens with an air of Mrs Beeton's 'Take six chickens'. 'I take a hundredweight of disintegrated or divided cotton waste or similar substances, and this is placed in an iron vessel called a converter,' he wrote. Nitric and sulphuric acid was then forced into the converter and after 20 or 30 minutes the resulting mass was dropped on to a perforated tray from which most of the remaining acid drained away. After another hour the cellulose nitrate was forced by hydraulic pressure into a hard cylinder. This cylinder of solid guncotton was subsequently broken up and mixed with a solvent. It was here that the real difficulties began. Many of the possible solvents were highly flammable; there seemed an infinitely large number of additives which could be used; and when Parkes found one that did the trick – camphor – he seems to have ignored its significance. What the camphor did was control or remove the contraction of the product during the later stages of its processing. But this seems to have been masked by the other ingredients and Parkes failed to recognize an essential factor in the production of what was a few years later to be registered as 'Celluloid' in the United States.

In the next stage, the guncotton was dissolved in the solvent to produce a malleable plastic mass, various resins and oils being added to give the end-product the necessary qualities of hardness or flexibility. It could then be processed into sheets, or moulded into shapes.

The versatility of this strange new material was outlined by Parkes, who noted that it could be used as an insulator on telegraph wires. 'It can be spread on textiles or other materials,' he went on. 'The layers of one colour may be spread on another and beautiful granular or marble effects may be obtained by rolling dissimilar coloured sheets together while in a slightly soft state.'

In practice, these characteristics meant two things. One, the cheap production of what the trade calls 'fancy goods', was illustrated by a display of products made from the new material at the International Exhibition of 1862. Here, in the words of the official catalogue, Parkes showed 'medallions, hollow ware, tubes, buttons, combs, knife handles, pierced and fret work, inlaid work, bookbinding, card cases, boxes, pens, penholders, etc.'. As if this were not enough, Parkesine, as it had now been christened, could be made 'hard as ivory, transparent or opaque, of any degree of flexibility, and is also waterproof; may be of the most brilliant colours, can be used in the solid, plastic or fluid state, may be worked in dies and pressure, as metals, may be cast or used as a coating to a great variety of substances'. Furthermore, it could be used to imitate tortoise-shell or wood, as well as to produce 'an endless variety of effects'. To men and women in 1862 it must have seemed that the millenium was on its way; Tennyson had been justified after all:

Men, my brothers, men the workers, ever reaping something new:
That which they have done but earnest of the things that they shall do.

In fact, it was a little more difficult than that. Parkes

A plaque moulded from 'Parkesine'

*Below* Ivoride head of Daniel Spill's own walking-stick

*Below right* Back of an ivoride hand-mirror made by Daniel Spill

claimed that his patented processes of making the new material reduced its cost from 130s ($16.00) a pound when he had begun experimenting to only 1s (12 cents) a pound by the 1860s. It was certainly a cheap product and during the later 1860s it was used to make, for the working classes, a whole range of imitation goods which would otherwise have been far beyond their pockets. But in fact, Parkesine was too cheap. The company which Parkes founded to exploit it had rushed too quickly into 'full-scale' production. Its raw materials, the cheapest it was possible to buy, were sometimes impure or contaminated, and from the scanty records that remain it seems that production problems were not carefully enough thought through. All this, quite apart from the maddening inflammability of Parkesine, added up to a recipe for disaster. Before 1870 the Parkesine Company was wound up.

While Parkes happily returned to the metallurgical and other fields where he was successful, the infant plastics industry was kept alive in England – but only just – by Daniel Spill, another minor inventive genius who could turn his hand to almost anything, and who had become Parkes's works manager. Spill made an improved version of Parkesine which he called xylonite. To exploit it, he founded the British Xylonite Company. His first products were coral jewelry and combs and these were followed by sheet xylonite coloured to produce imitation ivory and tortoise-shell. Next, the material was employed for the first of its 'social' uses – to make collars and cuffs which could be washed clean every night. The company had its ups and downs before eventually expanding into what was to become today's Bakelite Xylonite Ltd employing more than 10,000 people.

Spill's personal fortunes were dominated by his legal

battles with John Wesley Hyatt, an American who took over the plastics story in the United States as Parkes retired from it in Britain. Hyatt was a journeyman printer who in the 1860s settled in Albany, New York. In the spirit of the times he could turn his hand to anything that held out the prospect of great reward and he was attracted by an offer of Phelan & Collander, the local makers of billiard balls. Even a century ago, hunters were making their depredations on the big game of Africa, including the elephant whose ivory was the raw material of billiard balls. Phelan & Collander, looking ahead to the time when scarcity would send prices over the top, announced that they would pay $10,000 ($\pounds$4,200) to anyone discovering a substitute.

Hyatt was one of those who set to work. Legend, which runs riot even more frequently in the history of the plastics industry than in most others, recounts that having cut his finger he sought out the collodion bottle, found it had tipped over, and that the liquid contents had turned into a rubbery mass. This mass became malleable under heat from his hand but hardened again on cooling.

He had already experimented with a number of substances and now found that vastly improved results were obtained if the artificial billiard balls were coated with collodion. Whatever the truth of the story it is clear that he now followed in Parkes's footsteps. What Hyatt realized, however, was that the addition of camphor would eliminate shrinkage during the manufacturing process; from this he went one step further, cutting out the use of a normal solvent and relying instead on the solvent power of camphor when it had been liquefied by heat. However, the necessary temperature was higher than that of the safety limit for nitro-cellulose and the danger was only overcome by dissolving the camphor in ethyl alcohol rather than heating it. There seems doubt as to whether Hyatt won the $10,000, but in 1869 he took out a US patent for the manufacture of what was trade-marked in 1872 as 'Celluloid', the name derived by his brother from cellulose.

The next step was the formation of the Hyatt Manufacturing Company, soon afterwards transformed into the Albany Billiard Ball Company. Not all billiard balls are white and to give the necessary colour to the others these were coated with the thinnest possible layer of nitro-cellulose. For technical reasons only the smallest amount of colouring matter was added – with the result that the balls were covered with a film of almost pure guncotton. 'Consequently a lighted cigar applied would at once result in a serious flame and occasionally the violent contact of the balls would produce a mild explosion

Cover of a Xylonite catalogue showing the plastic collar of the time

Interior of the Albany Billiard Ball
Co., New York, showing
production of plastic billiard balls

like a percussion guncap,' Hyatt later wrote. 'We had a letter
from a billiard saloon proprietor in Colorado, mentioning this
fact and saying that he did not care so much about it but that
instantly every man in the room pulled a gun.'

Although such troubles were eventually overcome, Hyatt
was glad of a fillip given to 'Celluloid' from a different direction.
This came from the makers of dental plates who had been
using hard rubber as their raw material. But rubber manufacturers were sending the price soaring, confident that they
could do so in the absence of a suitable alternative. But could
not 'Celluloid' do the job? Hyatt decided that it could. The
Albany Dental Company was formed and from that moment
onwards 'Celluloid' was in business in a major way.

The new material was soon being made in France and
Germany, as well as in England, despite the number of patent

cases which began to come into the courts. Even with the best will in the world – not always present – and even in the absence of the high financial stakes soon involved, law suits would probably have been numerous since it was almost inevitable that different men in different countries would arrive at similar solutions to similar technological problems. Thus one impression created by the new industry was of somewhat bitter commercial dispute. Another, which hung for decades like a millstone round its neck, was that plastics were second-best substitutes. To a limited extent this was true for some years. Ivory billiard balls were *the* thing. White linen collars were also *de rigeur* and the celluloid alternatives which could be taken off and washed at the end of the day were for long, and however strongly the makers might claim the contrary, the sign of the man who could not afford a new clean collar every day. This feeling changed but slowly – in fact only when chemists began to produce plastics virtually tailor-made to specification. Tailoring for the job in hand not only meant that the substitute was as good as the material it re-placed, but that it could in some cases be produced with characteristics making it more suitable for a specific task than any naturally occurring substance.

However, the raw materials of these early plastics were not entirely synthetic since cellulose itself had natural cotton fibre as a base. The end-product came from the addition of acids or other chemicals under carefully controlled conditions, but the mere presence of natural-growing cotton rules out the word 'artificial' in its modern meaning. The same was true of two other early plastics which were first devised in practical form about the turn of the century and whose use continued in one form or another for two decades or more. These were cellulose acetate and casein.

The first attempts to produce a non-flammable celluloid by treating cellulose with something other than nitric or sul-phuric acid had been made in the 1860s. None of them was successful and it was not until the 1890s that Charles Cross and Edward Bevan, who had already discovered how to turn natural cellulose into an artificial fibre called viscose, found a satisfactory way of turning the same raw material into a transparent non-flammable sheet of cellulose acetate. Patents were taken out in many countries, but despite the attraction of its non-flammability, cellulose acetate might not have survived had it not been for the outbreak of the First World War. This brought a demand for a non-flammable lacquer which could be used to paint the frames of aircraft and stiffen the fabric of wings. Here two Swiss, the Dreyfus brothers, were the pioneers. When the war ended they realized the potential of cellulose acetate as a fibre and within a remarkably short time had put on the market a fibre under the name of 'Celanese'. It was the first of the really popular rayons, a generic name later used to describe all fibres made from cellulose and viscose; a name sometimes used, more debatably, to describe all man-made fibres.

Casein is the main protein in milk, and its discovery as a raw material for a plastic leads back to the probably apocryphal story of the German chemist's cat who upset a bottle of formaldehyde in his saucer of milk. When the hardened casein in the milk was found to be water-resistant a new off-shoot of the plastics industry was born. Whatever the truth of the legend, chemists in both Europe and the United States patented processes for turning casein into a useful plastic. With their ability to take up the most delicate shades of dyes, and the ease with which they could be processed, casein-based plastics quickly led the field in a limited range of applications, notably for buttons and buckles and fancy goods.

The next steps were so important that they are sometimes described as founding the modern plastics industry. They were taken by Leo Baekeland, a modest likeable man whose orderly organization of life was in strong contrast to the absent-minded scientist of legend. Baekeland was a Belgian who emigrated to the United States where his personal interest in photography led him on to develop 'Velox' printing-out paper. In 1899, at the age of 36, he sold his photographic interests for enough money to make him independent for life. Then, typically enough for a man of such restless interests, he returned to Europe for what he called a year's refresher course in electro-chemistry.

Back again in America, Baekeland began to develop new methods of air conditioning. He improved electrolytic cells. But in the early 1900s it was another task to which he turned – one which was to bring him world-wide fame. It was the search for a man-made material which could replace shellac, the yellowish natural resin secreted by the lac insect which on account of its insulating properties was being demanded in growing quantities by the expanding electrical industry.

At the start, Baekeland's idea was to build on the earlier work of Adolf Baeyer and Werner Kleeberg. Baeyer had announced as far back as 1872 that when phenols, a class of aromatic organic compounds, reacted with the aldehydes, another class of organics, the result was a resinous sticky substance. Nearly two decades later, when formaldehyde was newly available in cheap commercial quantities and one

Women workers doping aeroplane canvas before painting in a Birmingham factory, September 1918

particular phenol was coming from the developing coal-tar industry, Kleeberg found that he could get from their reaction a malleable paste that eventually set rock-solid. But both men, as well as those who read the papers describing their work, regarded these products as commercially irrelevant if scientifically interesting. Baekeland, probably leafing back through the literature in his methodical way, believed that he could do something with them.

His first idea was to produce a sticky residue from the reaction, find a solvent that would dissolve it, and then use the solution as the shellac substitute. But few solvents seemed to work satisfactorily. Why, therefore, Baekeland asked himself, should it not be possible to produce this sticky residue itself in useful form? Once the thought occurred to him he began to investigate earlier work, and he found that previous experimenters had apparently set about the job without exercising strict control over such factors as temperature or pressure.

A number of years passed before Baekeland was satisfied. He used raw materials produced in different ways, combined in different percentages, and in varying conditions of pressure

'Old Faithful', the still in which Leo Baekeland produced his first resins

and temperature. One of the keys to his final success was a piece of apparatus which he called a Bakelizer. 'Such an apparatus', he explained, 'consists mainly of an interior chamber in which air can be pumped so as to bring its pressure to 50 or better 100 pounds per square inch. This chamber can be heated externally or internally by means of a steam packet or steam coils to temperatures as high as 160°C or considerably higher, so that the heated object during the process of Bakelizing may remain steadily under suitable pressure which will avoid porosity or blistering of the mass.'

Baekeland worked on for five years. Not until February, 1907 did he file what became his most famous patent, the first of 119 concerning plastics, and the one which described how to make the material soon known throughout the world as Bakelite. It was not the world's first plastic, since Parkesine was that, but it did not require any natural material such as cotton fibre and was therefore the first entirely synthetic material to be put on the market.

There were three kinds of Bakelite. The first, Bakelite A, was made when the reaction was stopped while the material was hot and liquid; it set solid on cooling but was still soluble in the right solvents. If the process were allowed to continue without cooling, then Bakelite A was turned into Bakelite B, a solid which was soft when hot but hard when cold and thus admirably suited for moulding. The third variety, Bakelite C, was made by heating Bakelite B under pressure.

The new material had all the insulating characteristics which Baekeland expected of it, but it also had something more. It was the first of the plastics which, having been moulded in the hot state and then allowed to cool, would keep its new shape even when heated again. Almost as important was the wide variety of ways in which it could be used. In 1909, the plastics industry had not even started its ramifications. Even so, the famous paper which Baekeland read that year to the American Chemical Society in New York gave a hint of things to come. Wood dipped into liquid Bakelite could be given a brilliant coat of the material which was, he claimed, superior to even the most expensive Japanese lacquer. 'But I can do better,' he went on. 'I may prepare an A, much more liquid than this one, and which has great penetrating power, and I may soak cheap porous soft wood in it, until the fibres have absorbed as much liquid as possible, then transfer the impregnated wood to the Bakelizer, and let the synthesis take place in and around the fibres of the wood. The result is a very hard wood, as hard as mahogany, or ebony of which the tensile, and more especially the crushing strength, has been considerably increased and which can stand dilute acids or steam; henceforth it is proof against dry rot. In the same way I have succeeded in impregnating cheap ordinary cardboard or pulp board and changing it into a hard resisting polished material that can be carved, turned and brought into many shapes.'

The new plastic could be compounded with sawdust and wood-pulp, colouring matter or a wide variety of materials which would help produce special substances for special jobs. 'I cannot better illustrate this than by telling you that here you have before you a grindstone made of Bakelite,' Baekeland went on, 'and on the other hand a self-lubricating bearing which has been run dry for nine hours at 1,800 revolutions per minute without objectionable heating and without injuring the quickly revolving shaft.'

It was typical of Baekeland that he should end his account by saying: 'The opened field is so vast that I look forward with the pleasures of anticipation to many more years of work in the same direction. I have preferred to forego secrecy about my work, relying solely on the strength of my patents as a protection. It will be a great pleasure to me if in doing so, I may stimulate further interest in this subject among my fellow chemists and if this may lead them to succeed in perfecting my methods or increase still further the number of useful applications of this interesting compound.'

There was, in fact, to be an almost limitless number of useful applications. Bearings that needed no lubrication was only one prospect opened up. In the electrical industry the uses of Bakelite were soon going far beyond the replacement of shellac. The Westinghouse Electrical Manufacturing Company began using it to impregnate paper sheets made for insulating material while the infant motor car industry was quickly demanding Bakelite for junction boxes, distributor heads and the multiplicity of other parts which had to be chemically resistant, electrically insulating and capable of standing up to both heat and rough treatment.

Within a few years the use of Bakelite had become world-wide. Even so, many men in many countries were developing their own plastics in the years immediately before the First World War. One of the most important was James, later Sir James, Swinburne, a pioneer both in electrical engineering and plastics. Swinburne had the bad luck to apply for a phenol-formaldehyde patent shortly – some records claim only one day – after Baekeland had done so. He nevertheless persevered with different methods and eventually succeeded in the plastics field that Baekeland had first entered. Britain of the early 1900s was still the age of brass – brass fenders, brass fire-irons and brass bed-steads. All these needed much polishing, and a coating of shellac was often put on to reduce the elbow-grease required. Swinburne succeeded in perfecting a plastic lacquer whose quality was suggested by the name of the company which he founded to make it – the Damard Lacquer Company.

In the plastics industry the First World War divided separate stages of development quite as surely as it did in other fields. In some ways the German invasion of Belgium in August 1914 ended the 19th century; similarly, the war-time advances in the plastics industry marked an end to the old hit-and-miss, trial-and-error, methods which even the most scientific of the pioneers had tended to use. Baekeland and Swinburne, and the many men who did only slightly less important research in other countries, worked to fine tolerances of temperature and pressure; nevertheless, they realized their own limitations and well knew that if one set of ingredients did not provide what they were trying to make, then a pinch of something else might well turn out to give the answer. The reason, which they would have been the first to admit, was that comparatively little was yet known about the complex chemistry of the new materials they were making. All this was changed during the next two decades.

The change was closely linked with the new kinds of raw material which began to be available as the popularity of the petrol engine helped to open up the oil wells of the world. Before the war, coal had provided both phenol and formaldehyde. Cellulose had provided celluloid, cellulose acetate, and a variety of other synthetically made materials. With a small handful of other materials incorporated into such products as synthetic rubbers, this was virtually the entire list of substances which went into man-made materials.

Then came petrol. Or, more accurately, then came crude oil, a mixture of hydrocarbons and other organic compounds from which it was possible to separate, by distillation, by fractionation or by other processes, a huge number of different chemicals. Most of them are based on the simple constituents of carbon and hydrogen but most are more or less complex molecules. It was the study of this complexity which did much to make possible the impressive families of plastics which began to grow during the years between the wars.

One of the first realizations was that the physical characteristics of plastics were closely related to the size and complexity of the molecules of which they are built up. Thus cellulose, the constituent of the early plastics, consists of molecules in each of which six atoms of carbon, ten of hydrogen and five of oxygen have been linked together by the complicated chemical processes taking place within the living plant, the result being a molecule more complex than most of those met with in run-of-the-mill work in laboratory or factory. With the quickening pace of organic chemistry, three things were realized. The first was that it might be possible to take chemically simple materials and then turn them, in the chemical works, into molecules as elaborate as those produced by nature. The second was that the booming petrol industry might produce, as by-products, and in comparatively large quantities, just such simple materials. The third was that it might even be possible to tailor-make artificial substances with characteristics which could be forecast in advance.

The possibilities were increased by the work of one group of specialists, the polymer chemists, notably Hermann Staudinger in Germany and Wallace Carothers in the United States. Their story, that of polymerization, the chemical union of two or more molecules of the same compound to form larger molecules, has a history that goes back at least as far as 1872 when E. Baumann reported what was in fact the polymerization of vinyl chloride into what was to be known, more than half a century later, as polyvinylchloride or PVC. An earlier attribution gives credit to Regnault in 1835. However, it is not certain that Baumann realized what he had done. Eight years later Georg Kahlbaum polymerized methylacrylate. Even so, it was not until another 30 years had passed that the first polymerization patent was taken out. This applied to isoprene, one of whose polymers forms the bulk of natural rubber. A decade afterwards in 1920, the Belgo-American chemist Julius Nieuwland found that acetylene, the colourless gas with its molecules of two carbon atoms linked to two hydrogen atoms, could be made to polymerize into a giant molecule that had some of the properties of rubber.

Shortly afterwards Hermann Staudinger began to provide scientific chapter and verse for the macromolecules, or giant molecules, of polymerization which in all cases seemed to consist of large numbers of smaller molecules linked together into long chains. In nature, the chemical reactions of plant life produced the parallel unbranched chains of glucose units which were condensed into the fibrous structure of cellulose. In synthetic plastics, heat and pressure did much the same thing.

While Staudinger was investigating this theoretical basis of polymerization, the big American Chemical Corporation, Du Pont, took one of the first steps to study the industrial

*Above* Dr Wallace H. Carothers, who directed the Du Pont fundamental research programme from which came Neoprene synthetic rubber

*Right* Manufacture of viscose, showing the consistency of the material in an early stage of manufacture

possibilities of what was still little more than a chemical curiosity. Under the leadership of Carothers, it was found that if a chlorine atom was added to the polymerizing acetylene chain at the right point, the end-product was a synthetic rubber which had a high tensile strength and better heat resistance than the natural product. This was soon to be registered as Neoprene, one of the most important early synthetic rubbers, and one which was to help save the Allies after the Malayan rubber jungles were lost to the Japanese during the Second World War.

The advances in man's theoretical knowledge of polymerization, epitomized by Staudinger, merged with the practical industrial experience typified by Carothers. With both went the rapidly expanding supply of hydrocarbons from the petroleum industry. The outcome was the foundation not only of today's plastics industry but also of the closely allied industries making synthetic rubber and synthetic fibres. The links between these three empires are strong, for with few exceptions they turn members of the same family of raw materials into high polymers, the main differences in the characteristics of their end-products being the nature of the chemical forces operating between the chains of molecules. Put in a very over-simplified form, if these forces are weak, the result is rubber; if they are stronger, the outcome is a plastic; while if the links are really strong but the molecule-chains are long and slim, the end-product is a fibre.

However, no hard dividing line can be drawn between these various groups. Thus nylon was first produced by Du Pont as a result of Carothers's work – after the expenditure of $27,000,000 (£11m) and the efforts of 230 chemists and engineers – as a substitute for the silk of silk stockings, and is still most familiar in some form of thread, whether for sewing, for bootlaces or for climbing rope. Yet nylon is also produced in bulk and turns up as a family of polymers which can be moulded or extruded into a wide variety of end-products.

The word 'nylon' is also used as a generic name for any long-chain synthetic polymeric amide which conforms to certain specifications, a fact which highlights the confusion existing about many words, names and definitions in the plastics industry. One reason for this confusion arises from the fact that a specific chemical product can be registered under more than one trade-name. Polymethyl methacrylate has been known as 'Plexiglas' on the Continent, as 'Lucite' in the United States and as 'Perspex' in Britain. Quite as bewildering is the frequent use of what are really proprietary trade-marks for a far wider range of materials. Thus the word 'perspex'

A flame boils water, but a 1/1000 of an inch thick Kapton film between them remains intact. Kapton, developed by Du Pont, is an exceptionally strong and extremely resistant film with an unusual combination of mechanical and electrical properties. It retains high tensile strength as well as flexibility, cut-through resistance and resistance to cold flow over a wide temperature range. It has been used successfully in various applications from −269°C to 440°C. The Apollo lunar module used fourteen miles of wiring insulated with Kapton and it was used in the sun shield which helped salvage the Skylab space station.

itself is sometimes employed to describe all kinds of acrylic sheet; and 'fibreglass' is incorrectly used for many sorts of materials consisting basically of fibres of glass usually less than one thousandth of an inch in diameter, woven into cloth and then impregnated with resin. 'Bakelite' is often incorrectly used to describe a whole range of phenolic plastics while the trade name 'Formica' in the same way is sometimes incorrectly used to describe laminates that are not Formica.

The huge range of contemporary plastics has come into existence partly as a result of experience gained during the Second World War, when artificial materials were made with characteristics fitting them for specific jobs; partly because of the post-war demand for the lighter, cleaner, and eventually cheaper, products which plastics seemed likely to satisfy. It is also a direct result of the chemists' questioning of nature, of their persistent desire to find out more about the ways in which atoms of the various elements are bound together to form materials that are plastic.

Further there has been a good deal of luck, a classic example being the story of polythene, whose initial discovery 'provides an unusually clear-cut instance of the unexpected results that may come from research, and of the importance of the role of chance in such work.'

In the early 1930s Imperial Chemical Industries embarked on a research programme designed to investigate chemical reactions under very high pressures. These pressures were not to be the few hundred atmospheres of previous research, but pressures up to many thousands. Such work involved expensive apparatus and the spending of very large sums which might produce some results or none. It says much for the imaginative outlook of the firm that they went ahead with this project in the depressed economic conditions of the early 1930s.

In the United States J. B. Conant, later President of Harvard and the man who was to hold a number of key roles in the American war effort between 1941 and 1945, had discovered that polymerization was greatly affected by high pressures, and this was one of the effects which ICI began to investigate. At first the results appeared to be of little significance. However, early in March 1933 an attempt was made to react ethylene with benzaldehyde, at a pressure of 1,400 atmospheres and at a temperature of 170°C. 'There was no indication from change in pressure that reaction had occurred,' wrote Michael, now Sir Michael, Perring who played a major role in the series of experiments, 'and when the pressure vessel was dismantled the benzaldehyde was recovered unchanged.

The walls of the vessel were, however, found to be coated with a thin layer of a "white, waxy solid" to quote from R. O. Gibson's notebook record of 27 March. This material was analysed and found to contain no oxygen, which confirmed the observation that the benzaldehyde, present in the vessel, had taken no part in the reaction. The solid was recognized as a hydrocarbon and, apparently, a polymer of ethylene. A similar result was obtained when ethylene alone was subjected to this pressure but the amount of product formed was always extremely small.'

The researchers next did the obvious thing. They increased the pressure. This not only caused the ethylene to decompose but in addition produced a further and sudden rise so great that joints and gauges on the apparatus were blown open. It was clear that different and more expensive equipment would be necessary before the work could be continued, and in April it was decided that it should be abandoned for the time being.

In fact it was a lapse of more than two years. Work was dropped, then resumed, very great improvements in technique were made, and when experiments started again in the autumn of 1935 far higher pressures were possible without risk. This time ethylene alone was put in the reaction vessel before the pressure was raised and a series of experiments eventually resulted in a new material which was crystalline, of high molecular weight, and apparently of the long-chain structure which Carothers had already found in nylon. More important, it had characteristics which made it of great potential use in industry – it did not melt in boiling water, it could be formed into films and threads when heated under slight pressure, it was chemically resistant, and it had outstanding insulating properties.

Production of this polymer of ethylene, first known in Britain as polythene and now officially called polyethylene, was soon got under way, but the production first in ounces and then in pounds of what had so far only been made under laboratory conditions demanded immense, and expensive, development work. Despite this, by the outbreak of war, polythene was being produced by the ton. This was as well. One of its major uses was to be in the high-frequency equipment needed for radar. Soon after the war annual production of polythene in Britain alone had reached 100,000 tons.

The war speeded up the advances of plastics technology just as it spurred on the development of radar, and from the 1950s onwards industry was offered a growing range of man-made plastic materials, some tailor-made for specific jobs.

From the comparatively simple experiments of scientists

such as Carothers and the workers at ICI a host of different complicated manufacturing processes evolved. Most of them involve one of two different kinds of polymerization. In one, addition polymerization as it is called, a simple substance known as the monomer – ethylene in the making of polythene for instance – is subjected to specific conditions, usually heat and pressure, in the presence of a catalyst. The catalyst then helps to set off or speed up the joining of the simple molecules into long-chain molecules.

In the second kind of polymerization, condensation polymerization (or more simply polycondensation), two different kinds of simple molecule, each containing two chemically reactive groups, are heated together. The reacting ends of two molecules link up to form a larger molecule and a simple by-product such as water. But this larger molecule still contains reactive end groups, and the process can continue as heating goes on, with the molecules getting longer and longer.

These products, made only on a laboratory scale a decade earlier, were after the war produced by the ton in large chemical plants whose design and erection demanded great engineering and technological expertise as well as chemical know-how. They are made in various forms. Polyvinylchloride or PVC for instance is a fine white powder. Polyethylene comes as chips or granules. Other plastics consist of viscous liquids.

Other substances are often added to this raw plastic material, the stuff of a multitude of products found in every home and office, before it goes to the fabricating side of the plastics industry. Some plastics, such as PVC, require the addition of a heat stabilizer if they are to be processed above a certain temperature. Plasticizers can be added to produce a softer end-product, and so can dyes or pigments if particular colour effects are required. A fibrous inert filler can be added to the plastic either to make the end-product tougher or to make it cheaper.

The ways in which this raw material is then made into the plastic products of contemporary life depends to a very large extent on whether it is thermosetting or thermoplastic. This basic division among plastics, of paramount industrial interest, is a very simple one. Thermosetting plastics become soft and malleable when they are heated; but once they have hardened on cooling they cannot be made plastic again. In the case of thermoplastics the process of heating to make plastic can be repeated indefinitely.

With thermosetting plastics the most common method of processing is compression moulding in which the raw material

Typical narrow tube extrusion of polythene

is compressed in a heated mould. Another is laminating, in which the plastic is squeezed under heat and pressure onto and into layers of paper or cloth. Thermoplastics, on the other hand, are more usually formed into articles by extrusion in which the thermoplastic material is fed as powder or grains into a heated barrel and then, when softened, forced along the barrel and through the hole or die which gives it the desired shape. Various kinds of moulding are used – the blow mould-ing technique usually used for making the plastic bottles which are steadily replacing glass; or injection moulding used to make the complicated small parts of electrical equipment. Foamed plastics, the sponge-like products also known as expanded plastics, are produced by ensuring that a gas is given off as the plastic mass hardens, thus expanding the mass as the process continues. Plastic film can be made by the calendering process used in the paper-making industry. Articles can be given a plastic covering by dipping them in a fluidized bed of powdered thermoplastic, while many finished plastic products can be machined, cut, stamped, drilled or glued as though they were of traditional wood or metal.

Plastics are no longer substitutes. In their multitudinous guises they are an accepted part of everyday life and it is difficult for an open eye not to see them: in the office as the plastic telephone hand-set and a score of commercial articles; in the home the curtains of artificial fibre, on the river the plastic fishing-line and on the mountain the nylon climbing rope. The man with poor sight may well view life through plastic spectacles.

The qualities of lightness and durability are not the only ones which give such materials the advantage in an increasingly large number of fields. Another lies in the fact that they are biologically inert; specifically, they do not provide food for insects. Thus clothes made of plastics do not suffer from attack by moth; neither, in a different field, do the plastic jackets of books or the synthetic resins which for many applications have replaced vegetable and animal glues. Moreover these advan-tages, which spring directly from man's chemical control of his available materials, may very well be only the beginning. Molecules are made up of atoms. Atoms are also susceptible to human manipulation, and it has recently been found that man-made materials themselves can be further changed if subjected to the processes offered by the nuclear revolution of the last quarter-century.

# 5 The Nuclear Revolution

The conscription of the electro-magnetic spectrum to produce radio, television and radar in less than a century is a prime example of scientific discoveries being exploited by inventors for purposes which have radically changed the world. Only more important is the release, taming and use of atomic – or more correctly, nuclear – energy, a development whose principal stages have been carried through in only half a century but which represents man's most revolutionary step forward since the taming of fire. The story is a classic example of the way in which knowledge is first gained by scientists and then used by engineers, technologists and inventors. There has been the slow piecing together by men from many nations of different bits of the jig-saw puzzle; there has been the outside impetus – in this case war and threat of war – so often needed to interest non-scientists in what had been a purely academic affair; and there has been a long technological struggle, still continuing, during which pure science, applied science and engineering have all helped to create the hardware which fresh knowledge about the physical world has made possible.

The idea of nuclear energy – the energy locked within the nucleus of the atom – is intimately bound up with man's beliefs about the structure of matter. These beliefs hardened into recognizable form, as did so many others, as long ago as the days of ancient Greece. About 420 BC Democritus first asserted that matter was not continuous but was made up of indivisible and ever-lasting bits which he called 'atoms', or particles which could not be divided. The theory enabled him to explain the difference between various substances on the grounds that denser materials had their particles packed more closely together. A century later, Aristotle led an opposing school which asserted that all matter was composed, in varying proportions, of four constituents: solid earth, liquid water, gaseous air, and the element fire which successfully defied definition.

For some 2,000 years there seemed little chance of deciding between these two basic ideas. But for much of the period Aristotle's views held the field, while the alchemists unsuccessfully tried to turn base metals into gold by juggling with the proportions of their alleged constituents. Only with the birth of 'modern' science in the 18th century, with the growth of chemical theory and the chance of using controlled experiment to prove or disprove theory, did a rudimentary atomic belief again come to the fore, a belief which it was hoped would explain the mass of new facts by this time being brought forward by the chemists.

Newton, Robert Boyle, Antoine Lavoisier and Joseph Proust who had speculated that two elements could combine only in the ratio of whole numbers – 6:1 for instance but never 5.9:1 or 6.1:1 – were all men whose work led back towards Democritus's particulate theory of matter. It was left to the English chemist John Dalton, colour-blind and poor, to pull these separate strings together and to tie them into the atomic theory from which the nuclear revolution eventually emerged. Dalton outlined his ideas in 1803 and five years later gave them in full in his *New System of Chemical Philosophy*. The first tenet of his system was that the elements of matter – Dalton named 20 of them – consisted of invisible and indivisible particles for which he used Democritus's name of atoms. The atoms of any one element were always of the same weight, but the atoms making up different elements were of different weights. Furthermore, when atoms of different elements combined to form molecules of a compound, they always combined in fixed and simple ratios. As for the atom itself, Dalton saw this as a solid sphere – the hard billiard-ball of matter whose existence was accepted with little questioning for almost a hundred years.

Not until the last decade of the 19th century was doubt thrown on this simple and cosy idea of the atom. As early as 1875 Sir William Crookes had shown that when a cathode, or negative electrode, was placed under strong electric potential within a vacuum tube, there came from it an emission of what he christened cathode rays. At first the rays were thought to be merely a form of electro-magnetic radiation, although Crookes finally put them down to streams of electrically-charged particles, an idea which was met with extreme reserve by most other scientists. However, only two decades later J. J. Thomson, working in the Cavendish Laboratory at Cambridge, proved Crookes's point: cathode rays were in fact streams of negatively charged particles, now christened electrons. Yet these particles could have come from nowhere other than the

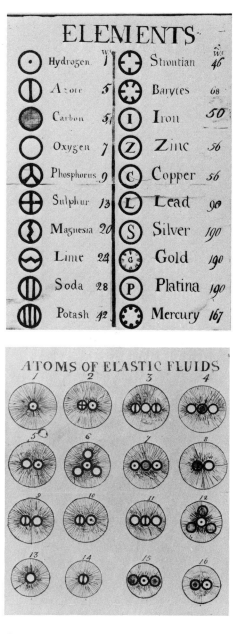

*Top* John Dalton's list of elements

*Bottom* Reproduction of lecture diagram prepared by John Dalton between 1806 and 1809 to illustrate his early conception of composition and relative sizes of atoms of gases and liquids

Sir J. J. Thomson with early
equipment in the Cavendish
Laboratory, Cambridge

metallic cathode – even though Thomson went on to show
that their mass was but a very small fraction, roughly 1/1837th,
of the lightest known atom, hydrogen. In one set of experiments he had thus destroyed the idea of the 'billiard-ball
atom'.

In Paris meanwhile, Henri Becquerel was also casting doubt
on the indivisibility of the atom after finding photographic
plates fogged by streams of particles thrown out by the rare
metal uranium. Marie Curie soon afterwards did the same
with her experiments on radium. Together, they made
scientists re-think their ideas about the basic structure of
matter.

Thomson had his own theory. For him the 'billiard-ball
atom' was replaced by the 'raisin-cake atom'. This was still
solid; but in Thomson's view it was a sphere of positively
charged matter, studded with just enough negatively charged
electrons – the raisins in the cake – to neutralize the positive
charge. This theory, which held the stage at the start of the
20th century, was soon to be demolished by the most brilliant

of all Thomson's pupils, Ernest Rutherford, the man perhaps most correctly known as the 'father of the nuclear age'.

Rutherford, studying the radioactive substances already noted by Becquerel and Curie, concluded first that the rays given off by such substances were of various kinds. There were the alpha rays, soon discovered to be streams of positively charged particles – in fact the nuclei, or central cores, of helium atoms; beta rays which were streams of electrons; and the gamma rays which were in fact electro-magnetic waves of very short wave-length.

It was with the first of these, the alpha rays, that in 1908 in the University of Manchester – after a short but fruitful spell in McGill University, Montreal – Rutherford began the experiments which yielded the vital clues to what the atom was really like. The crucial stage came with the 'firing' of alpha particles at a sheet of gold foil. The foil was only one fifty-thousandth of an inch thick, but it consisted of no less than 2,000 layers of atoms. The results were startling and almost contradictory. Most of the alpha particles passed straight through the foil, completely undiverted by any of the 2,000 layers, and impinged on the photographic plate behind them. To Rutherford this could mean only one thing: if the particles could pass through 2,000 layers of gold atoms and not be deflected by them, then atoms must be made up largely of empty space.

But this conclusion, staggering as it was, explained only part of the experiment's results. For while most of the alpha particles passed through the gold leaf without giving any sign of its existence, a few did completely the reverse: they were not only deflected by the foil, but deflected very sharply indeed, some of them even bouncing back from it. As Rutherford said afterwards, it was as though a big shell had been bounced back by a sheet of tissue paper. The experiment, repeated time after time, showed the same result and only one conclusion could be drawn: that somewhere in the atom there was an area of strong positive charge which, since like charges repel, brusquely repelled the positive alpha particle.

The picture that emerged was, with some modifications, that still seen today. At the centre of the atom, and forming its nucleus, there are one or more positively charged particles or protons. Circling them at a relatively immense distance are the negatively charged electrons, one for each proton under normal conditions. The numbers of protons and electrons in each atom, different for each element, range from one in the hydrogen atom to 92 in the atom of uranium – and 94 in the extremely rare plutonium 244 only discovered in 1971 – and the chemical characteristics of each element are entirely the result of these differing numbers of charged particles. To make this picture more up-to-date it is necessary to jump ahead to 1932 when the British physicist, James, later Sir James, Chadwick proved the existence of a third type of particle. This was the uncharged neutron, one or more neutrons being present in the nuclei of all atoms except those of normal hydrogen.

Rutherford's conception of the atom as a miniature solar system with negatively charged electrons forever orbiting a positively charged nucleus presented physicists with a number of problems. They were solved before the First World War by the Danish physicist Niels Bohr and by the end of the war the idea of the Rutherford-Bohr atom was firmly established.

Up to this point, research into the structure of matter appeared to have only theoretical importance, even though it was by now known that immense amounts of energy were locked up inside the atom. The existence of this energy became clear when it was established that the weight of the atomic nucleus was different from the separate weights of its component protons and neutrons added together. If it were thus possible to break up a nucleus into nuclear fragments that weighed less there would be a loss of mass. This in itself was

*Right* Lord Rutherford (*left*) and Niels Bohr with Lady Rutherford (*left*) and Mrs Niels Bohr photographed in the Rutherfords' garden about 1930

*Far right* Dr E. T. S. Walton (*left*) and Dr (later Sir John) Cockcroft (*right*) with Lord Rutherford after the first artificial transmutation of the atom

interesting but no more. What made it important was the size of the energy release given by Einstein's famous equation of 1905 – $E=mc^2$, which in the shorthand of science gives the amount of energy released when a mass of m grams is completely converted into energy. Now the difference in mass which might be possible in nuclear transformations would no doubt be very small. But Einstein's equation showed that the energy involved consisted of the mass multiplied by $c^2$ – where c is the velocity of light in centimetres per second. Little mathematical expertise was required to show that a very small amount of mass was equal to a relatively huge amount of energy.

On the face of it, the first step towards making use of this nuclear energy appeared to have been taken by Rutherford himself in 1919. Shortly before becoming Director of the Cavendish Laboratory in Cambridge he used the particles thrown out by radium to bombard a quantity of nitrogen. Very occasionally one of the particles would penetrate a nitrogen nucleus and transform it into the nucleus of an oxygen atom. Thus Rutherford had succeeded in carrying out the alchemist's dream of turning one element into another.

But what about the energy released? This was certainly greater than that of the alpha 'bullet'. But only about one

bullet in every million hit its target; the rest of them passed through the relatively large spaces which existed between the targets and their encircling electrons. Thus more energy had to be put into the nuclear stockpot than could be obtained from it.

This was still true 13 years later when two of Rutherford's workers in the Cavendish, the young John Cockcroft who was later to become head of Britain's first nuclear research station at Harwell, and C. T. Walton, succeeded in 'splitting the atom' as it was then called, by different and more sophisticated means. Whereas Rutherford used naturally radio-active radium to provide the bullets, Cockcroft and Walton used streams of hydrogen protons which they speeded-up by the use of high voltages to bombard small specimens of lithium, a light silvery-white metal. The result, in the almost throw-away words of their statement in *Nature*, was that, 'the lithium isotope of mass seven occasionally captures a proton and the resulting nucleus of mass eight breaks into two alpha-particles, each of mass four and each with an energy of about eight million electron volts.' But although the number of 'hits' was much greater than those in Rutherford's experiments of 1919, and although the phrase 'eight million electron volts' was enough to send shudders through the uninformed, the energy released in the experiment was still only a small frac-tion of that put into it.

The analogy between putting more energy into the nuclear stockpot than could be taken from it still held after Cockcroft and Walton's historic experiment. In fact Rutherford, naturally cautious and anxious not to encourage the wilder speculations, used an address at a meeting of the British Association to describe as 'moonshine' any hope of using atomic energy. Even so, the visionaries could hardly be held in check. As far back as 1903 Rutherford had made in a letter to Sir William Dampier what his correspondent had later called a 'playful suggestion that, could a proper detonator be found, it was just conceivable that a wave of atomic disintegration might be started through matter, which would indeed make this old world vanish in smoke.' In 1921 the Austrian physicist Hans Thirring had written after Rutherford's initial experi-ment that 'it takes one's breath away to think of what might happen in a town, if the dormant energy of a single brick were to be set free, say in the form of an explosion. It would suffice to raze a city with a million inhabitants to the ground.'

Less pessimistic dreamers forecast how a great liner might cross the Atlantic on the energy from a pound of nuclear fuel. More significantly there had taken place in London only a

few days before Cockcroft and Walton's experiment, the first performance of *Wings over Europe*, a play which like Wells's *The World Set Free* raised the spectre of nuclear weapons. 'The destiny of man', wrote Desmond McCarthy, 'has slipped (we are all aware of it) from the hands of politicians into the hands of scientists, who know not what they do, but pass responsibility for results on to those whose sense of proportion and knowledge are inadequate to the situations created by science.'

Frédéric and Irène Joliot-Curie in their Paris laboratory

McCarthy was before his time, but only by a year or two. By 1934 the next experiments leading mankind into the nuclear age had been made – although their significance had been missed. By 1934 a refugee Hungarian physicist had lodged with the British Admiralty a patent for a nuclear chain reaction of a type to be used in the first nuclear weapons. And by the spring of 1939, with world war only a few months away, Great Britain, France and Germany were mobilizing their physicists to discover whether it would be possible to make a nuclear weapon of gigantic power.

The events of those five years – in their results, possibly the most momentous five years that science has ever known –

follow one another in almost chain-reaction fashion. Early in 1934 Irène Curie, daughter of Madame Curie, and her husband Frédéric Joliot, discovered in Paris that by bombarding certain normally stable nuclei with alpha particles, these nuclei could be made radioactive. In England Leo Szilard, a Hungarian physicist who had studied under Einstein in Berlin a decade earlier and who has rightly been called the *éminence grise* of nuclear physics, had meanwhile been considering Rutherford's 'moonshine' statement. 'It suddenly occurred to me,' he later wrote, 'that if we could find an element which is split by neutrons and which would emit *two* neutrons when it absorbed one neutron, such an element, if assembled in sufficiently large mass, could sustain a nuclear chain reaction.' This was in the summer of 1933. Then, in the spring of 1934, came the announcement of the Curies' work. 'I suddenly saw,' Szilard said, 'that tools were at hand to explore the possibility of such a chain reaction.'

The reasoning was clear. In the earlier experiments by Rutherford, Walton and Cockcroft – and by others who had followed them – the initial nuclear transformation had been, as it were, a one-off operation. After it had taken place another million or so bullets had to be fired before a further hit was made on the target. What Szilard now foresaw was that if a neutron could be made to create a nuclear transformation and at the same time to release two neutrons these in turn might create two more transformations which in turn would create four; and so on. Furthermore, if these events took place quickly enough, the result could be an explosion which would make the energy-release of normal chemical explosions look puny by comparison. Within a year Szilard had filed with the British Admiralty a patent, sealed secret as it is called, since it was his conviction 'that if a nuclear chain reaction can be made to work, it can be used to set up violent explosions.'

In Rome, the Italian physicist Enrico Fermi had meanwhile been following up the Curies' work, finding that first one and then another element could be activated by bombardment with neutrons. Most of his results were explicable in terms of contemporary knowledge; particles were 'chipped away' from the nucleus and new elements were created. But in some cases, particularly that of uranium, the heaviest of the elements, with 92 protons and about 140 neutrons jostling together within its nucleus, there seemed to be some mystery. It was not altogether surprising. The material with which these early experimenters were dealing consisted of micro-quantities whose accurate identification by chemical test was itself something of a triumph. Fermi published his results. But he left it to others to

Lise Meitner and Otto Hahn in the
laboratory of the Kaiser Wilhelm
Institute in Berlin, 1925

discover exactly what happened when a uranium nucleus was
hit.

Among these others were Otto Hahn, Lise Meitner and
Fritz Strassman of the Kaiser Wilhelm in Berlin. And it is
with them, as the nuclear story gathers pace and world war
approaches, that the extraordinary ironies of the tale become
apparent. Enrico Fermi and Leo Szilard were merely two of
the nuclear physicists who played key parts in the tale – and
were forced to play them not in Europe but in the United
States, where they had finally sought refuge. And now, in
March 1938, the work in the Kaiser Wilhelm was grotesquely
disrupted by the German invasion of Austria. For Lise
Meitner was Austrian; she was also a Jewess, and the German
absorption of her country thus brought her under threat of
the concentration camp. She moved first to Holland, then to
Sweden. The work in the Kaiser Wilhelm had to continue
without her.

In this gaunt ugly building, soon to be laid in ruins by

British bombers, Hahn and Strassman went on with their experiments. They, like Fermi, bombarded uranium. The substance which they found in minute traces after the bombardment had all the chemical characteristics of barium, a silvery-white soft metal. What is more, Hahn the chemist could soon show beyond all reasonable doubt that it was in fact barium. But the nucleus of a barium atom contained only 56 protons; that left 36 protons of the 92 in the uranium nucleus – 36 protons, the number which it was known were contained in the nucleus of an atom of the inert gas krypton. If this process had occurred it was something very different from chipping away at the nucleus. Hahn himself was not quite sure what he had done and when he settled down in his laboratory on 21 December 1938 to write his report he described his results only as 'at variance with all previous experiences in nuclear physics.'

Before his report appeared in *Naturwissenschaften* on 6 January 1939 it had reached Lise Meitner in Sweden, for what was more natural than that Hahn should send it to his former collaborator? In Sweden Lise Meitner discussed it with her nephew Otto Frisch, a worker in Niels Bohr's Copenhagen research laboratory who was spending Christmas with his aunt. Walking in the snow-covered Swedish woods, they realized what Hahn had done.

'It took her a little while to make me listen,' Frisch has said, 'but . . . very gradually we realized that the breaking-up of a uranium nucleus into two almost equal parts was a process so different from the emission of a helium nucleus that it had to be pictured in quite a different way. The picture is not that of a particle breaking through a potential barrier, but rather the gradual deformation of the original uranium nucleus, its elongation, formation of a waist, and finally separation of the two halves. The striking similarity of that picture with the process of fission by which bacteria multiply caused us to use the phrase "nuclear fission" in our first publication.'

The news that Hahn had split the uranium nucleus in two was taken across the Atlantic by Niels Bohr who was fortuitously due to speak to the Fifth Washington Conference in January 1939. Events then moved quickly. Within a few days the Berlin experiments had been repeated in the Carnegie Institution of Washington, the Johns Hopkins University and the University of California. Frisch had already repeated them in Copenhagen. Similar work was carried out in Warsaw by a brilliant young Polish worker, Joseph Rotblat. The Leningrad Physico-Technical Institute announced a similar success in April, while in Paris a strong team of physicists working in the

Collège de France quickly answered one of the questions raised by the newly discovered fission process.

That process was dramatic enough. 'The picture,' as Frisch put it, 'was that of two fairly large nuclei flying apart with an energy of nearly two hundred million electron volts, more than ten times the energy involved in any other nuclear reaction.' So far so good. But this brief spark of nuclear fire had of itself little practical significance. The important thing was whether the spark could be kept alight. From the first it seemed that there was a good chance. For the two new nuclei were created 'in a strongly deformed and hence excited state' to quote Frisch. Thus they might expel one or more neutrons as they were created. But it was the impact of a neutron which had created the fission in the first place. Therefore, further neutrons could be directed to create further fissions – the chain-reaction which Szilard had envisaged four years earlier.

All now seemed to rest on the answer to the simple question: 'Did the nuclear fission of uranium create "spare" neutrons?' The French team in the Collège de France came up with the answer in February 1939 – and considered it so important that the paper containing it was rushed to Le Bourget airport so that it could appear in the earliest possible edition of *Nature*.

The answer was that nuclear fission did indeed produce spare neutrons. Thus it seemed plausible that under certain conditions it would be possible to detonate an explosion immensely more powerful than any caused by merely chemical reactions.

At this point, the European countries being sucked down towards the whirlpool of war began to act. The German physicist Paul Hartman wrote to the German War Office suggesting that nuclear weapons should be investigated, and shortly afterwards two groups in the Third Reich began work on 'the uranium problem'. In Britain, research on a nuclear weapon was brought under the surveillance of Sir Henry Tizard and with the support of the Committee of Imperial Defence Tizard tried to obtain control over the world's stock of uranium, a relatively uncomplicated matter since virtually the only important source lay in the Belgian Congo where it was mined by the Belgian Union Minière. And in Paris the Collège de France team was authorized to obtain another raw material then thought essential to the manufacture of nuclear weapons – the 'heavy water' produced exclusively by the Norsk Hydro Company at Rjukan in central Norway.

The apparent need for heavy water – a substance whose molecules contain oxygen and a rare variety of hydrogen called deuterium – underlines the fact that in the summer of

1939 immense practical difficulties still seemed likely to rule out the utilization of nuclear energy, for peaceful or for warlike purposes, even though a chain reaction in uranium was now seen to be theoretically possible. It was in this summer that Einstein signed the famous letter written by Leo Szilard, now a refugee in the United States, urging President Roosevelt to investigate the possibilities of nuclear weapons. But Einstein, like a majority of other leading physicists, was very doubtful whether such weapons could ever be built.

To appreciate the practical difficulties, it is necessary to ask why, since uranium is apparently 'fissile', the uranium stocks of the world did not blow themselves apart as they came into existence. The first answer is that the metal is found not in its pure form but as an ore from which it has to be separated. The second answer was supplied by Niels Bohr in the spring of 1939. Bohr put forward a theory – later found to be correct – based on the fact that uranium consists of a number of different kinds of atom each of which has a different number of neutrons locked inside the nucleus together with the 92 protons. Bohr suggested that it was only the uranium 235, whose atoms had 92 protons and 143 neutrons in each nucleus which was readily fissile. But these atoms formed only about 0.7 per cent of natural uranium, or roughly seven in every thousand. If any of the other 993 uranium nuclei in each 1,000 were hit by a neutron bullet, the chances of its being split were very remote; it would be far more likely to absorb the neutron, setting off a process of nuclear rearrangement which was interesting but which would not help to keep a nuclear fire alight.

Thus the first problem would be one of separating uranium 235 from the other kinds. The size of this problem, which for some time seemed to rule out any chance of using nuclear energy and which was eventually to demand the utmost ingenuity in invention from the chemical and the engineering industries, rested on the basic characteristics of isotopes, as the differing atoms of the same elements are called. The different isotopes of uranium – and of other elements – have the same number of protons in their nuclei but different numbers of neutrons. But, as with the various isotopes of other elements, the chemical characteristics of uranium 235 are identical with those of uranium 238. So are the physical characteristics with the sole exception of those determined by atomic mass. Thus for all the normal chemical processes which might be used to separate them they are as alike as two peas in a pod or two grains of sand on the sea-shore. In the summer of 1939 the practical chances of separating them in more than micro-quantities looked extremely remote.

But this was only one of the problems. Even if some way of separating the fissile from the non-fissile nuclei could be found there was a further awkward fact to be considered. It was soon apparent that two and a half neutrons were released on average by each fission. But even if these were released in a mass of uranium 235 not each of them would necessarily produce further fissions. Some would merely pass through the empty spaces, comparatively immense, which exist between the uranium nuclei and then escape from the lump of uranium before hitting a target. Others would almost certainly be absorbed by impurities which it was realized would remain in the uranium 235 however much care was taken in its processing.

It is at this stage of the argument that the heavy water comes in. It was known that the neutrons released in fission moved at a speed of about 10,000 miles a second; but it was also known that if they could be slowed-down the chance of their causing further fissions would be greatly increased. What was needed was a moderator – some substance which would not itself absorb neutrons but would certainly reduce their speed. According to calculations, heavy water would be a good moderator; so would graphite, a form of carbon; and so too would beryllium – all of these being light elements with only a small number of protons in their nuclei.

Even so, a uranium block of a certain minimum size would be needed for the nuclear fire to be self-sustaining. This was the 'critical size' and in this stage of nuclear research there was very great doubt as to what the size was. In addition there was the important matter of just *how* the fire would burn. In one set of circumstances the burning of the whole mass would take place in a minute fraction of a second, thus causing a nuclear explosion of immense proportions. But it seemed possible that in different, but perhaps inevitable, conditions most of the explosive force would be dissipated.

But before either of these contingencies could be taken further scientists had to discover more about the whole process of nuclear fission. They had to estimate, within fairly close tolerances, what the critical mass of uranium would be. And they then had to decide how they could separate the chemically identical isotopes of uranium – not on a laboratory scale where a few micro-milligrams had been separated with the greatest difficulty but as an industrial process which might have to produce hundredweights.

This was the situation in nuclear research when Germany invaded Poland on 1 September 1939. It appeared to offer a very faint hope of a vastly more powerful weapon, and an only slightly less faint hope of a new source of industrial power. What it certainly did present were problems, theoretical, industrial and financial, which would not have been tackled for years, or more probably for decades, had not the possession of nuclear weapons held out a hope of victory. Nuclear fission had been discovered in Berlin. Neither Britain, nor later the United States, could afford to let the Germans get the ultimate weapon first.

The story of the world's first atomic bombs is too familiar to be told in detail here. But there are some supremely important twists and turns to the tale that are hardly known and need underlining.

The first took place in February 1940 when Otto Frisch, who had by this time arrived in Britain, worked out with Rudolf, now Sir Rudolf, Peierls, what the critical mass of uranium was really likely to be. Sir James Chadwick, the discoverer of the neutron, was already at work on the nuclear problem in Liverpool University with Joseph Rotblat, who had been caught in England by the outbreak of war. Sir George Thomson, son of the J. J. Thomson who half a century earlier had helped to lay the foundations for the nuclear age, was already at work in Imperial College, London, and a handful of scientists elsewhere in Britain were investigating other aspects of the problem. Yet if any single act can be singled out as carrying the world across the watershed towards the nuclear age it is that of Frisch and Peierls in Birmingham, sitting down and working out, almost on the back of an envelope as it were, how big the critical mass of uranium would be.

Few men alive knew more about nuclear fission than Frisch and Peierls. Even so, their initial calculations, in the late summer of 1939, suggested a figure of tons. Only after an immense amount of work had been carried out in the university were they able to refine their calculations – and to discover in February 1940 that the figure was not measured in tons at all. 'In fact,' Peierls has stated, 'our first calculation gave a critical mass of less than one pound.'

This single calculation, whose result was later shown to be of the right order of magnitude, transformed 'the uranium problem' as it was known. Separating even a pound of uranium 235 was an undertaking of almost staggering dimensions but it was different from separating many tons. Filling an egg-cup with sand, grain by grain, might be a formidable task; but it was manageable compared with the fantasy of filling the Albert Hall.

Frisch and Peierls' discovery led directly to a committee

Four of the British team which
joined the Americans working on
nuclear weapons during the last
war. *From left to right :* Dr (later
Lord) Penney, Dr Frisch,
Professor (later Sir Rudolf) Peierls
and Professor (later Sir John)
Cockcroft

under George Thomson which in the summer of 1941 issued a
crucial document, the Maud Report which firmly stated 'that
the scheme for a uranium bomb is practicable and likely to
lead to decisive results in the war.'

This report was to have an immensely important effect on
events in the United States, a country then still at peace.
Here Einstein's letter to Roosevelt had led to the setting-up
of a Committee under Dr Lyman J. Briggs, director of the US
Bureau of Standards, and to work by the National Academy of
Science. But none of this had given much encouragement to
Dr Vannevar Bush or Dr James Conant, the two Americans in
charge of the country's defence research.

But the whole scene was changed by the Maud Report
which was shown to the Americans without delay. '[It] gave
Bush and Conant what they had been looking for,' says the
official history of the subsequent US nuclear effort; 'a promise
that there was a reasonable chance for something militarily
useful during the war in progress. The British did more than
promise; they outlined a concrete programme. None of the
recommendations Briggs had made and neither of the two
National Academy reports had done as much.' Within a
matter of days Professor Harold Urey, the discoverer of heavy
water, and Professor G. B. Pegram were on their way to
Britain. Within weeks the first steps had been taken to set up
what eventually became the Manhattan Project which, under

General Groves (*second from left*), head of the American 'Manhattan Project' which produced the world's first nuclear weapons, with Sir James Chadwick (*left*) and American scientists Dr Richard Tolman and Dr H. D. Smyth

command of General Leslie Groves, produced the world's first nuclear weapons.

Scores of technological riddles still had to be solved when the Americans decided – a few hours before the Japanese struck at Pearl Harbor – that they must try to make the world's first nuclear weapons. So had a mass of scientific questions. Only microscopic quantities of fissile material had so far been produced and many of its characteristics were not known, let alone understood. The whole subject of fission still lay on the extreme edge of scientific knowledge, and it was appreciated that before a bomb could be built that frontier of knowledge would have to be pushed forward an immense distance into the unknown. Only two things were clear. The materials would be more dangerous than any which scientists or industry had yet handled. And the effort demanded would involve more men, more money, and more scientific expertise than any other project which had ever been tackled, in the United States or elsewhere.

During the first months of 1942, three major question-marks hung over the enterprise which, it was realized in Washington, was in many ways an immense gamble. First of all, could a nuclear chain reaction really be created? In theory this was now possible, but even the men who said so admitted

that the imponderables were immense and that what had
seemed possible in theory might be impossible in practice.
Secondly, in view of what seemed to be the wildly immense
industrial problems involved, could enough fissile material be
produced? Thirdly, if it were possible to make enough
material, would it be possible to bring this together in such a
way that the resulting critical mass would explode? For theory
had suggested early on that if two lumps of fissile uranium,
each less than the critical mass but together forming more than
it, were united too slowly then the result might be a bomb
which, in the words of the physicists' lingering doubt, might
'swell up rather than explode'.

The first of these problems was put in the hands of Fermi
and under his direction there was built in Chicago during 1942
the world's first nuclear reactor. It was obviously not meant to
explode, and the uranium used in it was the natural metal in
which the fissile uranium 235 was effectively swamped by the
vastly larger amount of uranium 238. The neutrons released
by the fissions that did take place were slowed down by a
moderator consisting of graphite, a form of carbon, and calculations showed that under the right conditions these slowed-
down neutrons would create further fissions numerous enough
to keep the nuclear fire burning. If this were so, the device
would not only give practical proof of the physicists' figures;
it would also, it was calculated, manufacture [its own] quantities of what was correctly believed to be a second fissile
material. This was plutonium, an element not found in nature
until 1971, but one which would, it was estimated, result from
the nuclear reactions which would go on inside a successful
reactor.

Fermi's reactor – or 'pile' as it was at first called since the
graphite consisted of blocks which were piled up one on
another – gave a foretaste of the industrial problems to come.
Only a few grams of pure uranium metal had previously been
refined in the United States but more than six tons were
needed for Chicago. The graphite had to be of clinical purity,
and had to be processed into about 40,000 separate blocks, each
of which had to be finished to the strictest engineering tolerances. There were also the control rods. These were made of
the metal cadmium, which was known to be a good absorber of
neutrons. As the reactor was assembled from November 1942
onwards into an agglomeration of uranium and graphite, some
25 feet across, the cadmium strips were built into it, thus
effectively preventing the chain reaction from starting.

On 2 December 1942 the cadmium strips began to be raised
up by the complex machinery built around the reactor. Instru-

The world's first nuclear pile
consisting of graphite blocks and
uranium metal under construction
in Chicago in 1942

ments built into the reactor continuously recorded the intensity of the neutron-flow inside. And between 3 and 4 o'clock in the afternoon the needles on the instruments passed the all-important mark. Inside the reactor the nuclear fire was burning steadily. High officials in the Manhattan Project were given the news by an historic telegram which merely said: 'The Italian navigator has entered the new world.' Something quite as momentous as Columbus's landfall had in fact taken place.

The success of the Chicago reactor showed that a second fissile material, plutonium, was available but the reactor itself, built largely as a demonstration unit, had no cooling system, could be operated at only a low level, and could not therefore be used to make plutonium in practicable quantities. Even had it been able to do so, the whole reactor would have had to be dismantled to get it out. However, the Americans could now hope to produce their nuclear fuel in one of four ways.

First, it would be possible to make special plutonium-producing reactors – and the huge industrial complexes soon to be built at Oak Ridge and Hanford, costing millions of dollars and employing tens of thousands of men, were to make this element.

In addition to the production of plutonium, an immense industrial gamble whose success long hung in the balance, there was the separation of uranium 235 from its super-abundant uranium 238. This appeared to offer the three other

ways of producing a nuclear explosive. But the amounts of fissile uranium known to be needed were some hundred million times more than those that had been produced in the laboratory, and each of the different ways of separating the chemically identical atoms on an industrial scale involved its own appalling difficulties. One was gaseous diffusion which had been experimented with in England before the British effort was moved to the United States and Canada in 1943. The method rests on the fact that if a gas containing two isotopes is diffused through a porous barrier, the molecules of the lighter isotope will diffuse more quickly; thus the gas on the far side of the barrier will contain slightly more light molecules than are in the gas which has not gone through the barrier.

The difficulties were numerous. For various reasons the only practicable gas was uranium hexafluoride, or 'hex', a compound of uranium and fluorine which is solid at room temperature but is easily vaporized; but 'hex' was one of the most difficult gases that had ever been handled, extremely corrosive, extremely reactive, and of an intractability that brought tears to the eyes of engineers faced with building equipment to handle it. In addition, to provide an end-product rich enough in the rare uranium 235 the dangerous gas would have to be passed not through a few dozen barriers, not through a few hundred but through many thousands. Thus the gaseous dif-

A painting by Gary Sheahan showing the moment when the world's first nuclear pile went critical. Enrico Fermi stands next to the instrument rack near the balcony rail, slide-rule in hand, computing the rise in the neutron count inside the layers of graphite interspersed with uranium.

The U.S. Atomic Energy Commission's Oak Ridge Gaseous Diffusion Plant for the production of enriched uranium. Today the plant, built in 1943, produces enriched uranium for nuclear power plants in many parts of the world.

fusion plant eventually built at Oak Ridge contained hundreds of acres of diffusion barriers, spread across more than 50 acres of factory floor and connected by many hundreds of miles of piping – the whole unit, with its hundreds of joints and valves being built to a precision, and welded with a care which would previously have been unthinkable.

The second way of separating the fissile uranium from the rest was by the electro-magnetic method, a scaled-up version of the laboratory method which utilizes the fact that different isotopes in a stream of ions are deflected differently by electric and magnetic fields. But the magnets required are 100 feet in length, the electric supplies involved are enormous and the process demands the most exacting kind of high vacuum equipment.

The third method was a thermal-diffusion technique in which 'hex' was circulated between two concentric pipes, the inner being steam-heated and the outer water-cooled, a process which caused the uranium 235 isotope to concentrate near the inner pipe. Simple by comparison with the other methods, thermal-diffusion demanded such immense quantities of steam – and therefore of coal – that it was eventually considered impracticable.

Any of these means of producing a nuclear explosive would in normal times have been considered an almost reckless gamble, so small did the chances of success seem and so great were the demands on scarce men, materials and money. But so menacing did the threat of a German nuclear weapon appear that the Americans went ahead, simultaneously, with the production of plutonium and of uranium by all three possible ways. The outcome was that partially enriched uranium from the gas-diffusion and thermal-diffusion plants was fed into the electro-magnetic plant in June 1945. Within a month, enough bomb-quality uranium had been produced to make one weapon. And by this time the plutonium production plant had produced enough fissile material for another two.

Meanwhile other groups of scientists under Robert Oppenheimer had been solving the problem of how to bring the two halves of a critical mass together with sufficient speed. In the uranium bomb, dropped on Hiroshima on 6 August 1945 this was accomplished by firing one half of the sub-critical mass down a squat barrel at the target of a second sub-critical mass. In the plutonium bomb, as tested in the Nevada desert in July 1945, and as dropped on Nagasaki a few days after the Hiroshima bomb, the characteristics of plutonium fission ruled this out and made necessary an 'implosion' device in which a hollow core of less than critical mass was compressed into a critical mass by the explosion of encircling TNT charges.

The destruction of Hiroshima and Nagasaki revolutionized warfare and international relations. There had, of course, been few scientific secrets about the bomb, since the basic facts of fission had been published before war broke out, and the laws of nature were known to operate in the same way both sides of the Atlantic and both sides of the Iron Curtain. Only in the purely technological field were there industrial secrets which governed the ease, speed and cost with which 'the bomb' could be built, and it was no surprise to most nuclear physicists that Russia, followed by Britain, France and eventually China, exploded their own nuclear weapons.

Abandonment among civilized nations of the conventions which had previously protected civilians is not necessarily the most important outcome of the release of nuclear energy, although it is the most obvious and spectacular. Even so, two developments along the road from Hiroshima must be noted.

One is the hydrogen bomb in which the intense heat created
by the fission of a critical mass of uranium is used to fuse the
hydrogen nuclei in a surrounding layer of hydrogenous
materials into helium nuclei. Fission breaks apart the heaviest
nuclei, but fusion transforms the lightest. The energy released
by the second nuclear transformation is the greater, and the
explosive power of the hydrogen bomb is some 1,000 times
that of the first atomic bombs, a single one being more than
capable of completely destroying the largest city in the world.
At the other end of the weaponry scale has come the production of ever smaller atomic weapons and it is now claimed,
though with dubious credibility, that they could be used in a
tactical role on the battlefield without necessarily leading to
the use of strategic nuclear weapons.

While the new threat has within the last generation transformed diplomacy, the balance of power, and the credibility of
war as a plausible method for a nation to get its own way, the
release of nuclear energy has had immensely important
results in other fields. The most obvious of these is the
possibility that within the foreseeable future man may have
access to limitless power, first from electricity stations based
on reactors using nuclear fission, then on breeder reactors
which can actually create more fuel than they use, and finally
by nuclear fusion in which power would be obtained from the
nuclear reactions induced in the hydrogen from sea-water.

At the heart of all such power-producing schemes is the
nuclear reactor, the descendant of Fermi's 'pile' in Chicago,
and these reactors are also the starting-points for the production of radioactive materials which for the last two decades
have been playing ever-more important roles in industry, agriculture and medicine.

The scores of nuclear reactors which have been built during
the last generation, a great diversified family, have usually
been tailor-made for some specific task: for research and training purposes, for the production of fissile weapons material or
of radioactive materials for peaceful purposes, for the propulsion of surface ships or submarines; or, more usually, for the
production of power. Such reactors can be classified as either
heterogeneous, where the fuel and the moderator are separated
from one another in a carefully calculated geometrical
pattern, or as homogeneous where the fuel and the moderator
are mixed to provide a uniform medium through which the
fission-born neutrons will pass. Another classification, and
one more generally adopted in the nuclear industry, is based on
the kind of moderator used or on the kind of coolant which
carries off the fission-created heat; thus there are graphite-

moderated reactors and heavy-water reactors, boiling-water reactors and gas-cooled reactors.

As far as the production of power is concerned, all these reactors work in roughly the same basic way. The burning of the atomic fuel, whose intensity is governed by the insertion or withdrawal of control rods which absorb the fission-created neutrons, heats a gas or a liquid which is continuously passed round the central core of the reactor – much as a household immersion heater raises the temperature of water before this is drawn out of the taps. The gas or liquid heated by the nuclear fire is then used to produce steam; the steam operates a turbine and this in turn operates a generator which in turn produces electricity.

The method seems convoluted, and it is true that there are losses in efficiency at each stage of the operation. Even so, the energy released by nuclear transformations is so much greater than that in chemical reactions, that a single gram of uranium can in a nuclear reactor produce as much power as two tons of oil.

The problems in creating this power are very great. Vast quantities of water are needed for cooling, whatever kind of reactor is used, and as a result nuclear power stations tend to be sited on the coast, on wide estuaries, or on large inland lakes. Despite the safety precautions enforced where fissile material is present – precautions which in fact give the nuclear industry an enviable safety record – commonsense plus public opinion demands that large centres of population shall be avoided and this, taken with the previous requirement, lays the nuclear industry open to attack by the conservationists. Capital costs of a nuclear power station are much greater than those of oil-fired or coal-fired stations, and it is only recently that the costs of generating electricity at them have fallen below those of conventionally produced power.

There are also immense engineering problems, indicated by some typical facts and figures from British stations. Thus a reactor alone can weigh up to 50,000 tons, while the pressure vessel in which it is encased, and the necessary shielding, can bring the weight to 200,000 tons. The thousands of tons of concrete for the foundations must be laid to an accuracy of a hundredth of an inch. The 100,000 graphite blocks in one typical reactor had each to be made to the strictest engineering tolerances before being vacuum-cleaned, sealed in transparent bags and taken to the site. In another the fuel consisted of 42,445 uranium rods 19 inches long and 1.1 inches in diameter, each machined to within a few thousandths of an inch before being loaded into more than 3,000 channels in

the graphite core. Special steels, new methods of welding, and fresh ways of inspecting and handling at long range the dangerously radioactive by-products of fission have all had to be developed before nuclear power has become a possibility.

For the immediate future there is the power station which creates more fuel than it uses, typified by a prototype built at Dounreay on the north coast of Scotland. Here the nuclear core is only 3 feet long and $4\frac{1}{2}$ feet in diameter, providing enough electricity for a town the size of Brighton. Its fuel is plutonium obtained as a by-product from the operation of the earlier type nuclear power stations. Surrounding this is a 'blanket' of natural uranium. Not all the neutrons released in the core create the further fissions which produce the heat – carried away in this case by liquid sodium. Some of them travel on until they hit the natural uranium of the 'blanket'. What happens then depends largely on the speed at which they are travelling; but a percentage of the neutrons will hit the nuclei of U238 atoms in the natural uranium and convert these into nuclei of plutonium. Thus it is possible to look forward to a future in which not only the rare uranium 235 but most of the atoms of natural uranium will eventually be

The U.K. Atomic Energy Authority's prototype fast reactor at Dounreay on the north coast of Scotland, which produces considerable amounts of electricity for the North of Scotland Hydro-Electricity Board

energy-producers – the seven fissile atoms in each 1,000 being used in the earlier type nuclear power stations and most of the remaining 993 being converted into fissile plutonium and used in reactors of this later design.

There is also the possibility of thermo-nuclear power, the taming of the fusion process utilized in the hydrogen bomb. But this is still no more than a gleam on the distant horizon and before it becomes a practicability the mini-reactor is likely to become almost commonplace. The first nuclear-powered submarine, the US Nautilus, was launched as long ago as 1954 and the first nuclear-powered cargo vessel, the US Savannah, in 1959, the year in which the Russians launched a nuclear ice-breaker. Germany and Japan are other countries which have used small compact reactors for their ships. The Americans have developed under the SNAP (System for Nuclear Auxiliary Power) scheme, a whole series of miniature reactors, some of them as small as 14 by 13 by 18 inches, while the Russians have built a 'pocket power station' which can produce one megawatt for two years from a few hundred pounds of fuel – compared with the 4,000 tons of oil needed for a diesel engine.

All these increasingly small and increasingly versatile power-producers are straight developments of 'the boiler', as the peaceful possibility of fission was described three decades ago. But even the explosive force of the bomb is being adapted for peaceful purposes, and while the use of nuclear explosives for engineering is still in an early stage of development some experts believe that many projects which would be impractical or economically ruinous if planned with conventional explosives will be possible with nuclear charges.

The quantities of material which have to be moved in the building of canals, tunnels, dams and underground reservoirs are usually immense. But experiments which began as far back as 1961, when the American Operation Plowshare got under way, show that the back of the work can probably be broken by the underground explosion of nuclear charges. As in a nuclear weapon, the key lies in the immense amount of energy that can be released from a device which is comparatively small, comparatively light and, when weighed against the cost of moving mountains by chemical explosives, comparatively cheap.

Yet further application of the same technique lies in the nuclear mining of minerals, petro-chemicals and natural gas. In this an underground nuclear explosion loosens the geological holding layers and both speeds up the extraction of what is being mined and reduces the cost of the operation.

Preparation of radio-pharmaceutical compounds labelled with mercury-197 in a standard shielded cell in the laboratories of the Radiochemical Centre Ltd, Amersham, Bucks

*Left* The head of a reactor vessel being lowered into place on top of Sweden's Oskarshamn I boiling-water reactor

*Right above* The nuclear-powered U.S. Nautilus entering New York Harbor, 25 August 1958, after making a trans-polar voyage under the Arctic ice cap

*Right below* The launching in Leningrad of the 16,000-ton ice-breaker Lenin, the world's first nuclear-powered surface vessel

The radioisotope thermoelectric generator (*foreground*) left on the moon by American astronauts in February 1971

These and similar engineering uses of nuclear explosions suffer from the same handicap that has made the development of nuclear power more difficult, more dangerous and more expensive than it would otherwise have been: the need to deal effectively with the radioactive by-products of a chain reaction. The process does not only involve the breaking in two of heavy nuclei and the release of neutrons. This is merely the start of a long series of events. The sudden release of energy is the fact important to the success of the bomb or the boiler; but it is merely the beginning of a string of nuclear reactions which create a new family of radioactive substances. Their number, and their dangers, depend on a large number of variables, and while some radioactive materials are for practical purposes harmless, it is true to say that from the earliest days of the nuclear revolution the problem of dealing with the rest has caused a perpetual headache.

In the early years of the century it was found that X-rays produced by naturally radioactive materials could not only kill the malignant growths of cancer but could also cause damage or death if used without proper caution. In the early 1920s it was found that radium, painted on watch-faces to provide night-time luminescence, was accumulating in the bodies of workers who had licked it off their paint-brushes, and that its continuing radiation was affecting them. Further information accumulated during the last three decades has shown that the by-products of nuclear fission can not only cause illness or death but can also bring about mutations in the genetic material of living cells. Thus they can affect the characteristics handed down from one generation to the next, whether the cells are of fruit-flies or rabbits, of butterflies or humans.

The best-known radioactive by-product of nuclear fission is of course 'fall-out', the deposit of radioactive substances which descends on the earth from the atmosphere after the explosion of a nuclear weapon. In the nuclear reactor designed to produce controlled power, the radioactive substances are retained in the body of the reactor behind some form of bio-logical shield – one part of a complex series of safety measures incorporated in the design of all reactors. However, radio-activity is retained in the reactor, not destroyed there. Some of it will continue for thousands of years and the disposal of radioactive nuclear waste is one of the constant, and naturally growing, problems of the industry. Nuclear fission has given men the possibility of limitless power; it has also given them the problem of disposing of lethal waste.

Not all radioactive by-products can be pushed to the debit side of the nuclear account. Many of them are made use of by the growing battery of radioactive devices which during the last two decades have revolutionized whole areas of medicine, industry and agriculture. Thus radioactive strontium, pro-cessed from the spent fuel of nuclear reactors, lies at the heart of a new family of thermo-electric generators which power marine navigation lights, unmanned weather stations and aircraft beacons. The word 'spent' is comparative and the heat from the continuing decay of the radioactive strontium is enough to generate electricity in an assembly of thermo-couples. Outputs from a few milliwatts to several tens of watts can be obtained and the equipment will go on producing it, unattended, for more than a decade.

But it is not only 'unwanted' radioactive material that comes from reactors today. While the destruction of Hiroshima and Nagasaki was the apocalyptic sign that man had released nuclear energy, and the utilization of nuclear power was the sign that he could tame it, the production of many hundreds of

Measuring the uptake of iodine-131 hippurate in the kidneys at Edinburgh Royal Infirmary. The patient has been given an intravenous dose of iodine-131 in a form which concentrates it in her kidneys. The two scintillation counters measure the build-up of activity and two graphs, one for each kidney, produced on the recorder above the patient's head, show the concentration of iodine-131 and its excretion.

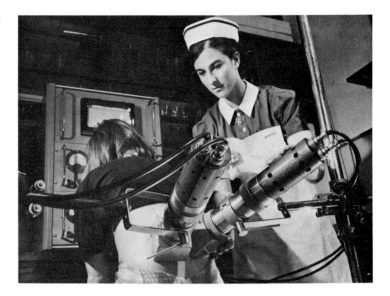

radioactive isotopes shows that he can fashion with the help of nuclear reactions a large number of new and almost unimaginably sensitive tools. This third result of the nuclear revolution is far less spectacular than the other two, and far less well-known or understood; yet it would be a rash man who claimed that in its long-term and all-pervasive influence it might not eventually be just as important.

Until the Curies began to make minute quantities of radioactive material in their Paris laboratory in the 1930s, radium was in practice the only radioactive material available. It had been used by doctors since the start of the century, and with some success, to 'burn out' growths in the human body. But radium had one great disadvantage, quite apart from its cost: the speed and other characteristics with which it disintegrated could not be controlled. Thus for the medical profession it served as a single tool with useful but somewhat restricted possibilities – much as if a carpenter had one single saw for his work instead of a range of them on which he could draw at will.

The release and control of nuclear energy altered all that. For from 1939 onwards it became increasingly clear that radioactive isotopes of many elements could be made by inserting samples of non-radioactive elements in a reactor core and there irradiating them. More important, it was possible to select the 'raw materials', and to treat them, so that the irradiated material gave off radiations of a kind and of an intensity which had previously been selected. The scope provided by this new technique can be judged from some simple figures: by the mid-1960s, one British centre alone was offering 150 radio-isotopes available in more than 1,000 chemical compounds and in more than 600 kinds of radiation appliance – a total of more than 2,000 items.

These materials could be virtually tailor-made. At first the tendency was to concentrate on their medical uses, a continuation and extension of pre-war methods. But just how such techniques could be refined by the post-war materials available is illustrated by one typical example from Sweden. Here rays from a number of different radioactive sources of the correctly selected intensity were directed on a growth in a patient's brain. Where the radiations passed individually through different parts of the skull, they had no effect; where they met, their combined effect killed off the growth.

However, it was not only in this way that medicine found a new tool in the radio-isotopes that first research stations and then commercial nuclear reactors began to produce. The radioactive material was chemically identical with the non-radioactive variety – even though it could be identified at a distance, without seeing it or touching it, simply by picking up on an instrument such as a Geiger counter the radiations which the radioactive version was constantly giving off.

As one example from many, this meant that doctors soon had a new diagnostic tool with which they could discover the metabolic processes of the human body. Metabolism transforms some substances very slowly. Only about 100 microgrammes of iodine passes through the average body each day and to trace its progress was out of the question until the advent of radio-isotopes; then it was possible to add a small amount of harmless radioactive iodine to the non-radioactive intake. How the body dealt with it could then be discovered with comparative ease. Such was the case with many other substances utilized by the body, so that during the 1950s and 1960s it became increasingly easy for a doctor to find out what portion of a patient's body was failing to change properly the various materials that it would have metabolized if healthy.

The medical uses of radioactive materials had to some extent been foreshadowed before the war. But a completely new use which followed the manufacture of tailor-made isotopes in the first post-war reactors was in agriculture. Here a common problem is to find out what growing crops do with different fertilizers. Until the mid-1940s this was virtually impossible; but when a small amount of radioactive material is incorporated in a fertilizer, its progress through the living body of a plant can be followed in detail. In exactly the same way the course of normal 'food and drink' can be traced through plants merely by ensuring that a small percentage of this is radioactive.

Also entirely new was the adaptation of radio-isotopes to industry in the post-war world. The point where an underground water-pipe leaks can be detected by adding a radio-isotope to the water and following the course of the pipe, above ground, with a Geiger counter. It is possible to incorporate small amounts of radioactive 'tracers' in the rubber of motor car tyres and then work out, by the disappearance of these from the tyres, just how much wear and tear is caused by differing conditions. When a radio-isotope is incorporated in metal piston rings, the amount of this later found in the engine oil indicates how quickly the rings wear under certain conditions. Radioactive ground glass has been used to trace the movement of mud in the Thames Estuary, and the movement of radioactive pebbles has revealed the currents which cause coast erosion. Radioactive materials released in the streams of an area picked for a new reservoir have provided an estimate of seepage from the site.

A different use for radio-isotopes in industry is in measuring-instruments which can indicate the thickness of a metal sheet or the density of a liquid. Here the radioactive source is placed on one side of the material and a detecting instrument on the other, the amount of radiation reaching the instrument showing the thickness of the material between. The same technique can be used to check whether packets on a production line are properly filled.

Another by-product of the nuclear revolution, quite important even though little noted in the shadow of nuclear weapons and nuclear power, is the new ability to sterilize materials by radioactivity which can inhibit or kill both the individual cells of living bodies or complete organisms such as bacteria.

One application is the irradiation of potatoes which are thus prevented from sprouting while in storage, and mobile units on which boxes of potatoes are carried through a 20-ton lead-lined drum and irradiated by radioactive cobalt, have been found successful in Canada. In the United States at least one factory is treating sea-food a ton at a time by the same process, and plans have been made for a similar plant in Germany. Soft fruit, fish, and tins of food have also been 'sterilized' in this way but so far no satisfactory method has been found of preventing changes in flavour. However, comparatively little is even now known about the biological and chemical problems involved; within a few decades, nuclear systems producing much of the world's power may well be helping the food industry.

Already the extraordinary effects of irradiation are being

applied in a host of unexpected one-off applications. In Australia it has been used to ensure that no anthrax bacilli exist on the goat-hair that goes into carpets. In Britain, medical syringes, scalpels and similar instruments are sterilized in large numbers by irradiation. New methods of pest-control have been introduced by the sterilization of insects, while the genetic changes induced by irradiation have been used to produce new varieties of flowers.

All these are comparatively little-known items on the credit side of the nuclear ledger. Perhaps most revealing is the number of them which impinge, directly or indirectly on the biological processes of living things, plants and potatoes as well as human beings. For if the nuclear revolution is now in full swing, the biological revolution, man's increasing ability to condition and control the life-cycles of many species, including his own, is only just beginning. In the long run it may well equal in importance the fresh control that man is beginning to exercise over inanimate materials.

Potatoes in the Brookhaven National Laboratory, Upton, New York. That shown top left was stored normally. The rest were subjected to various doses of gamma rays and the illustration shows how greater doses increasingly inhibited sprouting.

# 6 The Challenge of the Future

The nuclear revolution which took place between 1938 and the early 1950s after four decades of preparation by the world's scientists, may well alter the prospects for the human race more far-reachingly than any other development since man's taming of fire and his first deliberate sowing of crops. This is still the popular theory, and it is strengthened by the steadily increasing battery of uses to which radio-isotopes are being put, a process now affecting almost every aspect of life. Yet it seems possible, perhaps even probable, that the biological revolution which is already under way, may be even more important: it is, after all, giving man for the first time in history, a measure of control over his own biological future.

This revolution is perhaps more concerned with 'pure' science than those which have given man command of the air and the ability to produce raw materials to his own specification. It has possibly depended more on the intellect of man and less on purely technological advance than the steps which have enabled engineers to exploit the knowledge of the physicists and produce nuclear power. However, the work of the biologists in the age of the electron-microscope and irradiation is clasped tightly to the bosom of technology; and the discovery in mid-century of 'the double helix', the helical structure of deoxyribonucleic acid which is the molecular vehicle for heredity, demanded a unique merging of data and techniques from chemistry, physics and biology.

It is possible to trace back man's enquiring interest in heredity to the beginnings of the recorded past. 'Like begets like' is a saying which springs out of the mists of prehistory, an observation which throughout the generations men noticed was true of all living things, insects and animals as well as plants and men. Various hypotheses were put forward to account for it, as well as for the equally common fact that offspring could apparently show the characteristics of male parent, female parent, or both. However, as recently as a century ago Darwin himself was able to write: 'The laws governing inheritance are for the most part unknown. No one can say why the same peculiarity in different individuals of the same species, or in different species, is sometimes inherited and sometimes not so; why the child often reverts in certain characteristics to its grand-father or grand-mother or more remote ancestor.'

The vital clue to this tantalizing riddle which had intrigued man since he had first stood up on two feet out of four had in fact already been offered by Gregor Mendel when Darwin wrote these words. Mendel was an obscure Austrian priest whose story illuminates the truth that fact is stranger than fiction. Having failed three times to pass scholastic examinations which would have given him greater opportunities, he was forced to teach in the local school at Brunn – today Brno in Czechoslovakia. But he lived in the Abbey of St Thomas. And in the abbey garden he combined his interests in mathematics and botany by carrying out botanical research. This research consisted of breeding and cross-breeding pea-plants having characteristics which could be easily identified. First he used tall varieties and short varieties. When these were crossed he found that all the hybrids were tall; but when the hybrids were in turn crossed among themselves they produced 'offspring' one-quarter of which were dwarf and three-quarters of which were tall. The dwarfs, cross-bred in turn, all produced dwarfs. But when the talls were cross-bred about a third of them produced true-breeding talls, while two-thirds produced non-true-breeding talls. He next carried out comparable experiments with two varieties producing red and white flowers respectively. The results were comparable, with white and red substituted for dwarf and tall.

Mendel's conclusions were three-fold. It appeared that characteristics such as tallness or dwarfness, redness or whiteness, must be transmitted in some way from one generation to the next without dilution. It appeared that the transmission-mechanism must involve each parent-plant to an equal degree. And it appeared that some characteristics, such as tallness or redness, were dominant; but that the contrasting characteristic, dwarfness or whiteness, while recessive, did not disappear but could show itself in subsequent generations if not linked with the dominant characteristic.

Mendel carefully wrote up his experiments and sent his account to Karl Nageli, a Swiss botanist who was appalled by the mathematics of the paper, had little sympathy for an unknown amateur, and gave the Austrian little encouragement. Only years later, in 1866, did Mendel publish the first of two

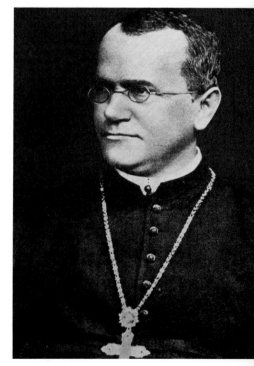

Gregor Mendel, the Austrian priest whose work laid the foundations of genetics

papers on his work, in the obscure *Transactions of the Brunn Natural History Society*. Then, appointed Abbot, occupied with administrative duties, and becoming too corpulent to continue properly with his gardening, he slid back into an obscurity that was not to be broken for three decades.

In 1900, by one of the chances of science, Mendel's work was discovered. Moreover it was discovered, quite independently, by three men: Hugo de Vries in Holland, Carl Correns in Germany and Erich von Tschermak in Austria. All worked in the after-glow of Darwin and all sought to explain the question that Darwin had left unanswered; how was it possible for individuals to vary in the way that they did?

All three men, searching over the literature after they had reached tentative theories, came across Mendel's papers and all, to their lasting credit, gave prominence to their predecessor and put forward their own ideas mainly as confirmation. De Vries, however, was able to make an important addition to what was soon known as Mendelism. Some years earlier he had collected a number of primrose plants that had been introduced to the Netherlands from America. In breeding these he found that on purely random occasions the plants would produce a 'sport', a variety differing in some main essential not only from its immediate ancestors but from any ancestor that could be traced. For some while there had been no obvious explanation. With the re-discovery of Mendel, however, it was possible to conclude that there was a sudden change, or mutation, in the mechanism of heredity. This, it was later found, was what actually took place.

Some details of the hereditary mechanism had been discovered more than a decade earlier even though their significance had not been appreciated. As with most scientific discoveries, the credit belonged not to one man, or to one team, but to a series of workers advancing upon the successes of their predecessors. Important among them were Walther Flemming, a German anatomist, and Edouard van Beneden, a Belgian cytologist. Between them, they helped to establish the existence of minute thread-like structures in the nuclei of living cells. Soon afterwards these structures were named chromosomes or coloured bodies, since they took up the colour with which cells were stained.

Early in the 20th century the work by cytologists, or cell-specialists, became united with the more theoretical work of those studying the mystery of heredity from the more theoretical angle. It became increasingly clear that inheritance was in some way dependent on the chromosomes. All living things were found to contain chromosomes, all the members of any particular species having the same number – from one to more than 100. A fertilized cell at first contains double the number of original chromosomes but after division, is left with the original number, half coming from the fertilizing cell and half from the fertilized.

This picture was increasingly seen to give a very simplified picture of the truth as, throughout the first decade of the century, scientists began to realize that inheritance was, as suspected, governed by the chromosomes. Among the most important of the men to give detail to the broad outline was T. H. Morgan, the American whose 'fly-room' at Columbia University became world-famous. Morgan in effect introduced a new tool of research in the form of the *Drosophila* fruit-fly. This insect could be bred in huge numbers without trouble, a fresh generation could be produced in a matter of days, while for the researcher it had the great advantage of having only four pairs of chromosomes, thus considerably simplifying his work.

Morgan discovered that the *Drosophila* was subject to mutations, showing that at least this part of the mechanism of inheritance was the same for the insect as for the plant-world. Together with other evidence, his discovery began to make it more and more clear that heredity in men was governed by chromosomes as surely as heredity in insects or plants.

However, it was here that one problem immediately loomed. Man was known to have only about two dozen pairs of chromosomes – for years 24 was thought to be the correct figure, now it is known to be 23. But if the multitudinous characteristics of the human race were to be accounted for, then a large number of these variables must exist as separate, discrete factors on each chromosome. A clue to the truth of this was presented by William Bateson, the English biologist who in the early years of the 20th century showed that some characteristics appeared to be inherited not independently but together, a pointer to the fact that they might be due to different factors on the same chromosome. Bateson's deduction led to the suggestion that the name for the discrete factor of heredity should be 'gene' from the Greek 'to give birth to', and that the study of heredity should be called genetics. It also led to much complicated work in Morgan's fly-room which eventually demonstrated that while specific factors on a chromosome were often inherited together, this was not always so. The explanation was 'crossing-over', a process in which portions of pairs of chromosomes were sometimes switched. This in turn led to the first 'mapping' of

Non-cross-overs 98.5%    Cross-overs 1.5%

Diagram to illustrate crossing over in a cross between a female fruit-fly with white eyes and yellow wings and a male with red eyes and grey wings. The blocks represent the chromosomes in which the two characters are linked and the genes are represented by the letters y and w. In this case crossing over between the genes has taken place in 1.5 per cent of the offspring, giving flies with red eyes and yellow wings and white eyes and grey wings respectively, instead of the normal linkage in the parents. (After Morgan)

a chromosome. For by studying how often two linked 'genes' became unlinked it was possible to estimate the gap between them on the chromosome; and, eventually, to decide what part of what chromosome was responsible for what inherited characteristic.

To a greater and greater degree this work involved complicated mathematics, a fact which drew into genetics the man who after the First World War succeeded in making the first map of a human chromosome. He was J. B. S. Haldane who marked the position on one particular chromosome of the genes causing colour-blindness, severe light-sensitivity of the skin, night-blindness, a particular skin disease, and two varieties of eye peculiarity.

Haldane's work on human genetics was only one piece of research from many which during the years between the wars helped increase man's understanding of the mechanisms governing not only the colour of a child's hair and eyes, and a multitude of other features, but also his or her susceptibility to certain diseases of which the best-known are probably haemophilia, Huntington's chorea and phenylketonuria.

In this field of human genetics research was carried forward over areas where facts were more than usually difficult to obtain, and more than usually contentious when they were obtained, the scientific data often being at the mercy of non-scientific interpretation. It was possible to question the respective importance of nature (or genetic inheritance) compared with nurture (in other words, upbringing) in such hotly disputed matters as intelligence. It was possible to ask whether living organisms could, as claimed by the Russian Trofin D. Lysenko, pass on not only characteristics which they had inherited but those which they had acquired, a proposition with fearsome political overtones. The answers to such dynamite-filled questions were rarely without sociological or political bias.

What had become clear by this time was that inheritance in all living things – flowers and insects, the lowest mammals as well as *homo sapiens*, was governed by particulate units, formed together to make long thread-like chromosomes, which duplicated themselves during the process of fertilization. And, despite the effects of random mutation, they did in general pass on inherited characteristics to follow certain laws which might be so complex that their details were difficult to unravel, but which were nevertheless statistical laws.

What was still in question at the start of the Second World War was the chemical composition of the material which acted as the mechanism of heredity, and also the way in which it transmitted the multitudinous characteristics of any one species.

The geneticists had at least something to go on. It had been known for some while that both proteins and nucleic acids were present in chromosomes and it was deduced that one of these groups of substances was in some way responsible for a genetic code. Until the early 1940s it was generally believed that the proteins were involved; then, however, it was found that one of the nucleic acids appeared to double its quantity between successive cell divisions and was reduced by half when a cell divides. This bore too great a resemblance to the replication of chromosomes to be coincidence; from this time on, attention was concentrated on the nucleic acids.

They had first been investigated by Albrecht Kossel during the last two decades of the 19th century and were known to consist of very large molecules which fell into one of two groups. Sugar was present in both groups; but in one it was a sugar called ribose which consisted of five atoms of carbon, ten of hydrogen and five of oxygen, while in the second group the sugar was of a different sort, containing only four atoms of oxygen and known from this as deoxyribose. These different varieties of sugar thus helped to christen the ribonucleic acids known as RNA and the deoxyribonucleic acids known as DNA.

After the war the general chemistry of the nucleic acids was worked out, notably by Alexander (later Lord) Todd. It was found that DNA contained, as well as the sugar, a phosphoric acid and four nucleotide bases – adenine, guanine, cytosine and thymine. They were, it was to be discovered, vital elements in the transmission of heredity.

During the years that followed the war, improvements were made in many of the 'tools' of research which could be used by geneticists. Among them was the use of X-rays to help discover how the atoms of complicated molecules were arranged. Earlier in the century Max von Laue and the famous father-and-son team of the Braggs (Sir William H. and his son Sir Lawrence) had shown that X-rays were diffracted by the regular spacing of atoms in a crystal, and that from the way in which this took place it was possible to discover the positioning of the atoms inside the crystal.

Maurice Wilkins, a young New Zealander who had been a member of the British team which had gone to the United States during the war to work on the atomic bomb project, was among the first to conscript X-ray crystallography in the search of the genetic code. Like many other physicists, Wilkins had turned away from nuclear work after the war; he

An X-ray diffraction photograph of
DNA in sodium salt

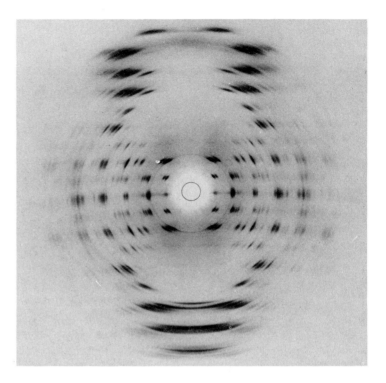

had been intrigued by a book on the riddle of life written by
Erwin Schrödinger, one of the founders of wave mechanics
in the years between the two World Wars, and had thus been
attracted to biology.

Wilkins typified a large number of physicists who after the
war were together instrumental in founding the new science of
molecular biology which utilized both physics and chemistry
to help answer the riddles of biology. Prominent among them
was Max Perutz, the specialist in the X-ray diffraction of
proteins who was, under Lawrence Bragg, to run the molecular
biology section of the Cavendish Laboratory.

However, one of the next steps forward – a phrase that is
something of a generalization since by the end of the 1940s
very many scientists were attacking the problem of the genetic
code from different angles – was made by a straight biochemist.
He was Erwin Chargraff who modified the new technique of
paper chromatography for the task. This method had been
used to discover details of the amino acids making up certain
proteins, and Chargraff now adapted it to determine the
amount of each of the bases in the nucleic acids. The results
were both intriguing and puzzling. For it was found that the
amount of adenine was always roughly equal to the amount of
thymine, and that the amount of guanine was always roughly
equal to the amount of cytosine. This was not all, for it was also

discovered that the amount of A plus T, in relation to the amount of G plus C, while always the same in any one organism was different from one organism to the next, the proportion being different in men from that in cattle, and that in other organisms being different again.

Dr James Watson (*left*) and Dr Francis Crick with their model showing the structure of deoxyribonucleic acid, whose molecular structure they discovered and announced in 1953

By the early 1950s a good deal of information had thus been collected over the years. The constituents of DNA were known but the riddle that remained was how these atomic constituents were arranged. How were the very large number of atoms making up the DNA molecules, which in turn helped to make up a chromosome, connected together?

The men who answered this riddle were the English biochemist Francis Crick and the American James Watson, two men who by worrying away at the problem eventually produced a theoretical answer whose correctness was to be amply confirmed by a decade of investigation and research.

Using Chargraff's chemical data, and the physical information yielded by Wilkins's X-ray pictures, Crick and Watson produced the double helix, a model of how the component parts of DNA were put together. Once described as 'a rope ladder wound up a spiral', the model was that of a DNA molecule in which each of the two helices was made up of the sugar-phosphate backbone which Todd had already shown to exist. The bases extended inwards from the backbones towards the centre of the model. Crick and Watson assumed that an adenine base from one backbone always 'stretched out' as it were, towards a thymine base from the other backbone; and that a guanine base from one always reached out towards a cytosine base from the other.

The model of the molecule did two things, quite apart from fitting all the available chemical and physical information. It accounted for the fact that the amounts of thymine and adenine, and of guanine and cytosine, were always the same. And, of yet greater importance, it allowed biologists to see, for the first time, how the replication of chromosomes took place. For it could well be imagined that in this process the two helices unwound, each then serving as a model for a complementary helix. A 'free' adenine would select a 'free' thymine, and a 'free' guanine would find a 'free' cytosine. Thus the first No. 1 helix would produce a complementary No. 2 and the first No. 2 would produce a complementary No. 1.

This postulated structure also made it possible to understand the variety of the genetic information passed on from one generation to the next by what at first looked like the beguilingly simple method of a single chemical. For just as the dot, dash and gap of the Morse code can be used to build up any number of letters and words, so the four 'letters' of the genetic alphabet, the A, T, G, and C of the bases, could be differently arranged in strings to make up an almost infinitely large number of different units of inheritance.

Knowledge of the more detailed mechanism of inheritance has increased immensely since Crick and Watson 'cracked the code of life' as it has been called. With this increase there has come speculation about 'genetic engineering', the ability to discover what chemical composition governs what specific inherited factors; and, from that, to make human beings to required specifications. It is difficult to rule out any future possibilities although most serious geneticists do not visualize the prospect within the foreseeable future, and many of them regard such speculations as nonsense. The most reasoned judgment is that any practicable development along these lines will require immensely more knowledge, and immensely more technique, than is available at the present moment and that it will come, if it comes at all, many decades in the future.

This is not, of course, to suggest that the problems and dangers should not be considered today. Already, in the United States, Robert Sinsheimer, chairman of the California Institute of Technology's biology department, has proposed

Eight radiation-induced mutants of the African Violet surrounding a normal specimen (centre of middle row)

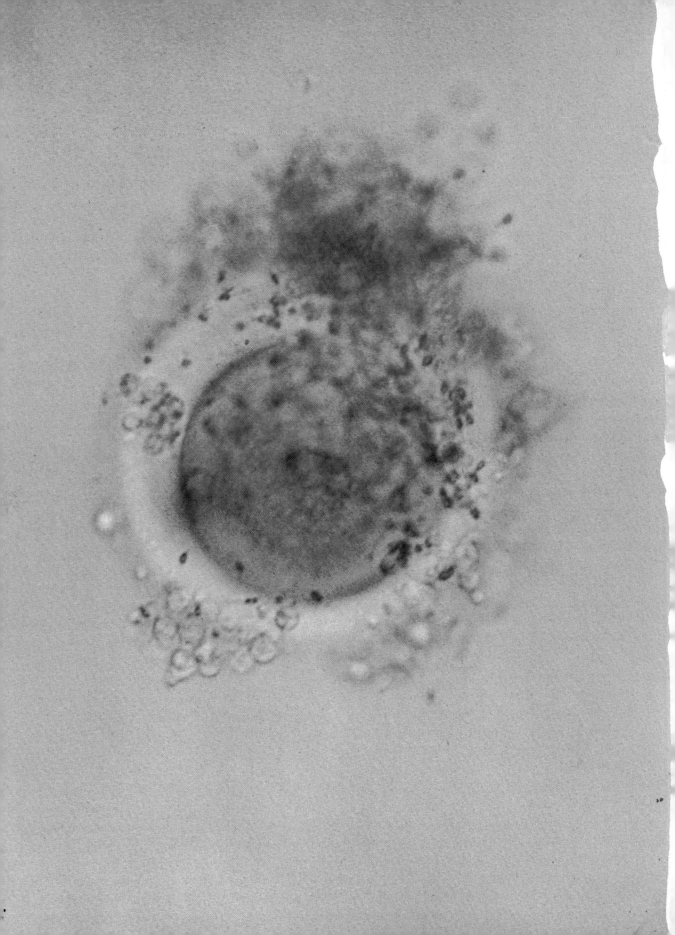

that only an international authority for human genetic research can furnish a safeguard against abuse. This, perhaps based on the unadopted Baruch Plan for regulating nuclear energy, would obviate an international 'genetics race' by ensuring that the results of significant research in the field were made available to all.

If a scheme of this kind were started its effects might well radiate outwards so that other aspects of biological and medical research began to be considered on an international rather than a national basis, a process already happening in the fields of nuclear energy and of space research.

At this point the biologists become intimately connected with the nuclear physicists. For it has now long been confirmed that the random transformation of genes known as mutation is speeded up when living matter is subjected to the radiation created by nuclear fission. So far, relatively little is known about the process of radiation-induced mutation. But just as it has already been used to breed new kinds of grain and of flowers, so may it be used in the future to breed 'tailor-made' humans. Such ideas are still the stuff of science-fiction – as much so as were the chances of using atomic energy when in 1933 Lord Rutherford described them as 'moonshine'.

The prospect of making humans to specification, dream or nightmare, is only one of many biological speculations which have been offered during the last quarter-century. Researchers have discovered more about the way in which the mind itself responds to purely physical, in particular chemical, treatment of the body. It has been found possible to cure by chemical treatment some forms of mental illness. New means of identifying genetic abnormality, and of forecasting its consequences, have suggested ways of identifying potential criminals. Thus biochemists have shown how human behaviour, both 'good' and 'bad', has a definite chemical base and may thus be susceptible to chemical control.

At this point the geneticists and the biochemists, the doctors and the mental specialists, step out into fields where their actions become inextricably entwined in ethical and moral arguments. Even so, the problem of where scientific advance *should* lead rather than of where it *can* lead, pales into insignificance beside another which is in some ways complementary to the understanding of genetic inheritance.

The breeding of 'tailor-made' humans, the control of potential criminals by chemical means, even the medical refinements which during the last few years have made it possible in exceptional circumstances to continue human life deeply into the penumbra existence where life merges almost

The follicle of the human ovary exposed to human spermatozoa in human blood serum. The outer material of the egg, the zona pellucida, can be seen breaking away from the nucleus. The spermatozoa appear as little black dots and can be seen trying to penetrate the egg.

imperceptibly into death, are never likely to affect more than a comparatively small number of the population. The Pill, the chemical contraceptive whose immense potential repercussions on human life are only now beginning to be realized, affects the masses of the world.

The desire to prevent childbirth at will is as old as the human race, and in primitive societies there have long existed beliefs that conception could be avoided if infusions of certain plants or herbs were drunk. These beliefs were based not on knowledge of the way in which such preventatives worked but on observations carried out over generations and handed down from mother to daughter. Indeed, the details of conception and birth, the chemical mechanisms which actually control what seemed to be a purely chance affair, continued to remain a mystery until the early years of this century.

Yet as far back as the 17th century biologists had begun to collect the information which a later generation would put to use in the development of the Pill. Thus in the 1660s Regner de Graaf of Delft gave the first reliable description of the *corpus luteum*, the yellow area formed in the mammalian ovary after the release of an egg in the process of ovulation.

More than 200 years passed before the significance of the *corpus* in conception began to be discussed at the end of the 19th century. It is notable that the sudden furore of interest – which, had technical expertise been available, might have brought the Pill to the 1900s rather than to the 1950s – came as physics was being shaken by its own revolutionary ideas. In fact the 10 years beginning in 1895 significantly paved the way for the mid-20th century in the air, in atomic research, the use of electro-magnetic spectrum and the production of man-made materials. It would be a rash man who claimed that any of these were potentially more important than the control over its own reproduction towards which the human race was now at last beginning to grope.

The first renewal of interest in the *corpus luteum* came in 1895 from Johannes Sobotta, an anatomist of the German city of Würzburg. Shortly afterwards John Beard, lecturer in Comparative Embryology in the University of Edinburgh, published a paper on *The span of gestation and the cause of birth*. Here, Beard put forward the idea that in the higher mammals the release of eggs during pregnancy was stopped by some mechanism that researchers should now try to understand, an idea which was taken up within a few years by Auguste Prénant, a Professor of Histology in the University of Nancy. Prénant took the thoughts of his predecessors one firm step onwards. The cessation of egg-release during pregnancy was, he suggested, the direct result of some substance or substances secreted by the *corpus luteum*; it was now up to researchers to find out what these substances were and how they did their job.

All this, it should be stressed, was still of a very theoretical nature. It was, moreover, concerned primarily with experimental animals. At this stage no one appears to have considered seriously the possibility of their research ending in a chemical contraceptive for humans. Yet a pointer to the future had already been given. Freud had written in the closing years of the 19th century: 'It would be one of the greatest triumphs of mankind, one of the most appreciable liberations of natural constraint, if one could achieve the elevation of the responsible act of procreation to an arbitrary and planned one and unbind it from its entanglement with the necessary satisfaction of a natural desire.'

During the first years of the 20th century, more than one worker in the United States and in Europe began to accumulate experimental evidence which supported the idea that, when mammals became pregnant, the very process of pregnancy started the production of an anti-ovulatory substance. But it was left to the physiologist Ludwig Haberlandt to provide really convincing proof. In 1921 Haberlandt found that the transplantation of pregnant rabbit and rat ovaries into non-pregnant animals induced sterility. More important, he found that the same results could be obtained by feeding or injecting ovarian extracts from the pregnant animals. Haberlandt went on to coin the phrase 'hormonal sterilization' since he believed that the substances which had the contraceptive effect were hormones produced by the mammalian endocrine glands. He also, rather daringly, suggested that doctors might try to use this method of contraception on humans. But in the 1920s there were no takers in the medical profession.

The caution was natural enough in the climate of the times. Birth control of any sort was still a barely mentioned subject, and in 1921 Marie Stopes had astounded the world by opening the first birth-control clinic in Britain. Even when the subject was raised, moreover, the birth-control devices discussed were little more than technological improvements on those used by the more educated members of earlier generations. The prospect opened up by Haberlandt and other workers in the same field was something radically different: a fundamental alteration in the functioning of the female body through hormonal activities of which very little was so far known.

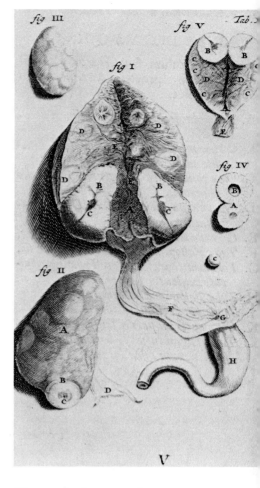

The reproductive organs of a cow from *Regner de Graaf: Opera Omnia* by Janus Leoniceus, 1677

Dr Margaret Sanger and her
sister, Ethel Byrne, in a U.S.
courtroom in 1916 during
Ethel Byrne's trial on the charge of
distributing obscene literature and
selling contraceptive devices.
In 1951 Dr Sanger arranged,
through the International Planned
Parenthood Federation, for the
first grant which started
Dr Pincus and others on their
fundamental investigation into
oral contraceptives.

For these reasons much of the research that went on during
the 1920s in universities throughout the world, and in the
laboratories of many pharmaceutical companies, has a slight
air of unreality. On the face of it, the work had few links with
humans and fewer still with human conception. If there was
any chance of the end-product being a chemical which could
bring about the temporary sterilization of humans, the fact
was scarcely mentioned.

The possibility was brought much nearer in 1929 when two
research workers, Allen and Corner, succeeded in isolating
a crystalline hormone from the *corpus lutea* of sows. Their
success, although they were not aware of the fact at the time,
was to be one of the key steps towards the Pill in its contemporary form. In 1929, any chance of the hormone being
available for more than research use seemed to be ruled out by
the difficulty, and therefore the expense, of making it. The
remains of many thousands of sows had to be obtained from
the slaughterhouses before even a few milligrams of the

One of Dr Marie Stopes's mobile clinics in the early 1920s

hormone could be manufactured. Years later, when it was found that it could be used to suppress ovulation in humans it still appeared to be impracticable for contraceptive purposes since a daily dose of no less than 300 milligrams was necessary. The structural formula of the substance was determined soon afterwards. It was found to consist of carbon, hydrogen and oxygen atoms linked together in rings to form a 'flat' molecule. Five years after Allen and Corner's discovery, the hormone was produced from an inert steroid of known composition, a success which threw a completely fresh light on its possible use.

By this time a number of other female hormones had been isolated, both in Europe and the United States, and it was becoming evident that some of them at least would be used medically. It was essential that biochemists throughout the world should agree to some measure of standardization and in 1935 a conference was called in London. The necessity for this is underlined by the fact that the same hormone was being isolated in the United States under the name of theelin, was being produced in Germany as progynon, in France as folliculin and as oestrin in England – an echo of the various names given to identical man-made plastics. So far, Allen and Corner's product had no name, although Allen had suggested progesterone without much enthusiasm. It was tried out by the British biochemist Sir Alan Parkes at a pre-conference party and met with success. 'The name progesterone may thus be said to have been born, if not conceived, in a place of refreshment near the Imperial Hotel in Russell Square where Willard Allen was staying,' Parkes later wrote.

Yet both progesterone and the other female hormones were still being considered almost exclusively as potential remedies for gynaecological disorders. Three barriers still barred the way to their contraceptive use. The first was the persisting difficulty of making them in industrial quantities rather than

Roots of *cabeza de negro*, the plant
that made the birth-control pill
possible, are chopped from the
ground by a labourer in the
Mexican jungle.

in the comparatively minute amounts required for specialized medical use. The second was the psychological barrier which still inhibited any serious suggestion that women might be allowed to decide for themselves whether or not to conceive and to implement their decision simply by making use of a chemical. Until these two barriers had been removed it was impossible to tackle the third; this was the disadvantage imposed by the fact that to be effective most of the newly synthesized drugs had to be injected rather than taken orally, a disadvantage which could be overcome only, if at all, by large-scale and expensive experiments which pre-supposed the acceptability of oral contraceptives.

The first of these barriers was removed by one of the most colourful characters in the entire story of the Pill. He was Professor Russell Marker, a Pennsylvania chemist who in 1940 turned his thoughts and energies to the problem of synthesizing progesterone in quantity. The traditional stories of folk-remedies to prevent conception had continued as a shadowy background to all the work of the biochemists, and in 1941 biologists working for the US Bureau of Plant Industry found evidence which confirmed at least one of them. For years infusions of the herb *Lithospermum ruderale* had been used as a contraceptive by Nevada Indians; tests with mice now showed that something in the herb did indeed decrease fertility.

Marker thought along similar lines but placed his faith in the Mexican wild yam which he garnered in quantities in the jungles of Veracruz. Finding American drug firms disinterested in his activities, he set up his own laboratory in rented premises in Mexico City. Within three years he had not only found how to synthesize progesterone from the Mexican plant; he had also, and with comparatively primitive equipment, made four pounds of progesterone – in an age when it was normally considered in milligram quantities. Legend claims that he then walked into a small pharmaceutical firm in Mexico City, asked if they were interested in making synthetic progesterone, and dumped down on the desk two jars containing nearly £50,000 (approx. $125,000) worth of the hormone.

Whether or not fiction has embroidered fact in this case, one thing is certain: Marker's work removed one of the barriers to production of a contraceptive pill. From the mid-1940s onwards, progesterone could be produced with only little more difficulty than the other female hormones known to affect conception in a variety of so far not totally understood ways.

Dr Gregor Pincus whose pioneer research helped to make the use of the pill a practical birth-control method

The next step came in 1950. In fact it was two steps in one since a definite decision to search for a revolutionary new kind of contraceptive was immediately followed up by a major experimental programme designed to find out whether hormones could be made to do the trick. Chance seems to have played its part, bringing to a major birth-control centre in New York Dr Gregor Pincus, research head of the Foundation for Experimental Biology in Shrewsbury, Mass. Pincus had been giving progesterone orally to numbers of rats and rabbits as part of an independent research programme not directly connected with birth-control. In New York it was emphasized to him that what was really required was a pill which could be taken regularly and which would stop ovulation over a period of time. No ovulation meant no free egg to be fertilized, and thus no conception. If a child was wanted, stopping the pill allowed ovulation to start again.

Five years research was needed before Pincus produced a pill, based on synthetic progesterone, which was orally acceptable and appeared to work. Only after that, in 1956, did he and two colleagues start the classic series of experiments which transformed the pill, with its small 'p' of a laboratory experiment, into the Pill which within a decade was being used by millions of women throughout the world.

For his tests Pincus chose the West Indies, where overpopulation was a major problem. One trial took place in Port-au-Prince, Haiti: two others in Puerto Rico – one in an agricultural area and one in the towns. Over a period of many months, each of the housewives taking part in the test was given 20 pills a month. The results were impressive: a reduction in pregnancies of 96 per cent. The final paragraph of Pincus's report noted that the data obtained 'would appear to demonstrate the finding of a highly effective oral contraceptive, usable in several different localities in the West Indies. It appears to be safe for use over a considerable number of months, has no deleterious effects on the reproductive tract nor on general health. Normal menstrual cycles occur regularly in the subjects taking the medication. Attendant on its use are certain side-reactions which appear to be in large measure psychogenic, and which minimize with continued use.'

The contraceptive pill Enovid was made in 1956 by G. D. Searle, the Chicago firm for whom Pincus worked as a consultant. The firm was the only one which dared to market such a product, and the climate of the times is indicated by the fact that when the US Food and Drug Administration approved it the following year it did so for treatment of menstrual difficulties and not as a contraceptive. But by 1960, when the

Giving a three-month injection of the contraceptive hormone, Depo Provera, in Thailand, 1972. Depo Provera has been approved for use as an injectable contraceptive in many countries although it is not available as such in the United Kingdom. An application for its use as a contraceptive is under consideration in the United States

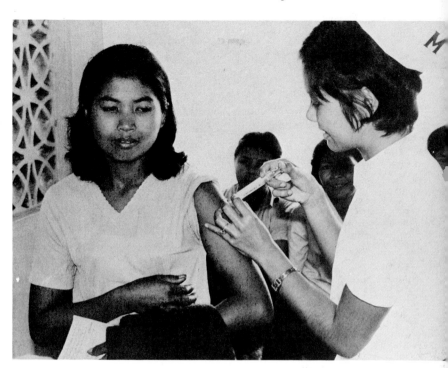

Administration openly acknowledged its contraceptive use, roughly 500,000 American women were already using it.

During the decade that followed the Puerto Rico experiment, both the Pill and public reaction to it underwent a transformation. The first effect was to encourage manufacturers other than Searle into making their own contraceptive pills. With the increased use that followed, there began to be built up a large mass of clinical experience; this in turn enabled the chemical make-up of the Pill to be so altered that it was more effective even though its side-effects were minimized. Side-effects have not been entirely removed. However, few unbiased observers who study the figures of the last sixteen years will deny that their dangers are considerably less than those of unwanted pregnancies.

One other fear has been removed by experience. In the nature of things, the greatest human and social benefits of a virtually fool-proof method of contraception would obviously spring from its use in under-developed countries, where education is minimal. Would women in such places use the Pill effectively? The answer has been 'yes' and is typified by one report from Ceylon: 'About 8–10 per cent never attended school,' says an account describing one group attending a contraception centre, 'but lack of education has not been a problem either in understanding the method or maintaining the record showing regular medication. One of the uneducated women of "low income" group said she will never forget to take her pill just as she will never forget to take her dinner, and accordingly to her "a pill a day after dinner, till the bottle is finished", is simple enough instruction for regular medication.' However, it is estimated that less than a tenth of Pill-users live in the developing countries. In some such countries the Pill is not part of the national family planning programme; when, moreover, it is only available on prescription it is in effect denied to most women, particularly those in rural areas where the doctor to patient ratio may be as high as 1:100,000.

There is no doubt about the sincerity of those who justify on ethical grounds a non-interventionist attitude towards over-population and an acceptance of the unhappiness brought by unwanted children. But the battle, determined though it may be, is a rear-guard one. With the easy availability of the Pill, the birthrate has begun to fall as dramatically in Catholic countries as in most others, and there can be little doubt about its gradual acceptance throughout the world. However, an important reason for the fall, at least in Latin-America, is believed to be an increase in illegal abortion.

But what comes next? One possibility is the injection of a hormone which would remain effective for three months, or perhaps for six. It is known that such injections have been used on many tens of thousands of women, although their use is not allowed in the United States by the F.D.A. or in Britain by the UK Committee of Safety on Drugs, as their toxic hazards have not yet been evaluated. It seems feasible, moreover, that research along these lines may be overtaken by something different. With the Pill, as with so many other 'inventions', advance in one field is aided by advance in another. In this case it is the plastics industry. At the end of the 1960s a young chemical engineer working for the Dow Corning Corporation mentioned to a doctor of the Population Council in New York's Rockefeller Center, that a new artificial rubber known as Silastic was being developed. One of its characteristics was that if certain substances were put in a Silastic capsule, they would diffuse out through the rubber over a very long period and, quite as important, at a constant rate. Would it not be possible, it was argued, for a capsule containing the chemicals of the Pill to be implanted under the skin in such a way that the diffusing chemicals would give contraceptive protection for five, ten or even fifteen years? The answer is not yet certain. But experiments made with female rabbits and monkeys have suggested that such capsules would not only work efficiently but could be removed at will and would produce no after-effects. Thus within the forseeable future control of conception will have been turned from a problem into a free choice unhindered even by the comparatively small inconveniences of today. Post-coital hormone preparations are also interesting, but will have little impact unless they are freely available throughout the world.

The next step, enabling a couple to ensure that a child will be of the chosen sex, has often been forecast, and more than one method of doing the trick has been proposed and investigated. So far, all have failed. But the problems of reproduction are being tackled on so many different fronts, the tools for research are increasing so quickly, that it would not be surprising if a way of handing this potentially disastrous choice to the human race suddenly appeared.

Yet not too pessimistic a view should be taken. The inventions and discoveries of the last hundred years which have been described and discussed are not only those which have in general had the greatest effect on human life – the reason why they have been chosen from among an immense number of candidates; in addition, each has posed its own threat and its own warnings of doom and disaster. In the case of photography it was perhaps nothing more than a fear that the art of painting might be driven from the face of the earth by the 'mechanism' of the camera – a phrase used by those unaware that in proper hands the camera could be an artist's instrument as readily as a paintbrush. The conquest of the air produced its warnings of the wrath to come, yet despite the undoubted menace of environmental pollution it seems likely that by the time manned flight celebrates its centenary the advantages will more than outweigh the disadvantages. Utilization of the electro-magnetic spectrum has produced its own challenges, particularly those provided by the threat of instant communication and its manipulation by small numbers of determined men. In their own way, synthetic materials were for long thought to be second-class products which might eventually drive out first-class natural materials – a threat whose lack of justification is only now beginning to be fully appreciated. Threats from the nuclear revolution need no stressing, although here, too, it looks as though mankind may already be turning the dangerous corner, so that the threat of nuclear extinction will become no more fearsome than the Darwinian threat of links with the apes that so terrified many Victorians.

There remains the genetic challenge presented by man's growing ability to control his own reproduction. It is a challenge which will probably be met as successfully as the others. It had better be.

# Illustration acknowledgments

Note
Pictures credited Science
Museum are from the
Science Museum, London.
The diagrams on pages 41, 44,
and 121 are by Howard Dyke.
For assistance in preparation
of the diagrams we are
grateful to Kodak Ltd (41, 44)
and Thorn Consumer
Electronics Ltd (121).
Jacket: *Front* Telefunken.
*Spine* Daily Telegraph Colour
Library. *Back, above*
Science Museum; *below*
Courtaulds Ltd.
Endpapers: Mary Evans
Picture Library.

13  From *De radio astronomico et
    geometrico liber*, 1545, by
    Reiner Gemma Frisius.
    Gernsheim Collection
16  Gernsheim Collection
17  Science Museum
18  From *John Leech's Pictures of
    Life and Character, from the
    Collection of 'Mr Punch'*,
    1842–6
20  Science Museum
21  Science Museum
22  Science Museum
23  *Both* Science Museum
25  Science Museum
26  Science Museum
27  Science Museum
28  Gernsheim Collection
29  *Above* Scottish National
    Portrait Gallery, by courtesy
    of the Free Church of
    Scotland College. Photo:
    Tom Scott
    *Below* National Galleries of
    Scotland
31  Science Museum

32  Science Museum
36  Kodak Museum
37  From *The Horse, Vol. 8*,
    1905–8, by Joan Wortley Axe
38  Science Museum
39  Science Museum
40  Kodak Museum
41  Photograph of tartan ribbon
    Cavendish Laboratory,
    Cambridge
42  Kodak Museum
43  Kodak Museum
44  Study for Le Chahut,
    Courtauld Institute Galleries,
    London
47  Polaroid (U.K.) Ltd
49  Institut de France, Paris
51  Courtesy Sotheby & Co.,
    London
52  *Left* Radio Times Hulton
    Picture Library
    *Right* Bibliothèque Nationale,
    Paris. Photo: Giraudon
54  *Above* Royal Aeronautical
    Society. Photo: Derrick Witty
    *Below* Science Museum.
    Photo: Derrick Witty
55  Flight International
56  Science Museum
57  Science Museum
58  Vickers Ltd
61  Science Museum
62  Library of Congress
64  Science Museum
68  Science Museum
69  *Above* Popperfoto
    *Below* Sport and General Press
    Agency Ltd
70  Hawker Siddeley Aviation Ltd
73  Office National d'Études et de
    Recherches Aérospatiales
74  Courtesy John Taylor
76  Imperial War Museum
78  United Press International

80  *Above* Vickers Ltd
    *Below* Flight International
83  *Above* Vickers Ltd
    *Below* Vickers Ltd
86  United Press International
88  Rolls-Royce (1971) Ltd
90  Camera Press
92  Royal Institution, London.
    Photo: R. B. Fleming
94  Deutsches Museum, Munich
98  Science Museum
99  The Marconi Company Ltd
100 The Marconi Company Ltd
104 *Left* Deutsches Museum,
    Munich
105 *Right* The Marconi Company
    Ltd
108 Imperial War Museum
109 Imperial War Museum
111 The Royal Radar
    Establishment, Malvern
113 Bell Telephone Laboratories,
    New Jersey
115 Bell Telephone Laboratories,
    New Jersey
116 Science Museum
119 Bell Telephone Laboratories,
    New Jersey
123 Daily Telegraph Colour
    Library
125 Science Museum
127 Science Museum
128 *Both* Ideal Home Magazine
    Photos: Clifford Jones
129 The Plastics Institute, London
130 The Albany Billiard Ball Co.,
    New York
133 Imperial War Museum
134 Bakelite Xylonite Ltd
138 *Above* Du Pont Company
    (U.K.) Ltd
    *Right* Courtaulds Ltd
141 E. I. du Pont de Nemours &
    Co.

145 Courtaulds Ltd
147 *Both* Science Museum
148 Cavendish Laboratory, Cambridge
150 Copenhagen University, Niels Bohr Institute
151 Central Press Photos Ltd
153 H. Roger Viollet
155 From *Foundations of Modern Physical Science* by G. Holton and D. Roller, 1958, published by the Addison-Wesley Publishing Company, Reading, Massachusetts
161 Daily Telegraph
162 Keystone
164 Argonne National Laboratory
165 Gary Sheahan. Photo: Chicago Tribune
166 U.S. Atomic Energy Commission
169 Studio Gullers A.B., Stockholm

171 U.K. Atomic Energy Authority
172 U.K. Atomic Energy Authority
175 *Left* Allmänna Svenska Elektriska A.B. *Right above* U.S. Navy Photo *Right below* United Press International
176 National Aeronautics and Space Administration, Washington
178 U.K. Atomic Energy Authority
181 Brookhaven National Laboratory
183 Radio Times Hulton Picture Library
186 From *The Mechanism of Creative Evolution* by C. C. Hurst, 1932, Cambridge University Press
188 Professor M. H. F. Wilkins, Medical Research Council Unit, King's College, London
189 Camera Press
190 Brookhaven National Laboratory. Photo: Robert F. Smith
193 Popperfoto. Photo: Landrum B. Shettles
195 From *Regner de Graaf – Opera Omnia* by Janus Leonicenus, 1677
196 Planned Parenthood-World Population, New York
197 International Planned Parenthood Federation, London
199 Time-Life Press Agency. Photo: Ezra Stoller
200 United Press International
201 McCormick Hospital, Chiang Mai, Thailand

# Index